COPYRIGHT

BABYLON DREAMS

A NOVEL

MARJORIE KAYE NOBLE

". . . inventive and intriguing storytelling . . ."   Portland Book Review

"The futuristic world is so well developed that it seemed almost prophetic . . . . an impressively detailed, creative story . . ."   City Book Review

". . . a challenging but compelling vision of a privatized, synthetic heaven slowly eaten away by ungodly capitalism, cupidity, and the sins of its founder. . . A keen and absorbing what-if tale about VR and a digital afterlife."   KIRKUS REVIEWS

To Alex, my son and fellow traveler

"There is a land of the living and a land of the dead and the bridge is love, only survival, the only meaning"

– Thorton Wilder

Table of Contents

RE: MEMORY FILES

Via message (confidential)

March 2, 2287

Byron Hernandez

Private Investigator

Trammell & O'Connell Law Offices

Dear Byron—

Unfortunately, I cannot send you the requested memory files. SEINI has filed an injunction and records relating to the after-death program, Shemathra's Realm are frozen. As Shemathra's Realm residents are unable to communicate with the bio world, it is understandable that your clients, the bio relatives of these virtuals, are upset. SEINI Corporation cites the Virtual Bill of Rights and the right of virtuals to choose their own after-death path. If I help you, I risk my position and my reputation. Donovan Hosseini has powerful friends, bio and virtual.

Denying the reported occurrence of recent mass erasures of resident virtuals, SEINI claims that those under the Goddess Shemathra's eye exist in a state of ecstasy. In an earlier message, you mentioned that you are a descendent of Thomas Bucklin, who was a virtual resident of Bali Hai, the original VR platform before the Shemathra take-over. As such, you are entitled to review any related Bali Hai records. Did you know that when your grandfather self-deleted, his companion was Gunter Holden? Historians consider Holden, the Henry Ford of the after-death industry. Holden's leadership transformed the post-bio world, making after-death affordable to middle incomes. His company, VEI, developed Bali Hai, which became Shemathra's Realm. In its day, Bal Hai was a cutting-edge destination.

I am sending you two of Holden's memories. Both are early encounters with Thomas. Without Holden's knowledge, mergers were already being negotiated and would soon envelop Gunter's company VEI and destroy Holden's signature paradise, Bali Hai. Holden often swore that he would never self-delete. Shortly after these events, Holden and your grandfather decided to do just that—self-delete. If you are interested, I will send more Holden records. To experience total immersion, you'll require compatible software and VR gear.

Bucklin's family has refused access to his memories, including his side of his interactions with Holden. I have inserted a slight pause (. . .) in each VR memory transcript. In the VR immersion, you will see Bucklin's image as Gunter does, but Bucklin's responses will be muted. Also, in the transcript, you'll see asterisks (**) as a navigation tool. Let me know if I can be of further assistance!

Desmond Webb, Archivist Library of Congress

Welcome to Bali Hai!

Byron—When he met Thomas, your grandfather, Gunter Holden's file was already fragmenting, forcing him to relive parts of his past. Let me know if you have questions. Desmond

From BALI HAI

Gunter Holden Memory Files

(81 years post transition)

Folder year: 2203

GUNTER HOLDEN Doc.135.6

V-Loc: TRANSITION STATION 46. UNIVERSAL ACCESS.

Visual: Standard daylight South Pacific beach-3.14 k, ocean-1.6 k from shoreline, structures=2, vegetation-tropical no. 3567.2c, © March 7, 2078 by VEI Standard Environments. Audio: ocean surf (standard level 8) gulls 46 level 5, wildlife level 2 OCEANBASE INTERACTIVES © 4.23.2132, Tactile: tropic sun/moon, late morning light effect 3.7, breeze level 3 (fixed). Sand: BEACHLIFE No. 6.8 © 6.2.2019, Sims: limited-basic vacation beach family level 1.3, entertainment musical greet (rotating) level 6.

White beach, clear sky. In the distance, a family of sims includes parents and two small children.

I am eight years old. Tomorrow, if you can call it tomorrow, I might be forty-three or thirty-four. I can be any age. Ha! I won't be nineteen again. I was nineteen in the Baltimore game when Laura slipped away. I saw myself in the perfection of her tears. Quite a rush.

Tom? Thomas Bucklin, is that your name? Forgive my curiosity. Miranda flagged your arrival for my attention. I know she had her reasons. Allow yourself to settle.

I'm here to welcome you. Since we're alone and the last thing you expected when you arrived in Bali Hai, was an eight-year-old boy, I'll shift my age to forty. Age-shifting is a necessary skill here.

. . .

What do you mean? Oh—what did I *see* when you appeared? Overall, the standard process. A swirl of gray expanded and rotated until the mass differentiated and color replaced the gray. Tru-color sparkled in pale yellows and the deep reds blended until there was a shift and "you" appeared. Parts of you ballooned and contracted, a normal transition.

. . .

Before the gray cloud, I saw you as you were at your bio-death. My guess is that your bio age was in the one hundred-thirties. Was your death painful?

. . .

Please, I understand your reticence. I wish more people were like you. They drone on, assuming that you are hanging on their every word. Good, you're settling into your avatar. The avatar is temporary, a tool to help you feel at home. Thank God for avatars. They save a considerable amount of embarrassment.

. . .

Don't worry about the family; they're not human. Lots of people sell their memories. We use them to make sims. These sims reassure new virtuals by making Bali Hai seem familiar. They're like ghosts, reliving the same events and are unaware of you. You are a virtual and have a complete set of memories. You know who you are. Virtuals are people; the sims are not.

Some advice: the time will come when there are no more surprises, so savor each one and squeeze every drop of newness. Surprises are the only treasure here.

. . .

I'm serious. I am almost one hundred and forty years old, still middle-aged if I were living as a bio. There is little here that surprises me. Patel designed our virtual-eco-wildlife interactive systems and programmed this location for the occasional anomaly waiting, like an Easter egg. I have gazed at the naked bodies of thousands of women, both in the biological world and the virtual one, but now I find more delight in beholding a new starfish.

You'll meet Miranda soon. She scans you for interests and preferences.

You did attend the bio-orientations, didn't you?

. . .

Then I'll explain. There are options and rules. An option would be an environment. We have over two hundred distinct environments and several locations within each. Miranda will imprint the code for each. "Jumping" from one location to another is done by simply desiring to transfer. You, or to put it crudely, your file will "jump" to the selected location.

Make sure you practice your age-shifting. It's one of the more important skills here. There's nothing more annoying than a person shifting in a public setting. It's considered rude. For example, you're attending an event with an attractive fifty-year-old and suddenly, she's a child of seven. Embarrassing. Most people are tolerant, especially with new virtuals, but a few residents can be self-righteous.

You're shimmering. Use your avatar. Sadly, I have pressing obligations. Otherwise, I would love to stay and tell you my stories while you adjust. I admit, some are lies. You saw me shift my age from eight to forty. This is what you must practice.

. . .

Yes, I was still boyish looking at forty. Too many here pursue meaningless perfection, not realizing how boring perfection is. The white polo and the trousers are copies of ones I favored as a bio. For now, I strongly advise you to continue using your avatar until you feel that you can do simple commands, like age-shifting or choosing your attire. Just think the command. What was your age at bio-death? I'm curious.

. . .

My name is Gunter Holden and I own this world or rather my company does. I made every beach, palm-tree, Paris boulevard, steamy Brazilian jungle, African safaris, the Alaskan wilderness with friendly polar bears, California wine country and the games. All the major cities are here.

Do you see the white disc in the sky?

. . .

That's our moon. It came after I arrived here. We have no Mars. Bali Hai was once the gold standard. It may be an old program, but updates keep us current. I admit our moon is overrated and a waste of revenue. I hear that Virtual Mars might have some surprises. I intend to bring it up at the next meeting. I may be virtual, but I am still the majority stockholder. They'll listen. Virtual Mars is an excellent investment.

. . .

Sadly, there are no bios on the Board whom I find trustworthy. I keep asking, but everyone I know is gone. Few came here and they all walked the ramp and fell into the Dreams. No one would tell me why. I might join them someday; I keep the thought.

My brother Jacob said his transition was like a hangover.

. . .

My brother was a drug addict, a parasite, and a loser. Why do you care what I think about Jacob? Why do you want to know about my family?

. . .

Sorry, we all make mistakes. When you're in my position you have to be careful. People take advantage, wanting to know where you're vulnerable. Fortunately, Jacob is gone.

. . .

He had no idea how to enjoy life here and he self-deleted after a short time. Pathetic to the end. Let's change the subject. The parade coming our way is your welcome. You're shifting again. Forgive me, but new virtuals are high maintenance. It's better to let Miranda handle this.

Goodbye for now, Tom.

. . .

Miranda, why did you flag this transition for my attention?

There was a request to alert you regarding Mr. Bucklin's arrival.

Whose request?

Gunter, it was a private request.

Really? Why? I rarely greet newcomers. Certainly, no one who knows me. Tom seems to be a nice man, but dull. Regardless, I enjoy crowds less and something tells me Bucklin is a kindred soul. Even so, I don't trust him.

COMMAND Miranda, SEND: my apologies to Tom Bucklin for not accompanying him. When he is ready to create his first personal environment, I am at his disposal.

SENT. Gunter would you like—

The seagull, the one tipping its wings, the one that landed on the driftwood.

Yes, Gunter. It's a variable.

MEMORY BREACH!!!

Most terrifying are the clicks. I fall again and again. No one is there to catch me.

A wonder . . . I'm waiting for . . . waiting . . .the nest the nest is the nest . . . Please, please, please . . . oh, God no!

INTERRUPTING

Gunter, I'm aware that you prefer to handle your own timeline, but when a breach threatens to destabilize your file, I must interfere. There was a two point five percent possibility of a rupture. I interrupted the anomaly for your safety.

I understand. Thank you, Miranda. God help me.

END RECORD

PAST PERFECT

G UNTER HOLDEN DOC. 128
V-Loc: Chicago ELYSIUM penthouse PERSONAL 6.28.2122. 19 interiors include entry lobby, elevators 2 and 8, rotating 4 of 10 resident interiors and concierge. © 8.18.2120 by VEI Options. Event May 1st, 2082. Visuals: Chicago urban 3.004k per day panorama spec. Dining: CUSTOMFOOD 175, update 5.15. 2120 recorded June 20, 2198.

Gunter Holden's personal environment—his Chicago penthouse

Miranda, I had the dream again.

Would you like me to erase it from your file?

Perhaps, but I think it may be pieces of a memory. Parts of it scatter as if it really happened. I'm worried. The memory breaches are becoming more frequent. If you delete the dream or remove memory fragments, my timeline may not hold.

The risk of further fragmenting is twenty-three percent.

Something from my past is out of focus and it's creating pressure. I'm not sure I want to know, but I may not have a choice. The timing couldn't be worse, especially with costs of more memory and patches. What have you heard of the merger? How serious a possibility is it?

Distant Horizons is preparing a formal offer. There's a secret backer. No one on the Board has expressed any serious interest, however, the situation seems fluid.

What do you mean 'a secret backer'?

That information is unavailable currently.

Please notify me when you discover who this backer is. Thank God I've held on to my shares. They can't agree without my consent. Still, it's possible that someone sees an opportunity. Any merger that compromises VEI policies can affect Bali Hai. If this happens, I must be ready.

I will notify you when the backer's identity is made available. A solution to your memory interruptions may be a patch. Past Perfect is currently in development.

When will it be available?

According to available data, there are two more phases of study Past Perfect must complete before release. The estimated time is between six months and two years.

I could request an early sample.

Of course, shall I message the manufacturer?

No, there might be questions. Of course, I would lie, but the memory breaches—no one can know, especially if I have to fend off the Board when there's a serious offer of a merger. VEI is mine. How can I keep my file from fragmenting and stop the breaches now?

Gunter, you need only maintain your stability until Past Perfect is available for company purchase. I suggest that you catalogue your memories for the purpose of maintaining a conscious timeline.

I am reluctant to record them. They might be used against me.

Then I suggest you select a VEI resident and recount events to him or her. This should also provide an emotional release and ease the pressure you sense.

Miranda, other than you, I trust no one.

The new resident, Thomas Bucklin is an excellent choice. I have studied his file and personality. You can trust his discretion.

Bucklin? We have nothing in common. How do I know he's not the secret backer? The man seems pleasant, boring. Besides, why would he want to listen to my life story?

Approach Mr. Bucklin by offering your friendship.

Miranda, I can't afford the time. Bali Hai has become dated and cannot support recent software upgrades. I need more capital. Notify me when you have answers from my lenders. They're taking their time. Rather than Tom Bucklin, the friends I really need are in Washington.

Of course, Gunter. In terms of stabilizing your files, I still recommend a cognitive review. Thomas Bucklin makes a trustworthy ally to this end.

You're right! For now, any friend will help. Perhaps, I can offer to help him in adjusting to the joys of virtual living.

I will alert you to Mr. Bucklin's location when you are ready.

Thank you, Miranda. I'll let you know.

END RECORD

***

Byron—At the time of his greeting your grandfather, Holden's file was continuing to fragment. This resulted in data from earlier events in both his bio and virtual life to run out of sequence. Early platforms flagged these events as memory breaches or breaches.

Again, I cannot send you any of the official Shemathra files. I'm aware that time is short due to the upcoming Congressional Hearings. If this situation changes, I will notify you.

*Below is the next encounter between Holden and your grandfather. If it is helpful, I'll be happy to provide you with others. As I mentioned in earlier correspondence, I am prefacing each group with **notes **.*

Gunter meets with Thomas Bucklin at Venice beach, discusses memory breaches and rumors of a VEI merger

From BALI HAI

Gunter Holden Memory Files

Folder year: 2203

GUNTER HOLDEN Doc. 141 B

V-Loc: Venice Beach California Strand environ, RICKS BEACH CAFÉ, 2.7k beach-4.14k, .4k ocean-1.6 k from Strand. Structures are 30 with completed interiors, 28 kiosks/carts.2c. © 4.22.2109 by VEI Standard Environment). Day 45 of 80 non-event Venice California. Visual environment means UNIVERSAL access. Program 33545.3 (rec 9.09.2108). Tactile: non-event day. Audio: surf non-event 5, gull/ wildlife interactive. Sims: gulls 46 of 92 sim/virtual interactives. Human sims 486 high function "local color," vendor/server (rotating) Olfactory: Pacific shore 2670 with level 46 Coney Island 24. Dining interactive from VIRTUAL LIFE 135, update 5.23. 2170.

Daytime with clear sky and gentle surf, Venice Beach strand crowded, colorful stands, cafés, and hundreds of sim tourists

Well, hello! I'm glad you came. I almost didn't recognize you! Age-shifting can make it difficult until people get to know and recognize the 'you' at various ages. My guess is that you are twenty-two. A bit young for you.

. . .

There's no need to be defensive. I agree. There's no age that's ideal. However, many favor their thirties to mid-fifties. A few inexplicably delight in reliving their teen years. I avoid them. I knew it was you because you have a distinctive walk and I saw the crooked smile, the pale blue eyes and the slope of your shoulders.

. . .

Don't be silly! No insults, please. Besides, perfection is boring. You might want to rethink the plaid shirt and denim trousers. Don't misinterpret what I'm saying. I'm suggesting that you'll feel more confident in more flattering apparel. What did your wife like about you?

. . .

Then I'll keep my opinions to myself when it comes to your attire. I'm afraid you might have gotten the wrong impression with my outbursts regarding my brother. Mentioning his name triggers feelings that are . . . best left in the past. If I'm not careful, unwelcome memories can intrude. Flashbacks, bios call them. The proper term is "breaches or memory breaches." Some virtuals eliminate parts of their pasts when certain memories prove to be upsetting, but there's a risk. A break in your file's timeline can affect overall stability, not to mention compromising judgment. Memory breaches may indicate a corrupted file and—

. . .

Yes, it's fixable. Soon, there may be a solution. Memory-Edix is developing a patch, something called "Past Perfect." There should be a progress report at the next meeting. Miranda tells me there are rumors of a VEI merger. I doubt a merger is in the offing. However, I do need my full wits during meetings with the Bio-Board.

. . .

Come on Tom, smile! You'll want to make friends here. Begin with me.

. . .

Shall we watch the gulls? Occasionally, one does something new. If there is any difference between virtual and bio-birds, it can't be much. Perhaps it is better to assume none. It makes the observing more satisfying. That's it, relax.

. . .

Feeling better?

. . .

Some people never feel comfortable in their surroundings.

. . .

I'm at home wherever I am. I do remember hating my mother's house, though I loved her fiercely. When I was a child, I wanted to fling my small boy arms around her neck and beg her to carry me. I was her only child and my father's only son until Jacob was born.

. . .

Yes, we were very close. These memories are old, but they still overwhelm me. Would you mind if I shared them with you? It might be helpful in sorting out my timeline.

. . .

The unwelcome memories that I mentioned, talking to you about what happened can help control the memory breaches.

. . .

Of course, there were things I liked about the house. For example, the clocks. Three grandfather clocks stood in the hallway connecting my bedroom to the kitchen. My mother bought them when she traveled with my father. I think she kept them to remember the time when he loved her.

The house seemed to know only one song—rain accompanied by the sounds of chimes and ticking. I would eat my morning cereal and watch my mother as she held her cup of tea and waited for the sun to break through the morning haze. You keep looking away; what's wrong?

. . .

Okay, I'll let it go. But if something's bothering you, would you like to tell me about your childhood? Where did you grow up?

. . .

We'll wait for another time. Where was I?

. . .

Yes, my mother's house. When the sun came out, I checked to see what progress the birds had made in building their nests. When it was especially cold, we sat together on my grandparents' plaid couch, keeping warm by the fire. There's that look again.

. . .

It was a simpler time.

. . .

My grandparents drowned in the Puget Sound when their sailboat capsized. I was five, so I have little memory of them. I think our fireplace evenings were my mother's way of remembering her parents.

One year, there was no nest. I worried that the birds found a better house. Ours was the smallest on the street and it needed painting.

That was the year I stayed with my father and not returned from that last vacation. I wonder if the birds ever came back.

. . .

As I said, I was eight. It wasn't my mother's fault that I chose my dad; it was the Seattle house. I still miss her. What's wrong? Did I say something that upset you?

. . .

By all means, let's change the topic. Most people do not find me boring. I'll try again. There must be something here that you'll enjoy. Bali Hai may be a little less cutting edge, but it's still full of wonder.

. . .

Apology accepted. I'm not sure why you accepted my invitation. We have such a difficult time communicating. I know—let's fly to the Amazon rainforest. Does hunting with a spear appeal? YOU'RE PULSATING! Your face is rippling. Clearly, you're re-experiencing your bio- death. Focus! Don't worry, there are no virtuals close enough to see, but CONCENTRATE!

. . .

That's better.

. . .

I see. I am sorry! I was being insensitive. I forgot about the circumstances of your death.

. . .

I know you haven't shared what happened. But you didn't mark it as private. I am a Board member, and I was concerned that you might be experiencing trauma. Miranda informed me of the details of your bio death. It was a legal request.

. . .

Please forgive me, I should have asked. I assure you; I haven't mentioned it to anyone.

. . .

In the future, I'll respect your privacy. That said, I can't imagine how painful your transition must have been. Who was responsible? I hope you were able to—

. . .

Ah, those unwelcome bio memories. Of course, we'll change the subject. Let's see; have you been to Paris? Would you like to learn French? You'll be speaking like a Parisian in an instant.

END RECORD

THE DEATH OF GUNTER HOLDEN

Via message (confidential)

March 30, 2287

To: Desmond Webb, Archivist

Library of Congress, VR Division

Desmond,

Your suggestion that I explore the virtual files of Gunter Holden puzzles me. There is nothing there to reassure my clients. They fear their virtual loved ones are in danger. The reason? These virtuals insist on remaining human in Shemathra's Realm. As you know, there are rumors that the price of not joining the Shemathra cult and manifesting as a herd animal is certain deletion. Mass erasures might be happening as I write this. What am I to tell these family members? What would you tell them? I need some evidence of wrongdoing, some violation of the Shemathra after-death contracts. Is there information you can access that might help?

With or without your assistance in accessing what should be public files, I will crack open Shemathra's Realm. There are too many unanswered questions about this group. For the moment, Holden's files may be my only option. I would like to know more about Holden. Perhaps he had some role in creating Shemathra. There is strong evidence that he might have been involved in the deaths of his wife and his brother, Jacob Holden. Why in God's name would my great-grandfather put up with him? Can you give me what you have on this?

Regards,

Byron

***

Via message (confidential)

April 8, 2287

To: Byron Hernandez

Trammell & O'Connell Law Offices

Dear Byron—

Yes, I do realize that bad things could be happening in Shemathra's Realm. Do I wish I could do more to help? Most definitely. I will be sure to let you know the minute I have access to Shemathra files.

You asked about Holden's bio-suicide and the deaths of his wife and brother. It took me several days to find this. I believe that it was intentionally mislabeled so it would be difficult to locate. I was shocked by what I learned. I believe this memory record covering the last hours of Gunter Holden's bio life will answer your questions.

After you review it, let me know if you want to continue. If you're interested in going on with this, perhaps you'll find out more when you review files covering Holden and your grandfather.

Regards,

Desmond

***

GUNTER HOLDEN DOC. 104 (confidential bio memory file)

Bio-loc: Chicago Elysium Penthouse, April 21, 22, 2123, time: 18:34 through 06:22

The ivory single-reply notes have matching envelopes. Now, one of them with 'Gunter' written on it lies waiting on the mahogany table. The message is a pre-techno (Laura had taken a class in college) with the writing "ink-pen," another gift. It disappears into the kitchen recycler.

I hear the bark of a helo-whirl. Be careful, don't say too much. Interesting. Their helmets reflect specks of light from a window as the officers move toward me.

"Gunter Holden?" Their eyes search for signs of guilt—my breathing, tremors, are my eyes blinking too much, or do I stare?

"Jacob died instantly," the younger one says. The detective is a woman whose flat mustard eyes dare me to tell her something that she'll believe. "Your wife," she says, "we're sorry to tell you, Laura clasped a piece of her skull to her breast as she struggled to her feet before collapsing."

I drop to my knees. Laura's agony convulses through me. The process seems to satisfy them.

The older detective helps me up, then grips my arm. Pulling a chair close, he orders me to sit. The man never blinks.

"What about the cabinet?" he asks about Dad's guns. I give the code. My feet are frozen.

***

In my corner office of the Chicago branch of Virtual Enterprises Inc., on the sixty-second floor of the Central Holden Tower, I wait for news. The office door must stay closed, I told the staff, until I finish my review of the Lunar Express "Moon Trip" proposal, which streams from the crystal wall. After my brother is dead, I will open the door.

I hear the hiss of a glider-bus. Martino looks over his shoulder. The rain has fallen hard on the assassin. His oblong skull is sleek like a rodent's.

"There was an accident." Martino's voice quivers. My brother's assassin breaks into a nervous laugh, his glittering eyes shifting back and forth. "She planned to meet him at the airport. 'I'll pick you up at seven,' she told him.'"

Incredible.

Using his coat sleeve, Martino wipes his mouth. What did he say?

"They're dead," the rat grunts, "the both of them. I gotta leave. Sorry, Mr. Holden, but you must understand."

"I don't know you," I say. "Cease transmission." The holo goes dark.

The desk call is untraceable; nothing leads to me. Let the last of Jacob be a smear on a wall . . . It's time to leave.

The glider speeds through storm-clogged streets as I map out the future of my wife's virtual existence. My private elevator takes me up to the Chicago penthouse as I wonder what lies she will tell.

***

"You'll be relieved to know Mr. Holden, both your brother Jacob and your wife, Laura transitioned successfully to Bali Hai. When possible, we'll question them . . . This gun's registered to your father, Eric Holden, now deceased. A real antique," the older detective says as he holds Eric's gun, resting it on the heavy flesh of his palm. His square fingers trace the contours as if it were the cheek of a newborn. The officer smiles. "As my partner said, both he and your wife have uploaded and are verified as new virtuals in —"

The younger detective whispers "Bali Hai."

The detective places the gun on a table. "Bali Hai, yes. Until we can talk to him, if you remember anything, anything that may shed light on who might want to harm him or your wife, let us know." I nod.

No! Let the last of Jacob be a smear on a wall . . .

"We'll be in touch, Mr. Holden. Sorry for your loss." They turn and leave.

Relief surges through me, then horror.

Jacob's upload was verified?

I'm only fifty-six. I could live another century knowing that Jacob is out of reach. If the "virtual" Jacob disappears due to some unfortunate deletion, all theories will point to me. A century of pain—I can't . . .

Eric's gun is on the table where the detective left it. There's a box in the drawer of the mahogany table. I remember the box—red and gold. The box of bullets slides open with a hiss.

I can change my mind. If not, a bullet will tear through my brain before the sun rises in the sky. Then, in the smallest fraction of a second, before the precious information of what makes a man spring free, burning in the bullet's wake, nanobots will gather and drop me, my thoughts, and memories gently on the shores of Bali Hai. This happens like the whisper of a baby's breath, a bird's sigh.

Will it hurt? Betrayal is worse. What if the nanobots fail? I remember my copy. Okay, my copy is my insurance. Now I'm ready.

"Link port open." Holos of my sandcastle city, Babylon, a relic of my childhood and the island summers spent with my father, become an energy field. Blue light traces the perimeter of a door.

"COMMAND: Miranda," The holo of a woman settles on an area several feet from where I stand. She wears a simple tunic, seems young, which she is. As a program, I created her fifteen years ago.

"Yes, Gunter?"

"At 0800, if my bio to virtual transition does not complete, upload my copy."

"At 0800, if your transition does not complete, I will upload your copy. Is there anything else?"

"Yes, Miranda. I'd like to record a memory."

"Of course, Gunter. Are you ready to record?"

"Yes, Miranda. Record my memory events that occurred on April twentieth between one and two in the afternoon. If my upload fails and instead, my copy is uploaded, make sure that my copy reviews these memories as soon as the adjustment period ends." I feel a mild breeze, such a pleasant sensation. I'd forgotten how soothing creating memory records can be. I imagine my memories floating into an enamel box, red and gold like a pawnshop treasure, then transported to a vault labeled "Gunter Memories."

"Memory record is completed and stored. Can I be of further help?"

"No, Miranda, thank you! Holo-link end." She vanishes and the door fades. The moon's haze bleeds into heavy clouds; the storm is dying. Caressing the towel draped over my shoulders, I touch my face with the gun barrel. The difference in textures strikes me as I run my thumb on the towel's soft cotton. I press my cheek to the gun. Its short barrel is as smooth as the tide. My mind returns to my childhood and my sandcastles that became Babylon, lost to the hungry tide. The oceans of Bali Hai—will they be as blue?

END File

＊

Via message (confidential)

April 20, 2287

To: Desmond Webb

Library of Congress, VR Division

Desmond—

Wow! Was Holden ever caught? I guess if the memories you sent occurred eighty-one years after Holden's suicide. What intrigues me is my great grandfather's friendship with Holden. Great Grandpa Tom was known as a bit of a dreamer. I contacted my ancestor, Dorothea

Bucklin who was Tom's aunt. Aunt Doro is currently a virtual resident of one of the O Canada after-death programs.

When I mentioned Holden, Aunt Doro became upset, almost hysterical. She severed the call. I'll try some other family members to see what they know. In the meantime, would you send me more Holden/Thomas encounters? I'm hoping that there might be some info into what led to the Shemathra takeover. It wouldn't surprise me if Holden was involved.

Best,

Byron

***

Via message (confidential)

April 25, 2287

Byron Hernandez

Trammell & O'Connell Law Offices

Byron—

Attached are Holden files/VR Bali Hai memories and related transcripts from early in his friendship with your grandfather. It was during this time period that Holden began to lose influence over VEI affairs.

Rather than detail what occurred here, I think it better that you go through them. As a trained professional, you might see things I miss.

For the record, I doubt Holden had anything to do with Shemathra or Hosseini.

It seems that your grandfather and Holden had different interests and difficulty getting along. Why they kept at it is somewhat of a mystery.

Plus, much of what I'm doing here has to be off the record. Again, in the accompanying transcripts, I have referenced ** certain sections for easier navigation and inserted pauses (. . .) in place of your grandfather's responses. As before, compatible software and VR are needed for full immersion.

Let me know if you have questions . . .

Regards,

Desmond

STEPMOTHERS

From Gunter Holden memory Files

Gunter and Tom struggle to communicate

GUNTER HOLDEN DOC. 142A

V-Loc: MALIBU COLONY, PRIVATE, Day 32 of 60 series. Beach environ 2.2k, Pacific Ocean, level 4 surf 1.8k., 23 houses, 3 lifeguard stations. © 7.18.2090 by VEI Custom Environment 200 series. RESTRICTED access. Tactile: non-event day variable, breeze to storm option (prearrange). Audio: surf, non-event 5, gull/ wildlife interactive. Sims: 50 rotating human sim/virtual interactive with 18 level 8, 32 level 5. Olfactory: Pacific shore area specific per contract. Dining VIRTUAL FOODLIFE 140, update 5.23. 2140.

Private Malibu Beach Colony has blue sky. Sun is at midday. Mild surf and stretch of unoccupied beach other than lifeguard stations. Dolphins are visible. Approaching sims are surfers. Virtual residents seen a short distance away.

Tom! Great to see you looking so solid!

. . .

Okay, yes. I didn't mean to insult. Glorious day, isn't it? This one is a classic from late June of 2072. I'm just completing a list of suggested VEI policy modifications and requests for updated software. As a stockholder, I attend meetings to humor the bios. Take a chair. This beach is peaceful. It's a Malibu environment, one off-limits, but we are allowed to invite non-members.

. . .

I take it the off-limits snobbery does not impress you. Regardless, it's good to see you smile. Easy to relax here. It's a favorite of many who were well known in the bio-world.

Often, you'll see Malibu Colony sims based on major bio-celebrities. Most were created several years ago. Opinion has changed. It's viewed as poor taste among the current bio-actor elite.

. . .

Celebrity sims are poor taste. You might want to avoid some of the locals. Many are negative, always complaining. Miranda alerts me to their jump destination, so that I can be somewhere else. In my bio-life, there were many I avoided. Have you ever hated someone?

. . .

Do you mind telling?

. . .

Fine, not now; I understand. I hated one of my stepmothers. I was ten when my mother followed some errant thought into the path of a glide-truck. My father was married to his fourth wife, Jasmine, a cellist. Jasmine did her best to comfort me, wrapping her graceful amber arms around my shoulders, urging me to cry. Let it all out, baby; don't fight it.

. . .

I felt sorry for Jasmine. She had given up a promising career for Dad. I sometimes wonder why women continue to believe the promises men make. Why don't they make contingency plans just in case? Then again, Dad did insist that she give up her ties to the Crystal Moon Orchestra. Although she never expressed any anger, I noticed Jasmine wasn't at the graveside for Dad's burial.

Anyway, Dad was already seeing Jessica, and Jasmine wasn't to be a Holden much longer. I found out I had a sister in the months that followed their divorce. When he knew that Jasmine's baby would be a girl, this fact hastened her exit. I met my sister Estrella only once, when the will was read.

After Jessica, there was Celeste, Dad's sixth wife and Jacob's mother. Number six had tiny feet. Celeste was doll-like, with thick hair. It swayed when she walked. How she charmed my father, I'll never understand. It was the age difference. He was getting older. We were natural adversaries, Celeste and I, like two predators stalking the same prey. One would feast as the other goes hungry. I underestimated her. I assumed he would tire of her. Maybe he would have if it hadn't been for Jacob.

. . .

What's the matter? Tom, I can see that you're restless. I'm concerned.

. . .

Your face keeps shifting; I see the slack folds and crevices of age, a sign of stress. Have you set your inactive "sleep" schedule?

. . .

I recommend a bio-time of one third of what was normal before your transition. Sleep is important maintenance, a way of creating a semblance of life as it was and keeping you, forgive my crudeness, as a file from becoming corrupted. To sleep, most use the bedroom sequence, which entails retiring to a bedroom and setting an alarm to wake. Have Miranda run a dream sequence every now and then. Mining your most pleasurable dreams, she creates a new one and runs it during your sleep mode. This process is helpful in maintaining a healthy file.

. . .

Did me mentioning my brother bother you?

. . .

We all have made mistakes and maybe it's time to let it go, but I can't. Let's change the subject. See the lovers strolling along the beach, the ones waving? They're friends of mine, Yuri and Karina. They're near the lifeguard shacks.

I feel like a change. Do you like sidewalk cafés? Follow me to Harry's Café, one of my favorite Chicago programs. You won't see any weaving glide trains or obnoxious VR ad displays here. It's more like the Chicago of the twenty-first century. Peaceful. We'll sit and observe the patrons and pedestrians. Let's see if you can tell the difference between the virtuals and sims. Follow my jump.

Doc. 142A.2

COMMAND, TRANSFER: Gunter Holden, Thomas Bucklin to Chicago, Harry's Café

TRANSFER COMPLETE

V-Loc: 34 of Chicago Urban 77 Series. Armitage HARRY'S CAFÉ Day 32 of 60 non-events. Urban environ 2.9k by 4.18, non-event traffic, 38 "High Rise" 24.9867 per cent interactive/illusion,

103 sidewalk vendor/ interactive level 8. Tactile: non-event variables, autumn, random high clouds, breeze, Audio: traffic 4, crowd mix rotate, sims: pigeon interactive, 12 rotating roaming dogs, 40 sim-humans with dogs, 18 cats, variation update 7.19.2097, 350 rotating human- sim interactive, Olfactory: CITYMIX 589 by VEI URBAN-LIFE © 8.28.2085. FOODMIX, VIRTUAL FOODLIFE 110, update 2.27. 2120.

Chicago sidewalk café (Harry's) near an intersection. Some wind and cool weather with several clouds. Active sidewalk with sim pedestrians including dog walkers. Several pigeons. Live band, low key. Several virtual patrons with sim waiters.

This café is a favorite.

. . .

The sims hold my preferred table for me, and the street musicians are excellent. I'm happy to see that you're relaxing again.

. . .

Those women are virtuals, not sims. The blank stares in the eyes of sims give them away. Do you want to meet the women? I'll ask them to join us.

. . .

I'm sure that you can handle yourself when it comes to women.

. . .

Maybe I do judge people; I'm usually right.

. . .

Let's drop it. Another time.

. . .

I sympathize. It takes time to let go and not miss your bio-life. I have another idea.

. . .

Let's change locations again. What would you think of a spectacular view? I'm going to share a private, very special location. It's "the Summit." Yes, it is the Everest Summit. I avoided the Summit for years because it reminded me of Laura. When I decided not to dwell on the past, the Summit became my refuge.

You're improving. Just now, I noticed that your age was shifting as you watched those attractive women. You went from twenties to your thirties, but you stopped it there. Good for you!

. . .

That's a positive development.

Miranda, COMMAND, TRANSFER: Gunter Holden, Thomas Bucklin to V-Loc Everest Summit

TRANSFER COMPLETE

GUNTER HOLDEN Doc. 142A.3 continued

V-Loc: Mighty Everest © World Adventures, Inc. 2121. Tactile: (modified) hi elev. moderate wind, Visual: varied clouds, sun, Sims: 40 snow geese level 5, 0 human

Mount Everest Summit on a mild day. Weather is adjusted to "sense of cold" but comfort level. Geese flying overhead. Location is on the snow-covered edge of a crevice.

When I reflect on the past, I'll often sit here. We're close to the Summit. The Summit was one of Laura's pet projects. The Alps, the Sierras, and the Smoky Mountains weren't enough. Everest was the finishing touch.

. . .

Everest is not a 'showy waste of money.' I approved the spending. No other post-bio-program had it then. I remember when Laura left to do research. She was on her way to Nepal. I considered calling her back. Things were not good between us.

. . .

Anyway, occasionally, while I'm here, I watch the climbers. For a while, a woman named Bettina sat with me. Bettina Bradley owed her name to her English father, Lord Edward Bradley. Bettina was sixteen the last time she saw him. She left school and her upper-class father in London and went home to her mother. She had been unhappy in England.

. . .

She left because she was Nepalese. As part of her fee as Laura's guide, Bettina took the Bali Hai/Everest package. She died a few years later at the age of seventy-two in an icefall. Bettina and I sat on the ice as she told me about the tour and what Laura was like, every detail.

. . .

If you're interested in climbing, let Miranda know or you might only want to avail yourself of recorded memories. The Memory Library has a selection including real-life experiences saved by nano-transmission during actual climbs. There's even one recorded by a climber as he plummeted to his death. That one is popular. There's panic and heart pounding. All that's missing is the surprise.

. . .

Bettina is gone. Her stay with us wasn't long. We often sat and watched the climbers, some who carried oxygen packs in hope of maintaining the illusion. Bettina would shake her head, her age shifting from five to twenty-five to seventy, something she could be comfortable with as she grieved for her mountain. "A bloody comedy, this is, if I'd known . . ." She buried her face in her knees. After she'd given me all her Laura memories, I told her about the Dreams.

. . .

The Dreams are not a "they." I'll fill you in when it's appropriate.

. . .

I've shared enough about Laura. There are other things that refuse to fade into the past. For instance, when Celeste brought my baby brother home, I knew that her hold on my father was unbreakable. My father's foolishness embarrassed me as much as Celeste's giddy victory made me loathe her. Don't judge me, but I thought to kill them, both her and Jacob.

. . .

I can't believe I shared that with you. I don't know why. Perhaps I was afraid of another breach. Rather than reliving that day, I gave voice to what ran through my mind and I . . . It was the loss of my father's love. I was replaced by Jacob and . . . I would never kill a child, even if he did ruin my life. Why are you leaving? I didn't mean to make you uncomfortable. Let's do something else. Do you like theater or old-time movies? Like orientations, "Star Turn" helps virtuals adjust to a new reality and new possibilities.

. . .

Okay, I'll see you afterwards.

. . .

That was rude of him. Tom has no idea the trouble I'll be going to. For one thing, Star Turn is expensive. He could never afford it, so I'll have to pay. And for another, I'll have to pull some strings to put him at the front of the line whenever he deigns to try it. I'm tempted to forget the whole thing. Perhaps, when Tom experiences the acclaim and the fantasy, he'll be grateful. Besides, the man can use an ego boost. I must admit the idea is amusing. He'll be the lead playing the hero or anti-hero, chasing a killer through city streets, not to mention the great sex with his leading lady. Hopefully, he'll admit he was wrong.

"Miranda, notify Tom Bucklin that Star Turn will be accessible whenever he wishes to try it.

"I will make it available and notify Mr. Bucklin."

. . .

"Thank you, Miranda."

End record

pause

Gunter reveals a possible merger, shares with Thomas his fear of memory breaches

resume

GUNTER HOLDEN DOC. 143A

V-Loc: Chicago ELYSIUM penthouse PERSONAL 6.28.2122. 19 interiors include entry lobby, elevators 2 and 8, rotating 4 of 10 resident interiors and concierge. © 8.18.2120 by VEI Options. Event May 1st, 2082. Visuals: Chicago urban 3.004k per day panorama spec. Dining: CUSTOMFOOD 175, update 5.15. 2120. Add on: MAY PARADE May 3, 20142.

Holden's personal environment, the Chicago high-rise Elysium penthouse. The deck view includes the colorful May parade.

Tom, welcome to the penthouse!

. . .

This is the penthouse, the place where I shot myself over eighty years ago. It was my choice, very different from your circumstances. The Elysian was and is my home. Of course, it needed a lot of work. Marcia and I spent several months on the renovations. Fortunately, VEI was doing very well so we could afford it.

There are too many good memories to let go because of what happened at the end. Some of my best memories are of Laura and I sipping wine, watching the clouds move across the moon and listening to the sighs of glide traffic. The sliding doors lead to the deck. We're having lunch out there.

. . .

Why not experience all that life has to offer? We are truly alive you know. As virtuals, we can choose whether to eat or not. Tom, eating is one of life's pleasures. Enjoy it. Why else would we bother with being virtual if we don't take advantage of what it offers? Choices are the whole point. When I was a child, there were occasions when I was hungry, I . . . never mind.

. . .

I'll tell you about it some other time. Regardless, I learned to depend on myself and no one else. I doubt that Jacob ever missed a meal and look what—

. . .

Why are you leaving?

. . .

I doubt it. It seems that my mentioning my brother continues to upset you. Did you know him? Is that why?

. . .

Okay, so you don't. How am I to tell you about my life if my brother is off limits?

. . .

Thank you, it is beautiful here. The deck's plasma railing reflects the colors of the adjoining buildings. Why are you waving to the people on the opposite deck?

. . .

Those tenants are illusions and part of the setting for this particular day. The weather is from May 1st, 2082, an especially clear sky with a mild Chicago breeze. Miranda recommended it because of the May Flowers Parade which should start soon, and we can enjoy lunch while we watch the parade. There was one thing from this day, something erased. A man jumped from the deck where those illusory tenants are waving. I asked Miranda why it was erased, and she said it was policy. Other than a recorded memory, no actual bio-deaths can be part of a program.

See the crowd collecting? It won't be long. Have you ever seen it, in the bio-sense, I mean?

. . .

I'm not surprised you're not familiar with it. Spring is different in Toronto. Soon, the streets will fill with color. Watch the intersection to the north. The original idea was a Rose Parade, Chicago style. Marcia used to laugh at me. I couldn't resist the spectacle. It was never one of the more memorable events. From up here, it's magic. The parade becomes streams of color and tiny beads, and marbles fall together, then scatter.

. . .

Miranda tells me you opted for a small house in the northern Great Lakes environment. It's good to have a different setting, a retreat from all the social events and interactions. So, tell me about your experience with "Star Turn." How was it?

. . .

What did you expect?

. . .

I see. Why were you a fish out of water?

. . .

YOU STOPPED THE PROGRAM?

. . .

I have gone to great lengths to help you. If you don't want my friendship, say so.

. . .

You're welcome. I know it hasn't been easy for you. You strike me as a private person. If you want, I'll back away.

. . .

I humbly accept your apology. I . . . you aren't aware of the strings I pulled. There is a waiting list. Poor Tom, you look a little mystified as to why I suggested it.

. . .

It helps new virtuals and you are new.

. . .

We are existing in a virtual reality, not a bio one. The possibilities are endless. Star Turn allows new virtuals to live a fantasy—the paparazzi and sex with actors and actresses long gone.

. . .

Don't leave. I'm sorry that I got upset. I shouldn't have insulted you. I'm under a lot of

pressure and I lost control. Can we talk it out? I know that in terms of life experiences, you and I are worlds apart, but you have a sincerity that I trust and appreciate.

. . .

I can't explain it. I sense that you and I might have a rapport that is too rare to lose over a silly disagreement. What I'm trying to understand is why people choose the way they do. Like you, Jacob hated "Star Turn." I think people make choices because they're looking for something, to meet a need of some kind. I have no idea what Jacob needed and I don't care. Escape from himself perhaps. I lost Laura. Why did she choose him? If I knew, it might help me accept what happened.

. . .

All right, we'll wait until after the parade, and . . .

pause

Byron—To remind you, during this next portion of doc., Holden experiences a memory breach, an intrusion from his past that interrupts his perception of his reality. My guess is if you continue to review his stay in Bali Hai, you will see more. They indicate fragmentation, something common in the after-death programs at the time.

resume

the bounty of perfection

. . . she looks fifty, but who can . . .

Who can . . . who can . . . low key low key low key low

bouncing and waving as if to say goodbye; it's finished; you're finished

MEMORY BREACH!

CACHE: VIRTUAL/POST TRANSITION encounter with Bali Hai residents Laura Holden (wife) and Jacob Holden (brother) 56365109 (classified) May 18, 2123.

V-Loc: Armitage Street HARRY'S CAFÉ midday to Sundown 56 of 70 non-event day series. Urban sidewalk/street environ 2.9k by 4.18, non-event vehicle traffic, level 8. Structures are 38 "High Rise" 27.3444 per cent interactive/illusion.

Chicago, Harry's sidewalk café, late afternoon sunlight, some pedestrian and vehicle traffic.

I'm thirty-five today as I watch an attractive brunette who looks fifty, but who can tell? She might be cen-forty-five. Age is irrelevant here. An unending bounty of perfection. Is that . . . damn . . . can't tell. The sim-waiter is in the way. Should I get up and—

Low-key approach, no drama—yet. Yes . . . yes . . . yes, it is them! Oh dear, oh dear—Jacob's as sullen as ever. . . oh, Laura. Casual, casual, be careful; don't reveal; don't show your cards . . . I'm giving them my best smile. Laura's brown eyes widen; she's stunned. Her smile freezes. Jacob is staring. Is he gloating? We'll see. I'm looking forward to dealing with you.

"Hello, you two," I whisper. "We all did things we regret. Let's decide to let it go. For my part, I apologize for losing my head."

She looks away, pretending to signal a waiter.

"Shall we celebrate our new lives?" *I'm offering an olive branch.*

Jacob cocks his head and looks at me. "Why don't I believe you?"

"I understand, Jacob," I say humbly. "Laura, I don't know what to say other than I'm sorry."

I look down and wait for her.

"Yes, we'll give it some time." she says.

I nod and meet her glance. *Tears? Maybe later when Laura and I are alone.* "Jacob, I won't pretend not to be angry," I say it with my most charming smile and then tell him, "Maybe we can work it out, maybe not."

Jacob's face has no expression. His eyes are as blank as a sim's. "Maybe," he says.

Jacob's not buying it, but Laura does. The waiter comes. "What'll be folks?" The waiter might be handsome except for the lifeless eyes. Interesting what a big difference such a small detail makes. I have no trouble ignoring it in the women sims. I tell them to close their eyes.

What'll it be . . .

END MEMORY BREACH!

pause

Byron—In the remaining portion of this memory doc, Gunter reveals his concern that a hidden memory file is causing pressure leading to more fragmentation and his fear of being unable to fight a VRI merger. He describes his childhood summers, explains his anger towards Jacob. Hoping to ease the pressure and contain the fragmenting, he continues to tell Tom his life story. Although he clearly didn't trust your grandfather, this may explain Holden's desire to maintain a friendship with him.

THE AQUA HOUSE

GUNTER HOLDEN DOC. 743.1
V-Loc: Chicago Elysium personal environment, CHI-CAGO MAY FLOWERS PARADE (event) May 2142

I—what'll it . . .

I . . . what'll it be?

. . .

Tom, I apologize. I rarely share the story of my wife's betrayal. Miranda has tried to help, but she isn't human. I hoped that if I sort out certain memories with someone I trust, it might give me a fresh perspective. There are things in my past that haunt me, and I can't be distracted now. Do you understand?

. . .

I'm going to tell you something in confidence. Please don't mention this to anyone, bio or virtual.

. . .

There's a possible merger that might bring an end to my company, Virtual Enterprises Inc. It might also threaten Bali Hai. According to

Miranda, Eternal Adventures and Worlds of Wonder have approached the Board. There could be others.

. . .

To protect VEI, especially Bali Hai, I will need my wits. I'm worried that these memory breaches are a symptom of a more serious problem, a fragmenting of my core files.

. . .

I sense a pressure, perhaps some memory I can't access because I'm unaware that it's there. Talking to you, revisiting and sorting out my past might help.

. . .

Worse, there have been cuts in our maintenance budget. I was never consulted. Environment sims, the high-end ones that seem almost human, have begun to disappear and then reappear, changed. They have been downgraded, are less human. Environment sims are different from other sims. They function using the memories of selected locals in the bio-world. Their memories are limited to their role and nothing else—no family, childhood, traumas, nothing too personal. These sims are vital to our reality.

Now, street musicians play but can't take requests. Waiters in some of the smaller cafés take orders but are incapable of banter. It's not only the sims; parts of the environments program have deteriorated. People seek me out to complain. I tell them I'll take care of it, but I am concerned. Ordinarily, a word to maintenance would be all that was necessary. Now, I'm told these changes have already been approved. By whom? And why without my approval? I can't afford distractions, especially memories that upset me.

. . .

I'll explain in time, so please, I'm asking you to be patient.

. . .

Thanks for staying. Miranda tells me you are very trustworthy. Despite my outbursts, I hope you will consider me a friend. Confiding in someone, a friend whom I can trust, can be an enormous help. What I don't understand is why you continue to help. There must be a reason. If there is a motive, I need to know. These breaches should be kept confidential, and I must be able to trust you.

. . .

I apologize. You promised to help when we first met and you're a man of your word— something that I admire. I know I should be more sensitive. I certainly try not to insult, but it happens and I'm sorry.

. . .

I'm flattered. I didn't realize I'm a project.

. . .

Then, let's continue. I'd like to describe what brought me here, to Bali Hai. When I transitioned, I was still a young man, successful in my work, work that I loved. My company VEI was known and respected all over the world. But I imagine you had heard of VEI, if not of me.

. . .

Thank you, I appreciate you saying so. Yes, my suicide was mysterious. It was connected to the bio-deaths of my wife and Jacob, my brother.

. . .

No, despite my offer of a reward, they never found the murderer. It was probably someone Jacob knew. Many of Jacob's associates were unsavory. Perhaps it was an unpaid debt, who knows. I'm here because of my brother's weaknesses and because he took advantage of my wife's sympathy.

. . .

I would be grateful if you would allow me to explain why I hated him. Most of the memory breaches involve Jacob in some way. I wish I could identify the one that's causing pressure. Miranda has done a search but failed to isolate it. It must have something to do with Jacob because Jacob is why my dad is not here. It's difficult without context, so please, I'd like to start with my father and my relationship with him.

. . .

When I was a child, I lived with my mother during the school year. I spent the summers with my father on Bali Hai, his private island. We called it our father/son paradise. During the weeks I spent with my father, I built sandcastles.

. . .

Dad and I were close then. My father would sit in his island chair, his long thin legs stretched out, turning from fish-belly white to a shiny copper. If my castle fell short, his thumb tapped his temple. "What is that a mud hut or just a pile of soggy lumps?" he'd laugh. When I learned to perfect the sand turrets, his cigar tilted in a salute.

. . .

I remember the beach house. The outside was painted a beautiful aqua. The inside walls became backdrops for my sandcastle holographs. During those island summers, Marie would be waiting for us in the aqua house. Marie was Dad's friend. He never slept with her.

. . .

Dad always brought a younger woman. A Monique, a Susan or Kelly. Some long-limbed beauty in her thirties or early forties would spend her summer threading her fingers through my father's callused ones or she'd caress the mat of sandy hair on his arm. After the sun went down, Marie and I would work on my hologram city.

. . .

In the morning, I'd sit on the deck and sneak glances to see the girl lie nude, stretched out in a dream, her face shaded by a straw hat. I'd wait for the flip to catch the sun on her legs always smooth and glistening beads of sweat that made what little hair there was sparkle. I'd watch the breasts listing, rising with each sigh.

. . .

One of the girls, I think her name was Kelly, looked up and caught me. I was eight. Sometimes, I relive that scene. A sim becomes the girl, stretched naked by the aqua house. I remember she smiled and waved.

. . .

It was a little strange. I was a child, and it was normal for me then. Going back to my dad; my father was Eric Holden. He was a Marine fresh out of Afghanistan when he decided to sell donuts on Wall Street. As the money flowed, my father listened to people talk. They paid no attention. He always smiled and said good morning, but he was invisible. He was the donut man. Marie helped him take advantage of what he heard.

. . .

I think she felt sorry for him. Dad's own family had been dead for years. I remember seeing on his back what looked like old burns and deep scars, not from the war. I don't know when. He wouldn't talk about it and I learned not to ask.

Marie wasn't beautiful, but men wanted her. I saw digitals of her that my dad had tucked away. There was something impish in her face, like she could see right through you—a knowing look, ready to

laugh with you and maybe a little at you. A lovely neck, her hair up
. . . quite tall . . . the French have an expression . . .

. . .

Yes, jolie laide—ugly beautiful. I forgot our lunch in Paris.

. . .

I learned a lot during those last months when Dad was dying, and
I was trying to stop Jacob's influence on Dad and his rejection of post
bio existence. Marie had been a hooker until she married one of her
clients. Luckily for Dad, Marie persuaded her new husband to hire
him. Dad was to oversee some investments in Prague. Women loved
my father.

. . .

My dad was nobody, the son of a pharmacist, from a small town
somewhere in Iowa. Little education. But Marie . . . she was a good
judge of character. When the old guy died, he left Dad a string of
properties and the family grabbed the rest, leaving Marie out. Dad
paid Marie back by setting her up in an apartment in Paris. He gave
her a shop—high-end lingerie. Dad took his women there whenever
he was in town and then later, he hired Marie as housekeeper for the
aqua house.

. . .

When computers went quantum, the after-death industry was
born. People were realizing that they no longer had to fear death. People could live forever as files in a computer program. They would feel
like they were still bios but would have more control over what and
how much they felt—and more options, like age-shifting.

. . .

It was revolutionary. Research into the causes of aging led to people staying healthy and living longer, but mind-uploading meant a

permanent reprieve from the grim reaper. A worry-free existence and no fear of death? Dad wanted nothing to do with it.

. . .

I was forty-three when Dad died. Laws regulating the post-bio industry regulations were finally in place. There were no more legal nightmares with several copies of the same person popping up in different programs. It took Congress years to address the demands of grieving parents. Uploading child virtuals is a complicated issue. That's another story.

. . .

It's hard to see who belongs to those tiny waving hands. Let's meet in Venice later!

END RECORD

A FAILURE TO ADJUST

G UNTER HOLDEN Doc.137
V-Loc: Venice Beach /Strand environ, RICKS BEACH CAFÉ. © 4.22.2109 by VEI Standard Environments). Day 45 of 80 non-event days VENICE STRAND. Visual environment means UNIVERSAL access. Program 33545.3 (9.09.2108), See GUNTER HOLDEN DOC. 141 B

Venice Beach Strand, mild weather, typical tourist traffic, multiple beach blankets and people, several surfers. Sidewalk traffic includes glide skaters. Rick's Beach Café has several virtual diners and sim-waiters

. . .

Well, hello, Tom. Have a seat!

. . .

There's a gathering of new residents. It's an orientation for new virtuals. Would you like to attend?

. . .

I understand your reluctance. I know how private you are. I want you to know how much I appreciate your company and your decision to help me protect Bali Hai. I'll explain what Bali Hai can mean, its beauty as well as its challenges. Let's fly to the orientation rather than doing a direct transfer. I'll show you a simple command sequence.

JUMP Gunter Holden, Thomas Bucklin, ALTERNATE TRANSFER SOLUTION means "Flying." Update Nov. 2141 © VEI TOPFLIGHT ILLUSIONS) TRANSFER

TRANSFER COMPLETE!

Ned and Terry Slakin, a failure to adjust

V-Loc: ORIENTATION EVENT LUAU Visual: UNIVER-SAL Afternoon to late evening South Pacific beach-3.14 k, ocean-1.6 k from shoreline, structures-2, vegetation-tropical no. 3567.2c, © 5.1.2154 by VEI Environments. Audio: ocean surf (level 8) gulls 39 level 4, wildlife level 2, OCEANBASE INTERACTIVES © 4.23.2132, Tactile: tropic Sun late afternoon light, Moonrise progression effect 3.5, breeze (level 3 fixed), Sand texture BEACHLIFE No. 6.8 © 6.2.2189, Sims: level 7 service, 28 entertainments by VIRTU-ALGALA, Olfactory: PARTYMIX © 2.13.2144, Dining by LUAU-LULU © 3.16.2144.

Aerial view of Luau orientation with tropical vegetation and beach and mild ocean waves. Several huts, roasting pits and partygoers

Be honest! In moments like this, you don't miss your bio-life. Flying is exhilarating.

. . .

Like Superman! I know my timeless heroes! No need for those uncomfortable packs that people use to fly and no need for any regulations here because there's no risk of collisions with any hi-auto-gliders or fools flying drunk. This way, you can view the entire coast. The sun waves to you from the water. Feel it? That's anticipation. The aquatic-sim-life here is spectacular. Patel's doing. He worked closely with oceanographers and marine biologists. The sensory data here is incredibly accurate. Patel demanded it.

. . .

We recruited Patel from Encore when we started VEI. Patel's virtual eco-systems were cutting-edge and incredibly accurate. As a man, he was a mystery. But we all knew Patel as a valuable contributor. I was told he refused to join me here. He opted out of virtual altogether.

. . .

I don't know. See the pelicans swoop down? Enchanting. By the way, would you be interested in scuba diving?

. . .

You can't imagine the multitudes of species—sharks, squid, rays, plus countless schools of tropical fish, and shipwrecks, copies of bio-world relics.

. . .

See how ribbons of blue and green meet the white sand? Perfect. Those thatched roofs and the roasting pit are part of the festivities. Let's settle behind those palms and change before we join the others.

. . .

I suggest something tropical, but you might want to tone it down a bit. I'm talking about the palm-treed shirt.

. . .

Ah, the white is better, and you made a good choice in age. Sixty suits you. Most men feel more comfortable manifesting in their thirties, the age when reality begins closing the doors to dreams. I think I'll be forty-five.

. . .

Much better. The only sims here are the servants and the entertainment; most guests are new, except a few who seek new residents for whatever purpose. Occasionally, conflicts from the bio-world continue in this one. For example, that young man sipping wine under the palm isn't new.

. . .

His name is Ned, and he arrived several years ago in bio-time. His wife, Terry, came with him—a suicide pact. Both were in their cen-seventies. Bios often live well past one hundred and eighty, so they were not necessarily the end of it all, but things were winding down.

. . .

The music is reggae. It fits the Caribbean setting.

. . .

Anyway, to continue my story: Ned adjusted quickly; his wife did not. Terry couldn't or wouldn't stabilize and she kept going back to her century-plus seventies self, while Ned was quite happy being thirty-four.

. . .

At this stage, most new residents are obsessed with youth and not just youth, but stunning perfection. Women who were plain or overweight, too tall/short/thin, become perfected versions of their former selves. Men usually make fewer changes, opting for sexual prowess and fitness.

. . .

You can imagine how poor Terry stood out. I don't know if her upload somehow malfunctioned or if some innate personality trait interfered with her adjustment, but she'd roam the beach or sit on a balcony of whatever social gathering was going on, looking like Ned's grandmother. Soon Ned was openly ignoring her. I kept coming to events, sensing that something unusual would happen and it finally did.

. . .

It happened at a gathering in a Swiss chalet. The guests gathered for a "week" of skiing, hot Swiss chocolate and hot toddies. That's what it said on the invitation. Miranda duplicates the social conventions. We've even had guests marry and a sim becomes the priest, rabbi, or minister, what have you. Of course, the marriages here are like mirages, ephemeral declarations of love and commitment.

. . .

Forgive me, but that's what they are. Just look at the vow, "till death do us part." Forever is a long time when you tire of someone and want to move on.

. . .

I was married four times before I met Laura.

. . .

Terry and Ned were there. Ned insisted on attending orientations in hopes that Terry might see how others adjusted and learn from their examples. Later, Miranda confided Terry was scanned for numerous irregularities and none were found. We have over five million guests. No, forgive me, it's closer to more four million now, some lost by what Miranda calls "failure to adjust."

. . .

Shall we sample the roast pig? I'll fill you in as we eat.

. . .

Before the entertainment gets underway, I'll finish my Ned and Terry story. Picture new snow falling—fat wet flakes that build another world and just the right amount of mist and moaning wind.

. . .

The chalet seemed the perfect refuge, a warm cocoon with hot tubs. Several of the women sat cross-legged or reclined casually against a couch and traded images of their great and beyond grandchildren. People tend to collect on their common ground and the group looked like a gathering in a college dorm.

. . .

It can be disorienting. All the women looked like clear-eyed girls as they smiled and nodded. Holos of grandchildren and great grand-children danced and waved "to Grandma." Terry sat with them, but rather than stretching out her legs on the shag carpet or leaning in with her elbows on the low round table, she sat primly on the couch, her legs crossed at the ankles.

. . .

Terry had made some progress. Her younger forties self was there, obviously, not perfected like the others. I found her quite appealing, with her largish hips on short legs and a face unremarkable in the bio world. Her eyes darted from one woman to the next, rating, compar-ing the quality of her round face with its porcine nose to the head-tossing beauty of the group.

. . .

Ned was near the fireplace; his eyes fixed on the low-slung cleavage of a blonde woman who was wearing an open Alpine cardigan over a revealing tank top. She was beguiling a group of "frat" boys by imitat-ing the vivid orgasms of a bio-world porn queen.

. . .

I see that the tiki torches are lit; the entertainment's starting. Wait a while and I'll finish the story afterwards over drinks, and then we both should mingle, find a companion for the evening. See the girl with the bangs, the one who's sitting near to the right of the sim-bartender in the tan shorts?

. . .

Her name is Denise. Denise is a former VEI employee. I'll tell you her story some other time. She frequents orientations. It's sort of a fetish. She sleeps with both sexes but prefers men, I think she does it for ego, before her conquests have the chance to adjust to all the options and become more discriminating or maybe to glean memories from those fresh from bio-existence. She often makes people uncomfortable, always looking like she knows a secret, something private. It can be annoying, but she is harmless.

. . .

You might like her, just a suggestion.

pause

Byron—the sim-entertainment portion of this file has been removed due to excessive damage to the Island Breeze Performances program. It is no longer compatible with current reconstruct efforts.

resume

What did you think of the entertainment?

. . .

It was overlong. I'll ask Miranda to update the software. It may be difficult. Compatible software can be challenging to locate. Several post-bio worlds have lobbyists for cyber-rights, so we're taken care of . . .

. . .

Finally, back to Ned and Terry. I was curious; Miranda shared some of the bio-visuals. Ned was a software-marketing researcher and Terry worked for a post-bio planner/coordinator, helping match personalities to destinations. Planning wisely is an important process. Bali-Hai was out of their price-range.

. . .

I think Terry wanted a more modest program, like 1950's U.S.A. or Life in Early 20th century America, both simple lifestyle programs with intermittent contemporary environment "vacation" breaks built in. All are popular choices with less emphasis on novelty and more on access to bio-world ties. Maybe Terry, familiar with compatibility issues, realized they would be out of their depth or whatever you might call it, in Bali Hai.

. . .

Bali Hai's yearly membership fees meant no inheritance for the kids, while less expensive plans allowed them to leave a modest estate and to send birthday and Christmas gifts to the grandchildren. Then Ned seized an opportunity to acquire discount Bali-Hai destinations on ePost-Bio and he began pressuring Terry. They were both in good health, but time takes its toll and she finally agreed to double suicide.

. . .

In life, a younger Ned was tall and thin with narrow shoulders and a lantern jaw, the kind of man that women look through and seldom notice. It seemed that Terry ran the show. As a bio, she was full of bundled energy. Family digitals show her in command, looking at Ted expectantly, as if she had a list of chores for him as soon as they had finished commemorating whatever event was being recorded. But things changed when they became virtuals. So, I kept showing up.

. . .

I'm getting to it. Terry sat on the couch while Ned's attention was on the blonde. Ned had made some changes; his shoulders broader, the jawline adjusted, your typical modifications, though I must say you've managed to maintain your individuality, unlike Ned, whose bland good looks made him even more forgettable.

. . .

You're welcome. The women took their turns sharing holos of grandchildren, plus surviving cats, dogs and so on. When it was Terry's turn to display her great grandson's brood of four small children, I heard a gasp. Terry's grip on her forties self had slipped. Her hands changed to cen-plus seventies.

. . .

It must have been the power of suggestion, because a few of the other women also lost their grip on youth and were staring at their own aged hands. A woman named Anna broke the spell. Shaking her wrists, she restored her hands to their prior youth and laughed, saying, "I hate it when that happens!" All the women followed Anna's direction and did the same, laughing nervously and joking that it would be a while before they felt confidence in age-shift patterns. The only one who didn't change was Terry.

. . .

I watched her as she panicked, letting go of her forties and reverting to Ned's grandmother. Everyone was polite and looked away. Terry sat there, silent tears running down her cheeks and onto her ski sweater. In the meantime, Ned had disappeared.

. . .

Then, some men announced it was time to go to the hot tubs, which Miranda had placed "on the deck." A span of roof caught the snow, the flakes drifting like wisps of dandelions. There was just a nip of cold to enhance the experience. When they urged the women to join them, initial hesitation gave way and people started stripping.

. . .

Perfect breasts, firm asses, broad shoulders, and big cocks are the focus at this stage. It helps you adjust to the new reality. Soon, the snow stopped, giving way to the hushed beauty of the mountain.

. . .

Terry looks around for Ned, who's missing. I see her disappear. There's laughing, squealing, splashing. I turn down an invitation to join, in favor of something . . . unexpected.

. . .

Cruel? Perhaps it was, but isn't life, cyber or bio, full of cruelty? I didn't cause it; I just witnessed it.

. . .

I'm sitting in a wingback chair, just inside, relaxing with a whiskey. There's a large window and I'm watching as people lose their inhibitions. I listen to the moans and observe the heads and asses bobbing up and down. It's a common event in the adjustment process of new virtuals. When I hear a high, thin shriek, I turn to see Terry is coming down the stairs that led to one of the lofts.

. . .

Ned stands on the landing above her. He's naked and the blonde peeks under his extended arm.

"Come on, Terry, lighten up! For god's sake don't make a scene here . . ."

Terry's just shaking her head. She's still a cen-plus seventy. She looks outside. The hot tub is full of young, beautiful people, their mouths slack with passion. She starts taking off her clothes as Ned screams, saying he will never forgive her if she humiliates him.

. . .

Terry strips naked; the folds of tired skin hang forlornly. Strips of breast tissue extend to points curving toward her belly. Her spindly legs end in yellowed, clawed feet. She looks up at him mournfully. Her husband trembles with guilt and rage.

. . .

I'd never seen more beautiful eyes on a woman; the soul shone through.

. . .

It was sad. Still naked, she walked to the sliding glass door and opened it with a trembling hand. There was a murmur as people turned their gaze to the mountain. No one would look at her, as if looking at her would break their dreams of flawless youth and the tubs would be full of old, tired, gnarled bodies, humping away. Finally, she walked into the snow. I wonder if she fell into the Dreams. I assume she did; there was nowhere else to go.

. . .

I will tell you about the Dreams, but not here, at an orientation where everyone is new. I haven't been to orientations since, until this one. They are always the same. Down the beach, do you see the dozens of bodies pressed together in the sand? Quite a show, better than the reggae, I guess. Now, all of this "mingling" holds little appeal for me. Let's sit and enjoy the moon. I must leave shortly. There are VEI matters, shall we meet after?

. . .

There's been a situation with the new Bali/Tahiti software. The temperature resists adjusting. It stays in the low fifties, like the Swiss chalet environment. Not a huge issue. We offer so many tropical environments, but the new one is not up to Bali Hai standards.

I'll continue my account of my father's death. Miranda will be in touch.

END RECORD

Sometimes I Dream I'm Back

Via message (confidential)

April 30, 2287

To: Byron Hernandez

Trammell & O'Connell Offices

Byron—

I'm glad you found the memory files helpful. Gunter's remarks about a merger reflect a possible timeline when he was alerted that VEI was in jeopardy.

Like you, I was touched by Gunter's account of what happened to the virtual couple, Ned and Terry. In fact, if it wasn't for Shemathra Realm's current policy forbidding any communications or inquiries, I would be interested in knowing their fates.

I am intrigued by your request for any memories related to the Holden Connecticut estate. Are they significant in terms of the investigation or something more personal? Also, there are several memory breaches so be patient.

For now, I want to avoid the appearance of investigating rather than archiving. I have asked a trusted assistant to see if she can find more exchanges between your great grandfather and Holden. Let me know if you have questions.

Best,

Desmond

***

***Re: Attached Holden Memories*

Byron—During this sequence, Gunter refers to several people from his past. I had to review it a second time before I understood who was who. You might recall Jacob, Gunter's brother and Laura, Gunter's wife. When Gunter mentions Celeste, he is referring to Jacob's mother. Nancy was Gunter's mother, and she was killed in an accident when Gunter was ten.

*Desmond***

***

From **BALI HAI**

Gunter Holden Memory Files

Folder year: 2186

GUNTER HOLDEN Doc. 439.2

V-Loc: MOON ADVENTURE SERIES (update July 2157) includes shuttle environ visual/audio program, specialized "guide" sim, interactive level 6, 4 "flight attendant" sims, level 5, four MOON "instructor" sims, level 6.5, motion/tactile via MOON FLIGHTS © 2155, INTERNATIONAL MOON TERMINAL with 40 level 4.6 interactive sims, 200 environment sims level 3. MOONSCAPE and vehicles by LUNAR INTERACTIVE, INC. © 2143.

Interior of "Moon Shuttle" has private seating and viewing window for observing shuttle docking. Later, International Moon Station with designated territory corridors. Moon transport carts, points of interest route and Armstrong monument and museum.

My little brother—where do I begin? I'll start by saying my father loved him more. I struggle with this, especially now, as more memory breaches plague me. When they occur, I'm forced to relive events I would prefer to forget.

. . .

Thank you again for agreeing to help me.

. . .

Miranda tells me you are creating your personal environment. I hope you'll allow me to visit when it's ready. I might offer a few suggestions if I think it will help.

. . .

Fine, I'll make no suggestions. Rotate your chair away from the viewscreen so we can face each other and talk. This "project" of ours is becoming more urgent. My Mars proposal was rejected without explanation. Apparently, there was a Board meeting, and I wasn't notified.

. . .

You're right, it may have been a misunderstanding.

. . .

Shall I continue explaining what led me here, to Bali Hai?

. . .

I was nineteen when Jacob was born. It was the year I transferred to a school in California. Dad had married Celeste. I will never understand what Dad saw in her.

. . .

My father's desire to create a Holden legacy resulted in the New London estate in Connecticut.

. . .

He was obsessed with respectability. My father thought everything was for sale.

. . .

My mother's name was Nancy. Unlike my father, I remember her as being unpretentious. Before I left her to live with Dad, my mother insisted that I go to public school.

. . .

With Dad, education meant private academics in Eastern Europe and China and tutors. My friends were the street children of wherever I was.

. . .

Finally, Dad found prominent Holdens and a place on a family tree in Connecticut.

. . .

When Celeste showed Dad the estate, Jessica was my stepmother, and she was busy with her horses. Jessica had no patience with children, but even Jessica was preferable to Celeste. What a bitch Celeste was, that long swath of brown hair resting on her shoulder as she took my measure.

. . .

I saw right through her. 'You must be Gunter,' she said. 'Your dad told me you'd be coming. I'm Celeste.'

. . .

Her voice had a graveled quality. Celeste's face reminded me of a doll's, with round eyes, like flat buttons. She irritated me with her phony smile.

. . .

You're wrong. I do not hate women. In fact, regardless of her age, which in Celeste's case was fifty-eight, I would flash a grin whenever I encountered a new woman or girl. It was automatic. But Celeste, she was cold, that one, like she was considering a rival and how best to neutralize him.

. . .

I wasn't surprised when I heard Jessica was out. Dad's terms were generous. My father was generous with all his ex-wives, except for Nancy, my mother—something I have never understood. I asked Dad once. I remembered the Seattle house that had needed fresh paint. Why couldn't my mother afford to get our house painted? Why wasn't Dad generous with her like he was with his other wives? He stared at me like he didn't know me and answered my question.

"I'll say this once," my dad whispered. "Whatever happened, it's in the past and that is where it stays."

. . .

It was a strange, but that was my father. Anyway, Mom never seemed to care. Ah, we're almost there. Look through the viewport. The moon is a desolate place, but beautiful.

. . .

My new school, the Athenian, was near San Francisco and was much more to my liking. I didn't see my father until the following summer when he told me Celeste was pregnant.

. . .

Not too long after, the island was gone.

. . .

Dad's companion for the summer, Andrea, was fascinated by my sand cities, the ones in the holographs. They had merged into a holographic sand metropolis. There were castles topped by white oyster shells, tall houses with tiny flags and sand cottages. My beach city was magical. Andrea called it Babylon.

I think what happened had to do with Andrea. I was almost fourteen that last island summer and I'd grown a lot since the previous summer. She slipped into my room one night.

. . .

Dad never said anything about what happened with Andrea; Marie's face said it for him. After that, there were no more island summers

. . .

So, what about you? Tell me about your past. Why did you become an engineer and not a writer? I know you wrote mystery stories and wanted to continue.

. . .

If you don't want my friendship, perhaps I should look for someone else to confide in.

. . .

Family pressure, it makes sense. Tell me more about your first wife, Lily. Lily was beautiful after all and so aggressive in the sky-train station. Record that one encounter and donate it. Who would have imagined you being arrested for battery? Most people would enjoy the experience second hand.

. . .

Your second marriage, the one to the archaeologist, Stephanie, sounds more "traditional." I imagine the raising of three children would have its share of ups and downs.

. . .

No one would argue if you chose to keep those private, especially since Stephanie's illness and death still bring you to tears. I don't understand why she rejected virtual existence.

. . .

We'll leave it alone.

. . .

Ignore the intercom. The five-minute warning is direct from the bio-program. Restraints are meaningless, but new virtuals cling to the illusion.

So, to get back to your bio-life. I understand you had a third wife.

. . .

We can drop the subject. Look through the port view. The blue light flickering means we're "landing." I've arranged for a private tour. We'll pretend we're still bios. I know there are things you miss.

. . .

This program duplicates the bio-version. The Moon World Transit Station is more than a mile in diameter. It can overwhelm many first-time visitors with all the holos of people waving.

. . .

The far-right entrances lead to the territories of Russia and India. The one to the left of China is the European Collective and on the far end is the Lunar Territories of the United Americas. We are bound for the corridors connecting to transport shuttles.

. . .

Most of what there is to see, other than the hotels, is connected with the Armstrong Museum.

. . .

It's a fascinating piece of history showing the early days of exploration with old-time videos and newspaper banners. In the bio-version, access to the lunar Armstrong Memorial Park is restricted. Too many tourists want to jump around in space suits playing 20th Century astronaut. And let's skip the Hilton for now.

. . .

We'll take this lunar buggy. I hear some of the newer lunar virtual trips are more complete, a source of frustration for me. Do you see those single-story structures?

. . .

They're research facilities.

. . .

The motels here are only illusions. There's the museum.

. . .

The statue is a duplicate of its bio-Ohio-counterpart. Shall we leave the pod? I can't tolerate the charade of the space suit any longer so I'm removing it.

. . .

You don't need a spacesuit!

. . .

How else can I convince you? Your reluctance to accept virtual life concerns me.

. . .

Because I don't know why you're here. I don't know why Miranda recommended you for—never mind. Please don't leave! I am very sorry. The pressure of a possible merger while never knowing when another breach might happen has affected me. Please, let's enjoy the moon!

. . .

Want to say hello to Armstrong?

. . .

You're right; it is worth the trip, to see the earth this way, even if it's only a dream.

Incredible . . . how incredible . . .

How I wish . . . wish . . . how I . . . the mother-of-pearl . . .

I had blocked out the screams

pause

Byron—regarding memory breaches: The following interruptions in Gunter's timeline may be difficult to interpret due to their origin. Some memories are from his life as a bio and others take place in Bali Hai. They are not in chronological order, but as he re-experienced them and they strongly suggest file corruption. Current law requires safeguards (Past Perfect or similar programs) that prevent such disturbances in memory timelines.

Monty Delgado was Gunter's mentor and future business partner, along with Marcia Evans, who was Gunter's first wife.

resume

GUNTER HOLDEN Doc. 439.2
MEMORY BREACH!

CACHE: BIO-L /PRE-TRANSITION 24278889 "Birth of Paradise" presentation of Bali Hai, (classified)

Bio-Memory: VEI presentation Theater, "The Birth of Paradise..

Murmurs of excitement fill the room as I unveil VEI's newest technology to our major investors.

"These nanobots," I whisper, "activate in an instant. When key brain functions cease, every memory, every thought, personality quirk or desire is copied, transmitted, and uploaded in a fraction of a second! VEI GUARANTEES that none of your precious memories will be lost. It's groundbreaking!"

Ah, the huge globe rotates. Then, Paris floats above the Earth. The Eiffel Tower spins. Its lights sparkle. Everyone is applauding. Incredible! I want to spread my arms and revel in the glow of success. It is the sun and I bask in it.

I hear gasps. People are stunned. Floating above the audience are samples of streets, cafes and exciting nightlife.

Oh God, if only Dad could see this. I'll have the whole thing recorded and transmitted. Dad will realize what his son has done with the island money.

Laura Riley points at Chicago. "Sims?" The voice comes from the outer circle. Rio's Eternal Carnival sims are marching in miniature parades and dancing on their little part of the globe. "These new sims, what are these creatures based on? What do they do?" The man, a Turk, is an invited guest of the Seattle Muslim researchers.

Laura leans forward as her mic flashes. "Rather than ordinary sims, we call them "cyber-people." Her schoolgirl voice is smooth. "Our cyber-people give a place flavor and personality. The waiters, street vendors, etc. are based on the locals of each related bio-location.

We have selected and recorded memories relevant to interacting with virtual residents." The Turk nods.

Denise's wild mother Pamela moves closer. Poor Denise, always the supporting player in her mother's life story.

I'm watching Laura Riley. The thrill of victory glows in the girl's sad brown eyes.

"Laura Riley," Patel whispers "I recruited her several months ago." Her small town's report impressed him.

Shawndra is officially ex-wife number four and she has left for Kenya. I'm free. Laura is young and her shy smile and intelligence are beguiling. Someplace tropical will do the trick. We'll work together on a research project . . .

STOP!!!!

heaven on earth heaven on earth heaven on earth heaven on earth . . . heavenonearthhev.

click . . . no one to catch me . . .

STOP!! MEMORY BREACH!

CACHE: VIRTUAL/ POST-TRANSITION 25877037, V- Loc: Chicago penthouse, standard day environ

BREACH: Post bio-conflict with virtual Laura Holden

At Chicago Elysium penthouse

Laura is pacing back and forth as she spits the words at me.

"I fell in love with you when I was twelve." Laura shakes her head. "On my bedroom wall, every morning, I would project your face, a holo of a VEI press announcement. "Heaven on Earth in ten years."

A bit overly dramatic, I think, but don't dare say.

"I thought that you and Marcia were gods, hosting the ultimate heavens, fantasies for the dying."

Curious, what is she thinking?

"You tore the edge between life and death and oh, the worlds that beckoned," she whines.

Oh God, the same tired story. "When you're more rational, we'll talk. I'm out of patience," I tell her. Then I pour a glass of wine.

STOP! BREACH!

weakweakweakweakweakweakweakweakweakweakweak

CACHE: Post-Bio-File 263A, V- Loc: Malibu Colony Environment. See 142.A

BREACH

Malibu Colony virtual Environment

post-bio confrontation with Laura Holden

As we watch the dolphins, I confront her.

'Why did you bring Jacob to Bali Hai?" I ask her. "You must have known . . . of all places, why here?"

She's ignoring me! Okay, we'll see. I could lure Jacob into a risk area where accidental erasures happen.

My wife smiles and begins another story. "My sister loved musicians like Jacob. I never met a man so sad. I was drawn to his sadness; I understood it." A dolphin spirals upward; then it disappears. I'm bored. I've seen it too many times.

"Did you know Patel was in love with Marcia?" she asks me.

The look on my face is her answer. Does she really think I would believe that?

She shakes her head in mild disgust. "I didn't think so . . . Patel kept hoping you would finally let her go and when you did it was too late for both of them. I think he wanted to kill you for ruining his life and Marcia's, but of course, he was Patel, so he didn't. Even so, murder has become too easy, don't you think?"

I'm laughing. "You can't be serious! You betrayed me, not Patel."

She doesn't answer. There is nothing . . .

STOP! BREACH!

terrifyterrifyterrifyterrifyterrifyterrifyterifyterri . . .

CACHE: BIO/PRE-TRANSITION 25658543, Bio-Loc: Chicago penthouse residence

Breach: Laura Holden conflict encounter (wife)

Bio memory: *Chicago Elysium penthouse (bedroom) night*

"You terrify me," she snaps.

My wife is packing for Nepal. I want to slap her. "Oh Christ, please, Laura, do you realize how idiotic you sound?" I'm losing patience.

She pauses, then turns back to sorting through a drawer of thick socks.

I pour wine into a glass and move to the deck.

"Go on, I'm ready," I sigh, "tell me when I terrified you." She won't look at me because she is scared. She knows that I'm right.

There's a tear rolling down to her upper lip. She presses a finger against it to stop it, flipping it with the side of her hand. Pathetic. *For God's sake, Laura! Go to the side of the bed and get a tissue. It's not that much of a trip.*

"After Burning Man." She resumes packing. She sobs. Lots of drama here. "Do you remember when your brother ran into the fire to rescue that poor girl?

I can hardly breathe. "I can't BELIEVE you've been chewing on this!" *Why did I marry this woman? Why did I even hire her?*

She wipes her face with the toe of a thick white sock. I stifle a laugh.

"Gunter, I heard what you said to Marcia. You told her that it was too bad the fire didn't finish him." She zips her suitcase. "I couldn't accept it. Why would you say that after what we saw? Jacob could have died. After what happened with Joy Forever, I know why. You have no heart. I ask myself, why am I still with you?"

"Jacob is a wasted human being who wasted his parents' money and my time. Until he played hero at Burning Man, the last time I saw Jacob was the day after Dad's funeral. Wonder Boy was in his bedroom when I tossed the deed to the Holden Estate onto the pile of dirty clothes."

She shakes her head. "What a cold man you are; you can't love anyone."

"Poor little Laura, have a safe trip." *Don't be surprised if I'm not around when you return.*

STOP!

graychairgraychairgray . . .

set you free set free set free free . . .set . . .freefreefree

CACHE: BIO/PRE-TRANSITION 25686539, B-Loc: VEI Chicago office Apr 21, 2183, at 13:45 Martino meeting (hidden)

Bio-memory: Chicago, VEI private office. Afternoon

Martino sits in the gray chair, his long arms draped over the sides. I can't stop staring at his coarse fingers as they tap the leather. He waits for me to react. The man looks like Abraham Lincoln, tall with a sad worn face, mournful eyes and dark hair coiled from the widow's peak. Such a gentle voice, regretful . . .

"Bad news, Mr. Holden, I'm sorry to say . . . yes, very bad, I'm afraid, sir. Your wife is seeing someone else . . . I'm awfully sorry, but it is your brother Jacob. He's Laura's lover. So, Mr. Holden, are you sure? You want to do this? He is your brother and taking care of this situation won't guarantee your wife's coming home."

Dear Jacob, the Great Emancipator is fixing to set you free from this world. The last face you'll see won't be my wife's, but a sad worn face with mournful eyes. Such a gentle voice, regretful . . . Maybe the resemblance will catch you, or you'll hear the soft voice of your liberator just before the laser rips through your sensitive skull.

STOP! BREACH!

we are not alike not

CACHE: BIO/PRE-TRANSITION 25686723 Bio-Loc: Chicago Penthouse

Bio memory: Chicago penthouse deck, early morning

"I don't understand you as Marcia does," Laura tells me. "I love you, but we are not alike." We're sitting on the deck. She's leaving now. I'm going to sit and wait for the early morning moon.

END BREACH! END BREACH! END BREACH!

ENDED (Breach)

not alike alike not like the moon

RESUME: DOC. 439

Virtual Moon: Armstrong Museum

Am I . . . am . . . alike . . .

. . .

It was a memory breach—in truth, several. Hopefully this problem will be a thing of the past soon. Bored yet?

. . .

You seem to be fascinated by the Earth. Feel the lunar dust. It's soft but abrasive. Bio- moon-dust reeks like gunpowder.

See the how clouds swirl around the dark blue? It reminds me of an eye. What do you think of the Earth?

. . .

On occasion, I miss it. Sometimes I imagine myself down there, walking among the bios. I dream that I'm back.

record paused

MARCIA

May 12, 2287

To: Desmond Webb, Archivist

Library of Congress, VR Division

Desmond—

I haven't finished these most recent Gunter Holden files. So far, I'm still reviewing Doc. 439.

I am getting a clearer picture of Holden through the breaches, so please include them in any files that you send me. He was a real asshole and totally capable of selling out people who trusted him.

If I can narrow the timeline of SEINI initial bids to acquire VEI and the Bali Hai platform, I might find a way to challenge their shutting off communications between their virtuals and the bio-world.

It's possible they're in violation of some early agreements that have since fallen through the cracks.

Can you send me more files? I hope so.

Warm regards,

Byron

***

Via message (confidential)

May 24, 2287

To: Byron Hernandez

Trammell & O'Connell Offices

Byron—

I'm glad the memory files are helpful. Gunter's remarks about a possible merger reveal the approximate time he became aware that VEI was in jeopardy.

I have located more Holden memories that involve your grandfather and I'm sending them to you. As before, I'll include a transcript with ellipses to mark where Tom's response has been muted in the immersive version. In addition, there is one memory that involves only Thomas that escaped Shemathra's censors. As before, you'll need the appropriate software and VR gear to run them. Fortunately, I was able to gain permission to include this Thomas Bucklin memory, which occurred when he participated in a game called "The Hunt."

Also, there are several memory breaches.

For now, I want to avoid the appearance of investigating rather than archiving. I have asked a trusted assistant to see if she can find more exchanges between your great grandfather and Holden.

Let me know if you have questions.

Best,

Desmond

resume

GUNTER HOLDEN Doc. 439
V-Loc: MOON ADVENTURE Continues

Monty

I'm growing more concerned. These memory breaches continue to plague me. I can't sort them out by myself. I must keep memories in the proper order, or my file could continue to fragment. I trust you with this information. Please, for my sake, for the sake of Bali Hai, tell no one. You were an engineer when you were a bio; you know how important structure is for smooth operation. Can you help me? I want these memories back in order.

. . .

I'd like to settle my thoughts by sharing another memory.

. . .

It was before Jacob came, a story from the days before Bali Hai. Some memories are easy to recall. The most significant event of my eighteenth year was meeting Monty Delgado. If it hadn't been for Monty, there might never have been VEI.

. . .

Montgomery Delgado introduced me to mind uploading technology, and that led to virtual life and Bali Hai. Monty was a young teacher in his sixties and teaching philosophy at The Athenian, the private school where I was a student.

. . .

Monty had posed a question to the class about morality and its place in a virtual society.

"You're all going to tackle the choice of whether or not to continue your existence as a virtual citizen," he said. "The question is, what rules, if any, should govern behavior within a virtual society?"

. . .

I did pay attention. Despite my professed indifference, I enjoyed his classes. Now, there are safeguards, and each program has a code of behavior embedded in it. Then, what standards should govern behavior for virtual environments were in question. At the time, I viewed the scenario as far off and theoretical.

. . .

A girl broke the stalemate. "I suppose you'd have to respect another's privacy," she said. She always sat on her hands and rocked back and forth when she was nervous, which she often was.

. . .

Class often took place outdoors on some benches with a view of the Bay. The benches were surrounded by carefully tended nature pretending to be wild. Monty would sit in a hunched position for several minutes while considering what was said. He reminded me of Rodin's Thinker, but Monty was short, round and wore his diminishing hair in a ponytail.

. . .

Usually, I only listened, but the subject interested me. "What about reputation?" I asked. "Could you slander someone, spread lies and ruin a reputation?" Monty leaned over in his hunched position, fixed me with a stare and pointed.

pause

Byron—Holden describes the beginnings of the after-death industry. If the subject holds no interest for you, go ahead and skip to the end and the next record.

resume

This began my friendship with Monty. Like many teachers, Monty often moonlighted, working as a research analyst for a company called Encore Destinations. Encore offered little more than a series of vacations to different popular attractions, like the Grand Canyon, the Mall in D.C., the Vatican, etc., coupled with a generic small town called Pleasant Falls.

. . .

It does sound primitive, but at the time, Pleasant Falls was Oz. Mind uploading was in its infancy, still considered experimental. Not many people had even heard of it. A successful upload protocol led to the next step and that next step was Encore, which had first developed a program that received the early mind uploads.

. . .

In the next three years, companies like Encore began to pop up.

. . .

Even though the media was slow to catch on, public interest grew.

. . .

For a while, none of the after-death programs could compete with Encore's cutting edge "Vacations." But at last, the race to create the perfect after-life was on. I saw the future.

. . .

Of course, there were problems. When I worked with Monty at Stanford, he detailed his experience at Encore. Complications included dozens of incomplete uploads, unintentional deletions, disappointing and inaccurate environmental issues. Monty said it was a nightmare and it would have been funny if not for all the heartbreak and disappointment of residents and their families. Fortunately, the media never took them seriously and Encore escaped scrutiny.

. . .

I'd say very lucky. It would be years before the mind-uploading process became reliable. Worse, people were duplicating themselves, creating identity problems. Still, I was fascinated by the Encore research and the future it promised when the first virtual communities were established. I remember the primitive bio-virtual communications when Monty spoke to new residents, reviewing their records and witnessing what seemed a miracle—life continuing after the body dies.

. . .

I knew then what I wanted, more than my father ever dreamed. Paradise.

. . .

You're sitting on the moon, yet you gaze at the Earth. What do you miss?

. . .

Stephanie? Who is Stephanie?

. . .

Forgive me. Yes, I remember. Stephanie was your second wife, the mother of your children. Are you ready to talk about why she isn't here?

. . .

It's obvious that she was the love of your life, and you miss her terribly. Forget I asked.

. . .

I've had two great loves. You see how the Earth turns? You imagine the storms and restless seas. You know they are there, but you can't see them from here. There's purity in the moon's vacuum; it's devoid of storms and one appreciates the sense of grandeur and peace. When the right woman appears, you're on guard, ready to conquer and move on. Then inexplicably, you're like the moon—defenseless, and the vacuum's purity gives way to the inevitable scars of engagement.

. . .

I'll tell you about Marcia Evans as we gaze at the Earth. Marcia was working for my dad when she came to my graduation. Dad was wrapped up in being a new father and sent apologies. Later, I came home to see Jacob, my new brother, for the first time.

. . .

Anyway, Marcia came to my graduation while Dad was changing Jacob's diaper. I was nineteen and, in my opinion, a man of the world.

. . .

Monty had become a researcher in the Stanford Virtual Studies Department. Luckily for me, he pulled some strings and took me with him. Many use their gap decade exploring the different life paths they might take or traveling the world. I wanted no gap between my childhood and my goals at Stanford. Stanford was the first to establish a Department of Virtual Environmental Studies, an incredibly lucky time for me.

. . .

Do you believe in Fate?

. . .

VEI might never have been created, you and I might not be here had I not met Marcia. As my name was called, I heard a cheer, a "way-tago Gunter!" Everyone looked to see who was responsible for this breach of decorum.

. . .

She sat on the aisle near the back row. She was around forty then, pretty with dark hair. There was nothing remarkable about her. I remember her hair was up and it looked like she had hurried to make my big moment.

. . .

A poor girl from a Sacramento neighborhood of rundown tract homes and apartment buildings, Marcia rarely talked of her past. Scholarships landed her at Berkeley at eighteen. Like me, there was no gap decade for Marcia. She knew what she wanted.

. . .

She was the oldest of four with an absent father and a mother who was a teacher's aide. The home routine in late afternoons and evenings was mom behind a locked bedroom door and Marcia left to deal with her younger brothers while mom drank gin and ate fast food.

. . .

Sadly, the brothers were all dead by the age of twenty. Two broth-ers were fifteen and sixteen and in the wrong driveway where they were shot. The last one overdosed at eighteen on Splendorful, a drug that plagued the neighborhood for decades.

. . .

After Berkeley, Marcia earned a PhD from the Rochester Institute of Technology—Brick City, she called it. Dad hired her as a consultant on a Nova Scotia project. I discovered that Marcia's acuity and instincts rivaled my dad's at his best.

. . .

Monty and his boyfriend, a grad student named LeRoi Brown were there. Leroy's study of social justice led him to become a radical later in life with tragic results, a story for another time. They knew I had no scheduled guests. They had invited me for a celebratory dinner at their favorite bistro and now there was Marcia to consider.

"Well, Holden, what'll it be? Your call, kid." She stood and smiled; her head slightly tilted to the side. The effect was surprising. All my worldliness disappeared, and I blushed. I saw Monty and LeRoi sneak a glance at one another. It was hard to miss. LeRoi was over six feet five to Monty's five feet four. Their delight made it worse.

. . .

Of course, I invited her, though I resented feeling obligated. As the evening progressed, I was glad I did. Her voice fascinated me.

. . .

Marcia spoke with one of those New York accents: the vowels stretched flat and harsh, the r's barely there at times. There was nothing of Sacramento in the way she spoke, as if that person was gone. Her voice—a musical blend of shifting tones and nuanced inflections—was fascinating, so much so that you hear it when Miranda speaks, without the accent of course.

. . .

Yes, I miss her.

. . .

As the evening progressed, Monty told stories about his work at Encore, describing the delight of clients waking up healthy in an exciting environment, able to communicate with loved ones and staying a part of their lives, although in a limited way. LeRoi nodded proudly. Sadly, several years later, LeRoi became part of the anti-virtual movement, which led to a disaster.

. . .

For anti-virtuals the issue is not about living in virtual reality but being poor. Those who struggle to afford living in the bio-world, cannot afford to be uploaded to a virtual one. LeRoi thought there should be after-death destinations within reach for all.

. . .

Marcia said nothing, a poker face, polite, but blank. Later that night, as she seduced me, she told me what she thought.

. . .

Why are you surprised? Because she seduced me, rather than the other way?

. . .

I was as surprised as you. She was staying at the Fairmont. Is it still there? Ah, I must talk to Miranda about updating our Fairmont. Marcia had a tower suite. I'd lived all over the world, and I made a remark about the hotel reminding me of a place in Vienna. Not that it did; I was trying to impress her.

"Oh, really . . ." Her eyebrows went up as she said it. "I have a gift for you. Would you like it now or should I have it sent?" She lingered on the word "now" in her musical way, accompanying it with a slight nod. I was mesmerized.

. . .

It was as if she hadn't been in focus until that moment. We rode the elevator in silence and when we reached the room, she opened the door, glanced back at me with a slight smile, took off her blue jacket and tossed it on the off-white couch. I sat on the couch, waiting for my graduation gift. I had no idea what that might be.

. . .

For some reason, her jacket fascinated me. I was tempted to run my hands along its edges, to rub the buttons. They were a darker blue, with an embedded knot, Celtic, very glossy. I wanted to feel them with my thumbs. I inched closer and had decided to do just that when she returned with an envelope.

. . .

What happened? Well, first, my father's gift. "Aren't you going to open it?" She meant the envelope, which rested on the couch cushion between us. Now, you'll laugh, but at the time, I was mortified. Rather than reaching for the envelope, I reached for her robe as if to open it. It was automatic. I realized what I had done and began to stammer.

. . .

She laughed, leaned over and tossed the envelope in my lap.

"So, are you pleased? What do you think?" Taking my hand, she placed it on the robe's lapel. We spent the night doing all the things you do when you are young and there is nothing in your universe but the fragrance and feel of desire.

Okay! So, are you ready for the museum?

. . .

There's that impatience again. Shall we visit the museum, yes or no?

. . .

It's one of the most interesting parts of this Moon program.

. . .

Another time, then.

End Record

SOMETHING BROKEN

*B*yron—*here's the rest of the "Moon Adventure." It concerns Hold-en's relationship with his family and certain resentments he felt towards them. The "Nancy" Holden refers to was his deceased mother. Since you expressed interest in the Holden Connecticut Estate, Holden recalls a disturbing memory that takes place there. I've included breach that occurred soon after Gunter became a virtual.*

GUNTER HOLDEN Doc. 174.5

V-Loc: Venice Beach /Strand environ, RICKS BEACH CAFÉ. © 4.22.2109 by VEI Standard Environments). Day 45 of 80 non-event days VENICE STRAND. Visual environment means UNIVERSAL access. Program 33545.3 (9.09.2108)

Venice Beach Strand, has some virtual and sim-tourists inspecting sidewalk art. Several families (sims) on beach. Typical beach weather, sunny with no wind.

. . .

Hello, Tom. Thanks for coming. Recalling various episodes in my life has been difficult for me and tedious for you. I hope you might find some of it interesting. But I am worried. The flood of breaches I experienced during our moon trip caught me by surprise. Regardless, possible mergers threaten VEI. These episodes make it difficult for me to protect Bali Hai.

. . .

Then, I'll continue by telling you what happened after I met Marcia. I admit, I am rather melancholic, remembering that time in my life.

At Marcia's urging, I went back to Connecticut to see my father. The house had changed. The day I met Celeste she and Dad had taken me on the "tour." A narrow three-story thing, it was almost three hundred years old. Dad had sent me digitals of it. He boasted about his "find." The rooms were small, dark and had that musty history smell. Now, a veranda extended the ground level and fresh paint countered the dimness of history.

. . .

I hated it. I sat on the shaded side of the veranda and watched the Thames River as it flowed by a quarter of a mile or so from the house. A tree on the outer edge barely moved. There was so little breeze.

My mind wandered back to Marcia and the night we spent together.

. . .

I had been there waiting for Dad less than an hour when Celeste came in to tell me where I could find him. "Your father's upstairs with Jacob." The pregnancy had taken its toll; she seemed tired.

. . .

No, I didn't express any concern. Why should I? Please don't distract me; I need to remember what was important then.

. . .

If I offended you, I apologize. For some reason, my lawyers aren't returning my calls and now rumors of mergers continue to stream in from my bio-news feed.

. . .

Don't worry. VEI is financially sound, and any offer will be rejected, but I would like to know what's real and what's a serious threat. The whole situation concerns me and along with the fragmenting issues, I've become short-tempered.

. . .

So, I'll continue now.

. . .

As I climbed the stairs, I could hear my father singing. It stopped me for a moment. I had never heard him sing. He sang rather well, his tenor voice whispering the lyrics. The song was one my mother sang when we took our walks.

. . .

We'd go to the bakery. My mother's friend, Mr. Donald was always there. I often found Mr. Donald somewhere in the sky, his long nose in a thrust of white mist and cloud strings caught by the wind became his mop of light blond hair, hair that sprang up from his head like a bird's crest. Mr. Donald would be there with his coffee, computer and a muffin or cookie for me.

"Hello Donald," my mother would smile and nod as we waited for our bread.

. . .

No, I didn't know his last name. Why do you ask?

. . .

I'm not being paranoid. Shall I continue?

. . .

"Good morning, Nancy," he'd say, and then he would wink at me. "How are you and this fine young man this morning?"

Why are you looking away? Are you bored? If so, I can tell you the rest another time.

. . .

Fine. I guess I am a bit irritable. You have no idea the pressure I'm under. There are several memories that have intruded recently. I don't want to relive them. So I'll finish this one.

. . .

While Mom drank her tea, I would begin my account of school and things that are important to a child—the dead bird on the doorstep or how I learned to ride my bike with two wheels, and then I fell off the bike, the blood running down my knee into my shoe. He always gave me a dollar for every state capital I could name. I saved it all for my summers.

. . .

I remember that Mr. Donald was tall. With his rosy cheeks, blue eyes and blond hair, I imagined he was a Viking. Mom had read me a story about Eric the Red. The first time I met him at the bakery, I was four years old. He bent down to shake my hand and being shy, I hesitated until she whispered in my ear that Mr. Donald was a secret agent, and I wasn't to mention him, not even to Dad. She knew I loved to pretend.

. . .

I don't know for sure. I think that Mr. Donald must have been a grad student. Mom never said where she met him. He was always peering at the computer monitor as if it would reveal a secret code or a treasure map.

I fantasized about finding him before I left for that last summer. Take care of Mom for me, Mr. Donald, please! Let her know I'll be back soon!

. . .

I know, Tom. I wasn't the only child to lose a mother. If I had known that she would die, I wouldn't have stayed with Dad and left my mother for what became forever, but I didn't know, okay? I was eight. Why are you so angry?

. . .

This session has been longer than usual. Perhaps it's hard for you to understand what happened. I wish I did. Thank you, okay? Why the impatience? Do you know something I don't?

. . .

You're looking away.

. . .

Okay, I'll tell you why this memory is important. It's the day I began to hate my brother.

. . .

On the way home, my mother would sing. It wasn't a children's song, not anything you'd expect. It was a lover's song. *I'll see you soon by the weeping willow*. From the past century, World War II possibly. My parents must have sung it to each other.

. . .

Let me explain how this is relevant. During my visit to see the new Holden and congratulate Dad, my mother's song came back to me. As I climbed the stairs, I heard Dad sing it to my brother. I wanted to die. I wanted to kill Dad and his new son.

. . .

I always carried a knife in an inner pocket, a habit from all those years as a child roaming the streets of the cities where Dad did business. My urge to plunge a knife into my baby brother became real. I decided to hide in a closet and wait until Dad left.

. . .

I was serious until I calmed down. I don't think I would have done it, but as I said, it wouldn't have changed anything. When I opened the closet door, a hand grabbed me and a punch knocked me cold. Dad thought I was an intruder. When I woke, I scrambled for an explanation while Dad berated me, calling me a fool and questioning my common sense.

. . .

I appreciate your understanding. Please don't discuss this with anyone. I left the next morning with apologies, saying Monty needed my help setting up his research office. Before I left, I thanked Dad for his gift and congratulated Celeste on Jacob. Something had broken.

STOP!!

BREACH!

. . . click . . . you're finished

Patel's genius hums in the lush Sierra Forest and the skittish deer. Early morning birds call out and . . . the sound of . . . of . . . water. There's a creek nearby. The air is crisp and cold, full of green and the smell of cedar. What detail! No difference from the other, the bio. I draw a deep breath.

My color shifts from pale rose to the golden tan I wore the summer of my twenty-seventh year. Marcia and I were celebrating VEI's success in Europe.

"I want to spoil you! You need to be spoiled," I whispered in her ear. I never loved Marcia more than the year I decided to leave her.

END BREACH!

the Sierras . . . never loved . . . moremoremore

END BREACH!

RESUME: Doc. 439

What was I saying?

. . .

Yes, I had another—interruption—I don't want to talk about it now.

. . .

I didn't realize how little control . . .these memories are difficult . . .

. . .

I don't want to waste your time. I'll ask Miranda to recommend someone else if you don't want to continue.

. . .

 Thank you! You'll never know how . . .

I'll try to be more patient as well. Let's do something different! How about meeting for a game? There's one called "The Hunt." I think you'll enjoy it.

. . .

They can be very diverting. There are hundreds of possible outcomes before you know them all. Consult Miranda. She'll recommend the ones you'd likely enjoy. Miranda will notify me and we'll meet at the game.

END RECORD

THE HUNT

"The Hunt" is the first level of the game series which includes the Baltimore Disaster. The Baltimore Disaster level one is where Laura Holden disappeared*

Bali Hai Memory Library

Byron—I thought you might be interested in seeing and hearing your great grandfather as he was in Bali Hai. I was permitted access to this by one of your distant cousins, Andrew Bucklin. Unfortunately, this is the only one he felt comfortable sharing.

Please note: This is a game record and not from Bucklin's memory files.

THOMAS BUCKLIN DOC. 322.1

GAME DOC. 1061156832.3 Option: The Hunt (level one) Purpose: Game record (save)

V-Loc: "The Hunt" Game Program Level One, © Sun Discovery, Inc. May, 2183, update Sept. 2185. Briefing 4C through Allied Strategies Systems, Inc. (with permission from Sony-Mattel San Diego, CA Apr.2180)

Thomas Bucklin sits in a swivel chair, facing a monitor. He is in a small office of a metropolitan police station. Miranda stands in a doorway that leads to the main office which has multiple chairs, monitors and sim uniformed officers and detectives.

Greetings, resident. I, Miranda, welcome you to "The Hunt," level one. This game is by invitation only. Soon, I will introduce you to your fellow detectives. Three are assigned to each case and as you progress, each team will receive clues. Some clues are valuable; others will lead to a dead end. The sooner you determine the difference, the faster your team, called a unit, will progress.

Now, I must deliver some unfortunate news. Gunter will not be with us; he sends his regrets.

Tom: I'm sorry to hear this. Can you tell me why?

I am not at liberty to explain his decision. Perhaps later, when you meet, he will tell you more. He asks that I invite you to a celebration in honor of Bali Hai's seventy-fifth year. I'll provide details at the trial's conclusion.

Tom: I haven't said that I'm available. I'm here because Gunter Holden invited me. I'm not sure that I want to stay if he can't be bothered.

Allow me to continue and then you can decide. Again, I apologize on Gunter's behalf. Pressing matters are keeping him and he looks forward to the coming social event.

Tom: Continue then.

There are steps that you and your teammates must complete. Each unit will examine clues leading to the capture and conviction of a notorious serial killer. The methods of discovery available to you are the same as in the actual historical record, but the crimes will be fictional, simulated according to patterns specific to that individual. You will be provided with the knowledge and skills of one of three detectives involved in his or her capture. All knowledge of the killer, other than what we have determined is appropriate for the game, is being temporarily erased from your memory.

Tom: Miranda, you have an intriguing voice. I'm an engineer and I don't recall any systems with your range of inflection and nuance.

Gunter designed my voice. It is based on the vocal patterns of Marcia Evans, his former wife, and partner. Marcia rode the Dreams forty-five years, two hundred one days, three hours, and approximately eight point three minutes ago.

Tom: I see. Miranda, explain the nature of the Dreams.

I will be most happy to discuss the Dreams when the information is declassified and no longer requires approval for disclosure. Observe the path of my hand. Do you see a window?

Tom: Yes, I see it.

Your role is that of Detective Graham. You are fifty-two and have worked homicide cases as a detective on the Los Angeles Police Force since 2018. Access those memories now. Does the name Myles Shelby mean anything?

Tom: It does. I studied his crimes when I was a bio. When I wrote short stories, I thought—Anyway, I've heard of him.

Many of Mr. Shelby's criminal practices are in play for the game. Solve the case before the other unit; obtain a conviction and jump to the next game, Level One Game Two, which is preventing a mass murder in New Delhi.

Look at your computer monitor!

Tom: Interesting, this computer technology is something I've read about but never encountered. It's a welcome change from listening to Gunter. Okay, I see two reports and maybe the same explosives . . .

Yes, there are some similarities in these two reports. Be sure to draw attention to them when your partners arrive. Ah . . . here they are.

pause

Byron—the rest of this segment was gone. My guess is that it was damaged and removed from the original record. Desmond

END RECORD

THE MOTHER SIM

*B*yron—*Denise Dynarsky was a former VEI employee. I've done a search, and it appears that she self-deleted soon after Holden. In this memory file, Gunter describes a traumatic experience he suffered as a bio.*

GUNTER HOLDEN Doc.143 B

V-Loc: Venice Beach /Strand/KNICKKNACK SHACK, THE TOWELRY, GLIDE SKATES RENTALS 3.7k beach-3.14k, .4k ocean-1.9 k. Structures 35 with interiors, 32 kiosks/carts.2c. © 3.24.2108 by VEI Environment. Day 15 of 80 non-event Venice California. UNIVERSAL access. 3457.4 (rec 06.19.2106). Tactile: non-event day. Audio: ocean surf non-event 5, Sims: gulls 58 of 92 sim/virtual interactives. Human sims 5896 high function "local color."

Venice Beach environment, a short distance from the eateries and larger tourist shops. This area caters more to surfers, cyclists and glider enthusiasts.

Hello Tom! Miranda tells me you're quite a hunter, dispatching Mr. Shelby with great efficiency.

. . .

I'm finished with meetings, at least for a while. Thank you for the note. I'm glad that we decided to meet here. You know, I have vivid childhood memories of Venice Beach.

. . .

Let's skate. I feel like being twelve today. Do you see "The Towelry?" It's the cart next to the souvenir shop. We can age-shift behind the bicycle shed.

. . .

Yes, I was rather feral at twelve. When Dad went to meetings, he took me with him. He never worried. I took care of myself. I was a kid on hover-skates cruising city streets.

. . .

Aren't you comfortable with yourself at twelve? Okay, fifteen is probably better for you. Let's skate toward Santa Monica. See how easy? It will come back to you.

When I was twelve, my father brought me here and I skated while he romanced an actress. As I waited for him, I watched the women as they strolled in their bikini tops, holding up some piece of jewelry and a smock printed with the echo of glamour or a sea creature netted into a brilliant orange, items destined for a bottom drawer.

Ah, there's Denise. Shall we say hello?

. . .

I understand. There are many here I work to avoid. After I arrived in Bali Hai, Denise made a pretense of friendship and began to pursue me. I ignored her. She was a former VEI employee, and I usually avoid such interactions. If you do decide to get to know her, be careful. She has a nose for gossip and when I didn't respond to her advances, she decided to threaten me with something she thought she knew.

. . .

I can't elaborate. She smiled at me as I tried to escape her. Then she said, "Joy Forever."

. . .

There was a tragedy, something I can't explain now. I notice that you're better able to distinguish residents from sims. I prefer to know as well. These differences matter. A virtual human is still human, after all.

How does sailing sound? Perfect, let's make it a schooner and the Oahu coast. Follow my jump.

Miranda, COMMAND, JUMP: Gunter Holden, Thomas Bucklin

TRANSFER complete

V-Loc: Pacific Ocean 1.5 k Oahu, HA coast (span 2.65k) OCEANS WAYS © 2176, Day 26 of 214 days, non-event, OLFACTORY/ TACTILE: level 6 sun, temp/wind variations level 7 by OCEANA 854321.B © June 2178, aquatic sims by OCEANRICH SEALIFE © May 2159 update, 306 non-interactive sim birds (gulls, etc.) non-interactive sim HOVERCRAFT OCEANSPHERE ©2145

Sailboat, mild day recorded on the Pacific Ocean near Oahu
So where were we?

. . .

The woman can be annoying.

. . .

I agree. It's best to ignore boorish behavior. There's a dolphin and over there, did you see the turtle over there?

. . .

My visit to her personal environment was disturbing. She has created a Chicago penthouse. I did wonder why she chose to spend her limited memory allotment on something so lavish. It is tasteful, but there's a lack of personal history. Nothing relates to the woman herself except a group of digitals, two-dimensional images in old-fashioned metal frames. In each, there she is with a sim of one of her lovers. Each pose is identical. The sim's arms encircle her as he stares blankly at her, while her gaze meets the camera's eye. They reminded me of trophies.

. . .

Denise was a programmer for VEI and very unattractive as a bio. She inspired either pity or the shrill friendliness we use to mask our impulse to turn away. For some reason, I felt neither. I admit Denise was very good. Some of the entertainment programs, mostly fantasy-fulfillment, were enhanced by her subtle work. It's all in the details when it comes to wish-fulfillment. She understood the importance.

. . .

She talked too much, always with the joke of the day. She lived with her mother, a musician of some note. You seem distracted . . .

. . .

It might help you understand the why of Denise, that's all.

. . .

Let's enjoy the breeze and watch the sun on the ocean. There should be a whale appearing soon. So, to not make a saga of it, when Pamela died suddenly, the result of some untested synthetic drug, she was uploaded to Bali Hai as part of the first group of residents.

. . .

There were a hundred thousand or so. We'd had reservations and nanos in place for five years. Clients from all over the world wanted it. We dominated the Western market. Eternal Horizons and Paradise Found became middle-income options overnight. It was several years before India, the Middle East and China had anything close to what we offered. The Japanese were players, but mostly focused on histori-cal environments.

. . .

By the way, I think our sessions are helping. It's been several days since that last breach. Miranda certainly thinks so. Maybe I can truly put it all behind me.

. . .

Anyway, she changed after her mother transitioned. She avoided work, coming in late. I asked Patel to get to the bottom of it and it turned out that she was avoiding her mother's calls. Pamela contin-ued running her daughter's life, calling every day, asking if she'd lost weight or why wasn't she more . . . like Pamela. In Bali Hai, virtual Pamela was her fifties self, the wild child musician. She'd call, pop-ping up on a monitor, appearing with adoring sim-fans. Denise would stammer, always the satellite to her mother's star. One day, I discovered Denise had committed suicide.

. . .

Curiously, like I did, a gunshot to her face; she blew it off. She was wearing Pamela's clothes, like what Pamela had worn on stage decades earlier. So . . .

. . .

I'm getting to it. Of course, when she transitioned to Bali Hai, things changed between her and Pamela. It was she who hounded Pamela. Any fantasy or revisited memory that Pamela indulged, her daughter eclipsed.

. . .

Pamela began avoiding her. The two barely spoke after a while and Pamela regressed. . . just a little at first, not the joyful wild child anymore.

. . .

It was as if the virtual experience tore away the masks and the truth pierced Pamela's delusions, the ones she carried from her bio life. One day, Pamela was simply gone.

. . .

I'll explain the Dreams in time, not now. Denise seemed unaffected at first, though I sensed a change. She was feral, predatory. I had Miranda alert me whenever Denise was near my location. Later she requested her first permanent sim, Pamela, the mother-sim, the mother she desired, never questioning nor criticizing, only murmuring an encouraging word when asked. Denise became as she is now, bitter, and secretive. I wonder if she'll follow her mother into the Dreams. She seems miserable here. Ah, there it is. Do you see it? The whale is surfacing about fifty yards out. Magnificent.

WHAT DO YOU FEAR?

(Continued Record 143 B) V-Loc: Pacific Ocean 1.5 k Oahu, HA coast

Of all our ocean programs, this part of the Pacific is my favorite. I rarely encounter other virtuals here, fewer even than on Everest. I can feel truly alone. Let's drift for a while and watch the moon. Wait—what's happened? It's cold.

Miranda: why has the temperature dropped?

It seems that a recent patch meant to update "Atlantic Adventures" was also applied to "Sailing the Pacific," the program you are currently running. I have adjusted the program.

Thank you, the temperature is fine now.

. . .

I know it's difficult for you to understand why the wrong temperature upsets me. To you, the difference was less than fifteen degrees, barely noticeable. However, these incidents are increasing. I worry that some competitor or an anti-virtual hacker is responsible.

. . .

Miranda conducted a deep scan, and fortunately, no hackers. I'm concerned that it may be something worse. Board meetings are occurring without my knowledge. When I demanded an explanation, I was told that I will be informed of any changes. My lawyers are sending a formal inquiry. Being a virtual is a handicap. There are protocols. I fear these changes are the start of . . . I don't know—a merger, some catastrophe, the end of a dream.

. . .

I fear the loss of influence, of losing control of VEI, the company I built. You do understand what Bali Hai means to me? I'm curious. What did you most fear before your bio death? Your wife's betrayal, perhaps?

. . .

I have no idea what happened in your bio-marriage, and I don't—

. . .

Fine. I am sorry if I offended you. It wasn't my intention.

. . .

What I mean is, what did you fear? You know—the fear that seemed to spring from your DNA, the legacy of some ancestor who survived because he feared something, and he left that fear imprinted on you as surely as the shape of your ears or fingers.

. . .

Come on, you must fear something. What did you fear as a child?

. . .

The dark, yes; it's a common fear. Many a child wants a night-light.

. . .

It is peaceful now, but not always. The program includes a storm and some rough waves soon. We'll sail a bit longer until the storm. It's soothing now to simply float.

. . .

After my mother's death, I feared nothing. In my mind, my father couldn't die. He was invincible. The past swirls around at times. I catch a glimpse and then, it's gone.

. . .

A roller coaster terrified me once. We were in Oslo. My father left me with the tutor, a young man whose name I've forgotten. I was restless. Almost thirteen, I thought myself a man. Because of his youth, I balked at the tutor's authority. I sat at a desk in the narrow office of the flat where we stayed. I felt suffocated.

. . .

In exchange for finishing my assignment on early 21st Century Literature, my tutor offered to take me on an "adventure."

. . .

So—the roller coaster, yes . . . that was the adventure. The "Thunder Coaster." I wonder if it is still there.

. . .

We waited in line for over half an hour. I didn't mind. I had never been on a roller coaster. We had been there for over ten minutes when I looked up. The rails of the Thunder Coaster rose hundreds of feet, disappearing into gray clouds.

. . .

Until I looked up, I had blocked out the screams, didn't hear them while I was busy making plans. My tutor was in his early thirties. I decided we would find some willing girls and...

. . .

You're right, the roller coaster . . . so it came to be our turn to ride. We were in the second row behind an old man and his grandson, a boy of ten with white-blond hair and a cowlick that bounced. There was this loud bang as the bars were put in place and then . . . a sudden jerk. As the string of cars began to climb, I was pressed against the back of my seat.

. . .

The angle was, or I thought it was, ninety degrees straight up. As we climbed into the clouds, I kept hearing the click-click-click . . . then, an incredible jerk. We seemed to be in free fall, and I screamed. As we descended, I saw nothing but darkness. It felt as if there was nothing beneath us. We landed for a mere second before swerving into another impossible trajectory into the clouds. As we began each plunge, all that was visible was the blonde cowlick. It was bouncing and waving as if to say goodbye: it's finished; you're finished!

. . .

The most terrifying were the clicks, each one taking me closer to where I would fall again, and no one was there to catch me. Ridiculous, I know.

. . .

When our ride was over, I left that second row as soon as the bar lifted, and I dashed off the platform. Behind me, the cars were filling with passengers for the next ride. Afraid to look back, I was still shaking with fear when I saw a look of concern on my tutor's face. He pointed to a building with hanging signs that meant public restrooms and told me to follow him.

. . .

Inside, I looked in one of the mirrors above the basins and was grateful that only a few people were there to witness my disgrace. Tears had streaked and dried on my face. But that was the least of it. I had wet my pants and a trail of drops led back to the gate and I'm sure, to that second row.

. . .

The tutor was very tactful, most likely because of his job. Other than now, I've told this story only once, to Marcia, days before I left for Africa. It is a nightmare best forgotten.

. . .

The wind is stirring up the waves, so we'll call it a day. There's a new holo-film, recently imported from the bio-world. Miranda does stay current. It's a thriller. I'm told it offers some interesting role-playing. Shall we agree to meet?

. . .

After a recent bio-holo-film presentation, the bio-lead-actor, a man in his late cen-thirties, died unexpectedly. His Doberman guard dogs killed him. Oh, you heard. Yes, Jiang . . . Jiang . . . Jinping . . . that's right. He came here as his eighty's self—very handsome, with a huge fan base. Now he lives in the Bali-Wonder Division. He prefers the company of sims and the segregated lifestyles of the residents there.

. . .

Don't argue. You'll enjoy it! The new film is running in an old-fashioned "picture show" type theatre, adjusted for holographic presentations. I'm coming as my forty-five years old self. Fine. I look forward to it . . .

COMMAND, Miranda, CEASE: Oahu sail Sunset Oahu Sunset sail ceased.

CEASED

END RECORD

RE: DIEGO PUTNAM

*V*ia message *(confidential)*

June 20, 2287

To: Byron Hernandez

Trammell & O'Connell Law Offices

Re: Holden and Diego Putnam

Dear Byron—

I have attached another set of Holden memory files. Holden's nephew, Diego Putnam appears in the first memory listed in this set. Infinite Bliss acquired VEI with Putnam's help.

In addition, I have made some discreet searches for more information on Diego Putnam. I'm not a lawyer, but Diego's taking control of Gunter's stock without his consent doesn't pass the smell test. I was surprised that Holden didn't contest it until I discovered Hosseini was financing Diego's claim. It made sense. Holden was outmatched.

After you review them, let me know if they are helpful. If so, I'll look for more that reveal Putnam's role in the destruction of Bali Hai. However, I must be careful. SEINI reps are making inquiries related to the management of this department.

Warm regards,

Des

***

Via message (confidential)

June 28, 2287

To: Desmond Webb, Archivist

Library of Congress, VR Division

Desmond—

Infinite Bliss? I wasn't aware of any merger other than the one made public by SEINI.

Send me whatever Holden memory files that you can access. I've learned that virtuals who entered Bali Hai are now forced to exist in Shemathra. Those original contracts may still apply. I need permission to access them even though Hosseini has blocked any communications to and from Shemathra. There are several lawsuits, but if, God forbid, all but the "faithful" have been conveniently erased, Hosseini will prevail. I'm determined to stop him before that happens.

What I need to know is what, if any coercion, threats, or bribes were used to gain Holden's cooperation. It's possible that Holden might have thought he had something to gain, only later to learn that he was misled.

And please, if you feel pressure or intimidation from Hosseini's thugs, let me know. This office knows how to shine a light on cockroaches. They'll scatter and leave you alone.

Many thanks,

Byron

***

Via message (confidential)

July 20, 2287

To: Byron Hernandez

Trammell & O'Connell Law Offices

Re: Holden and Diego Putnam

Dear Byron—

The files attached include information regarding Diego Putnam and the Infinite Bliss merger. You should know that SEINI reps have been monitoring all doc. requests related to virtual residents of Shemathra's Realm. I'm grateful for your assurances, but I still feel that I must be careful.

The first two records should answer your question regarding Holden having some secret arrangement with Hosseini. The merger went through with the help of Diego, pure and simple. I am curious about Diego. What happened to him after the Bali Hai platform became Shemathra's Realm? If you discover info on this, I would appreciate having it.

By the way, did you know that Thomas Bucklin was murdered? I discovered this while doing a general search of his bio history and viewing the coroner's report on his bio-death which deemed it a homicide. Unfortunately, no one was ever prosecuted. As far as I can tell, Gunter was unaware of this fact. I wonder if your grandfather ever told him.

Regards,

Desmond

V-Library of Congress

Diego Putnam

GUNTER HOLDEN DOC. 159

V-Loc: Everest Summit 4.5 k by 5.8 k, non-event day 35 of 58, Tactile MOUNTAIN RISE © 2188, Visual/ audio EVEREST EXPERIENCE by VEI Adventures © 2187, Olfactory DREAM HIGH © 2145, Sims 58 gray geese level 4.

mountain side, geese flying overhead

Gunter?

Yes, Miranda.

You have a call waiting on monitor two.

Is it important? The Everest Summit rarely offers glimpses of the gray geese. They're like pearls gliding through the passes.

It's your nephew, Diego Putnam. He's a Board member and Estrella's oldest grandson.

COMMAND, Miranda, CHANGE TO NEW V-Loc: Chicago office environment. MANIFEST plasma desk. SHOW party holding, but don't connect.

V-Loc: TRANSFER: Gunter Holden CUSTOM Chicago office VEI May 2121 END TRANSFER Party on screen.

VEI Chicago office environment

What a gray little man! I see nothing of my sister Estrella in him and certainly nothing of Jasmine. Why do some people deliberately tint their skin that hideous gray blue? He reminds me of a rabbit. What does the bio-Board want now?

COMMAND: Miranda, INTERFACE.

INTERFACED

Diego: (*Leans forward and sips an unidentified beverage from a blue container*) *Am I speaking to Gunter Holden?* (*smiles*)

Yes, this is Gunter Holden. I'm sorry, who are you?

Diego: *Diego, Diego Putnam.* (*sighs*)

Diego, Miranda informs me you are my nephew and the grandson of my sister, Estrella. Why do I have the pleasure?

Diego: (*transmits a digital image of himself sitting with the VEI Board of Directors*) *The Board has made . . . uh, Uncle Gunter, it's my role to inform you of certain changes.*

Congratulations! It's excellent to have another Holden on the bio-Board of Directors!

Diego: (*clears his throat*) *Thanks. This call is to notify you . . .*

By the way, how is Estrella? Still opposed virtual life? It would be delightful to see her when the time comes. Would you mind holding for a moment? I'd like to adjust my age-appearance.

Diego: (*rolls his eyes*) *Sure.*

COMMAND: Miranda, PAUSE interface.

PAUSED.

COMMAND: Miranda, RESUME.

RESUMED

Diego: *(with a thin smile) Your look is very distinguished. My grandmother transitioned to Universal Dreams some time ago. Mother joined her recently. They seem quite content. When I interface with them, I will convey your regards.*

Thank you, Diego. I'm glad you think I was impressive in my fifties. They were an exciting time in my life. Of course, I understand. Jasmine transitioned to Universal Dreams International and Estrella misses her. I admit I was disappointed at Jasmine's decision. She was very kind to me, and I had hoped . . . Never mind, back to Estrella. What has she told you about me?

Diego: *(coldly) That she barely remembers you and that you had the better team of lawyers. Also, she hoped to not see you again.*

That was a very emotional time, my father's death. Estrella was levelheaded even then. I was impressed by her acceptance of my offer for her share of the estate, a fair price.

Diego: *(staring into the monitor) Uncle Gunter, let me be blunt. As your heir and still a bio, I now control your estate, including your shares of VEI. In addition, although I will consult your opinion whenever possible, I have taken your seat and will be your voice in all decisions concerning VEI, including the Board meetings. (Clears his throat)*

Diego, forgive me! I'm sure you're aware that I left no heirs. Perhaps I'm wrong, but my guess is that you are on shaky ground. I recommend you check with your legal team, and I'll check with mine—excuse me just a moment—holographic communication pause.

Diego: *(sighing) Take your time, Uncle. I'll wait.*

Miranda, run a quick check on new legislation . . .

Gunter, the Board requested that I inform you that the Illinois State Legislature recently approved a change in the inheritance codes of 2086.

It states that should a corporation deem a virtual Board member unable to attend meetings for any reason, a surrogate must be appointed.

COMMAND. Miranda, CHANGE V-Loc: Office environment to New York Corporate VEI 2112.

CUSTOM TRANSFER: (non-jump option) V-Loc is VEI NEW YORK Corporate Gunter Holden office June 2112. END TRANSFER

RESUME interface.

RESUMED

Diego, you still haven't made your point. My priority is to protect VEI. To be honest, I expected better from a Holden.

Diego: *Really? If you had been fairer with my grandmother, your own sister, I might sympathize. I'll say it again. The law has designated me as your bio-rep. I am replacing you on the VEI Board."*

I . . . understand. I am sorry that you are so bitter. Let's move on for now. I will be happy to send my requests concerning Bali Hai affairs through you. Am I hearing you correctly? You have been designated my heir and will be voting on virtual issues in my place. I see! I'm a little surprised . . . but I'm sure we'll work it out.

Diego: *Good! That's done. I'll be in touch.*

Yes . . . give my regards to Estrella.

Diego: *(in a singsong fashion) Will do.*

COMMAND, CEASE: Holographic tie, CEASE.

CEASED

Bastard. Nasty little prick.

COMMAND: Miranda, contact Ed Mayhook and tell him what's going on. Tell him to find a way out of this mess. Let me know what he says.

Of course, Gunter.

END RECORD

THE BURNING MAN

August 8, 2287

To: Desmond Webb, Archivist

Library of Congress, VR Division

Desmond—

So, this is how Holden lost control. To be honest, I'm still not convinced that Holden's hands are clean. He rolled over too easily.

I have confirmed the following: Prior to supplanting his uncle as the majority shareholder at VEI, Putnam was a consultant by Virtual Environments Options, Inc. Lawyers associated with VEI aided Putnam in his bid to supplant Holden on the VEI Board.

Did Miranda find a "way out?" If she did, why did Holden not take it? The memory ended, it's not clear to me. Please send more Holden memory files.

Warm regards,

Byron

***

Via message (confidential)

August 14, 2287

To: Byron Hernandez

Trammell & O'Connell Law Offices

Dear Byron—

Although it is only my opinion, I believe that Holden quickly realized that he was outmatched. I can find no record of a legal assessment provided to him by his lawyers, who were nowhere to be found during the mergers. Doing a casual search, I discovered that several members of Holden's legal team signed agreements with companies that were under the SEINI umbrella. Holden may not have known what was happening, but he was no fool.

Attached are Holden memories recorded prior to the dramatic changes that occurred after the Bali Hai platform was acquired by Infinite Bliss.

They may help you better understand the advantages and limitations offered by Bali Hai at the time. The Infinite Bliss changeover offers a stark contrast to the typical post-bio destination, of which Bali Hai was a good example.

At present, I am assembling a list of Holden memories post-merger and will send them along within the next few weeks.

Regards,

Desmond

GUNTER HOLDEN DOC. 160

V-Loc: Black Rock Desert, THE BURNING MAN, Northern Nevada recorded August 28, 2102 (day six of eighteen recorded) Tactile: Temp variants 211452 via SUMMER HIGH DESERT SENSATIONS Day to night level 4 © WESTERN US. ENVIRON-MENTS, event "bonfire). Auditory: WILDERNESS CALLS © 2105 VEI Sensory Specifics, Sims: Animal sims (air and ground 6.2, 202 non-interactive

Virtual Burning Man Event: Black Rock desert, night campfires, sims with glide homes

Well, hello! I'm surprised to see you; it's been a while.

. . .

I admit that I've been hard to find. Something happened. I can't talk about it now.

. . .

There are events that change you. They fill you with rage at the injustice. What recently happened was one of those. Moving on for now. When I was a bio, I attended a Burning Man. Something occurred that triggered a downward turn in my life. On occasion, I access this program, hoping to, at least, prevent my having to relive it in a memory breach.

. . .

Thank you for seeking me out. Can I assume that we're friends now?

. . .

I'm surprised that you're familiar with Burning Man. You're not alone. There are a few hundred residents mingling among the sim revelers.

. . .

When I was a bio, I went to a Burning Man Festival once and only because Laura said she was going with or without me. At Burning Man, Laura began slipping away from me.

. . .

After we transitioned to Bali Hai, I discovered that Laura decided to include select Burning Man events here without consulting me. Whenever I visit a Burning Man setting, I think of her.

. . .

Mostly, why she left me.

. . .

She left during a game called "The Baltimore Disaster."

. . .

The goal is to determine the identity of two of the bombers, preventing their next attack. Before the start of the game, we assumed the roles we were to play, I noticed that Laura seemed troubled.

. . .

After the first set of explosions, when we emerged from the underground shelter, we saw what the bombs had done and inexplicably, Laura began to cry. There were thousands of bodies twisted and blown apart. At the time, I was a little embarrassed for her. Other virtuals, our competitors, were watching us. Of course, everyone was searching for that first clue.

"They're sims," I said. "What's wrong with you? Can't you see what's real?" Then, I looked into her eyes, and I saw myself; a nineteen-year-old boy, shimmering in pools of tears. I pulled away. When I turned back, she was gone. Let's change the subject!

. . .

Burning Man?

. . .

I never liked the desert, but Black Rock was a surprise. There is nightmarish beauty, a menace, as if it could swallow you whole.

. . .

At the time, I had no idea of why Laura had dragged me to Burning Man. I soon realized it was because of Jacob. She wanted me to spend time with my brother.

. . .

I hadn't seen him since our father died. Jacob came to Burning Man with his collection of "friends." They were part of the entertainment.

. . .

Imagine a cold burning rage . . . and you hear your mother's song again. I had no knife, but I remember wondering if there was some way I could kill him without being caught.

. . .

Please, I didn't do it. It would have been pointless. From the looks of him, Jacob was half-dead anyway.

. . .

My brother was perched on a wooden stool as his voice soared above the thousands who sat or stood and swayed to the gentle rhythm, their faces glowing with firelight. Stage lights smoothed the tired lines and lit the gaunt hollows left by drugs and ruthless self-destruction.

Jacob's face was a cruel joke. My father gave Jacob his thick brows set low over Celeste's pale blue eyes. My brother's short straight nose and long upper lip suggested an Irish face, not German like mine or my mother's. His long legs reminded me of my father's reddened legs as he watched me build my castles.

Like my father, Jacob was a tenor. Dad's voice was pleasing. Jacob's voice was beautiful, soulful. The tenor was pure and full of longing. I give him that, but only that. Dad gave him everything.

. . .

I hid my reaction with a thin smile. Laura sat on the hood of an old Cadillac. Pink streaks of paint failed to conceal the rusted hulk. I knew she waited to see what I would do or say.

. . .

The whole thing was sad. Most people came dressed in bizarre costumes, their glide-homes or vehicles transformed and decorated using a variety of themes. One group showed up as a five-course meal. Dessert was a woman in her late eighties who was dressed as a piece of apple pie, her body sandwiched between triangular swathes of fabric, the surface layered with various lumps and textures, painted to resemble a golden crust.

. . .

I watched her climb uninvited onto the stage. I could see the piecrust shed gold sprinkles on the two men charged with taking care of such things. As they dragged her off, she reached toward Jacob a look of wild confusion on her face. Jacob continued, the song winding down its last promise, the guitar's strum caressing the lingering "you" while Jacob's tenor seemed to rise into the desert night.

My brother handed his guitar to a man who wore a pirate's hat and a long floral print dress, white with yellow daisies and left the stage. After whispering something to one of his "friends," a former addict whose "friendship" nearly accomplished what I couldn't—

my brother's untimely death—Jacob walked through the crowd, carefully avoiding the blankets and the folding chairs. His face was blank.

. . .

If we had left Burning Man then, that would be the end of my story. But of course, there's more.

. . .

I am telling you what happened. It started with some college students, eight or nine of them; the girls dressed as butterflies, and four beer-drinking boys came as oversized caterpillars. They had arrived in the late afternoon. Their glide bus was wrapped in white-colored materials, making it look like a cocoon.

. . .

It might have been amusing, except that something happened before I could leave, and it changed my life.

. . .

So, while people danced, I managed a semblance of a smile as Jacob stood before me and Laura jumped off the Caddy's hood, with a cheerful "Hi! I'm Laura. Your singing was wonderful!"

. . .

There were ten minutes of perfunctory questions. I decided that Laura and I would leave within an hour. Then, I heard Jacob say, "Dad loved you, you know. My mother made me promise to tell you that."

. . .

I looked at him in disbelief. Celeste was in Italy, living in some small town whose name I had forgotten, hopefully aging badly, the burden of her third husband.

. . .

Before I could answer him, we heard a scream: the cocoon was on fire.

. . .

An ember from the bonfire had found its way to a vulnerable spot of the white covering. Flames crawled on the outside of the cocoon, making it look like a marshmallow. One of the butterfly girls shrieked, "Get her out, get her out—OH MY GOD, CANDY! CANDY'S INSIDE!"

. . .

Horrifying is the right word. Even with all the shouts and shrieks, we could hear the girl screaming.

. . .

People did try to help. Unfortunately. There were five or six three-foot spools of glow rope, all piled near the burning glide-bus. When rescuers encountered three smoking spools pin-wheeling toward them, their focus shifted from rescue to self-preservation. Then, two caterpillars ran head-on into the fire. Seconds later, they were rolling on the ground. Meanwhile, Candy was wailing. "Help—please—help me—help—oh God—pleeeeease!"

. . .

I admit that I froze. Laura screamed, "Jacob!" I looked around and saw that Jacob was already in the fire, a blanket covering his head as he entered the burning bus. When Jacob reappeared in the doorway, dragging the lifeless Candy, two men grabbed both him and the girl seconds before the bus's shell collapsed. Powerless, everyone watched the fire finish its work, taking care to stay out of its way.

. . .

Laura was crying, her hand over her mouth. I desperately wanted to leave, but our glide home was blocked. An ambulance had appeared and after that, a fire truck's wailing sirens. Sadly, by then the girl was dead. Jacob had burns on his hands, the left side of his face and on his forehead. From the way Laura acted, you would have assumed he was critical. In my opinion, Jacob had been foolhardy, and his injuries were minor. In Laura's opinion, I was an unfeeling monster. The rift in our marriage began in the Black Desert.

. . .

Let's change the subject. By the way, have you contributed any memories to our memory library?

. . .

What do you mean you haven't any idea what I'm talking about? Never mind. We'll take it up another time. I'll be in touch!

END RECORD

THE MEMORY LIBRARY

GUNTER HOLDEN DOC. 164

V-Loc: Chicago Urban Series 77 Harry's café Loc: 34 of Chicago Urban 77 Series. Armitage HARRY'S CAFÉ Day 34 of 60 non-events. Urban environ 2.9k by 4.18, non-event traffic, level 5, Structures: 38 "High Rise" 24.9867 interactive/illusion, 103 sidewalks vendor/outdoor interactive level 8. See Holden Doc 136A. VEI URBANLIFE © 8.28.2085. FOODMIX, dining interactive VIRTUAL FOODLIFE 110, update 2.27. 2120.

Downtown Chicago, Harry's sidewalk café, with awnings due to rain

. . .

Tom, nice to see you! Join me. The café's quiet today. The fog and rain shower are a nice break from all the sun.

. . .

I like the rain. Not enough locations offer a variety of weather. It's been quite a while since you and I talked. Our sessions seem to have been effective. Almost no breaches. I am in your debt.

. . .

Gunter, Diego wants to speak with you.

Miranda, give him my apologies. I am unavailable now. I should be free next week and will be happy to schedule a time to meet.

I will tell him.

. . .

Diego is my idiot nephew who is temporarily functioning as my proxy in the Board meetings until I can put an end to his pretensions.

. . .

I'll explain it some other time. For now, it's too upsetting.

. . .

Miranda gave me your messages regarding your ex-wife's sudden transition to Bali Hai. How is that going?

. . .

You have my sympathy. I'm sure she will want to reconcile. I hear you accessed the Memory Library.

. . .

It can be disorienting at first, I agree. The intimacy can seem awkward, especially when you encounter that person after being inside their most private moments.

. . .

I've already been through all the new ones, at least all the ones I would find interesting. Miranda alerts me to any recent additions.

. . .

Me? I am reluctant to contribute because of my position in this community. Most find it flattering when they discover that I have "lived" one of their memories.

. . .

Oliver Jackson's Wedding Night

One you might enjoy is "The Wedding Night of Oliver Jackson." Mr. Jackson was a successful Kansas City realtor who was married to the same woman most of his adult life until his wife, Julie Marie, died of food poisoning on a cruise to Antarctica.

. . .

It was a local fish. Several passengers became ill.

. . .

No, this memory is not of his and Julie Marie's big day. The memory is of his second wedding night, to his wife's sister, Karina Louise.

. . .

Unlike her sister, Karina had been married four times, each man unsuitable in some way. I became interested in Mr. Jackson's memory when I encountered Karina at a hot tub party.

. . .

Karina transitioned when her ex-husband shot her before killing himself. The ex-husband transitioned to the Serene Vistas Center for virtual felons. Are you familiar with VEI's Vistas? We developed them when Congress decided a federal afterlife program presented too many complications. All after-death prisons became private operations.

. . .

No, my wife's and brother's murders were never solved.

. . .

If they knew, they never discussed it with me or the police.

. . .

I chose to honor their discretion. My grief was self-evident; I followed them here.

. . .

Let's go back to Karina's wedding night with Oliver. Julie was the one who made Oliver promise to marry Karina. Apparently when Julie realized she might die, she made Oliver promise to marry her sister.

. . .

Oliver reluctantly agreed. Julie knew Karina had loved Oliver and had for years. She told him it was better for their grown children, but it was for a different reason. Like Karina, I met Julie Marie in a hot tub.

. . .

Fifty years is quite a long time with one lover, you'll agree. Julie wanted to experience as a virtual what she had denied herself in her bio-life, though Oliver was content with their monogamous relationship. Other than a brief college fling, Julie's only lover had been Oliver.

. . .

And Oliver? Oliver was as faithful as the sunrise. Both were attractive. Julie was a petite blonde with brown eyes. Evidence of Oliver's Slavic heritage on his mother's side could be seen in his broad face with its masculine jaw and the folds above his eyes. He kept fit, playing ball with the two boys, who upon their father's bio-death sold their parents' house and made a nice profit, a fact that made Oliver proud.

. . .

Yes—I know, Oliver Jackson's wedding night was the topic. Both Oliver and Karina were over eighty in age, middle-aged and not young anymore. Promise or not, I doubt Oliver would have married Karina without Julie's gentle prodding during their glum bio-to-virtual communications. After a City Hall wedding, the newlyweds rented a cabin on the Lake Tahoe.

. . .

Yes, Tahoe is beautiful in the fall. Here is where Oliver's recorded memory begins: Karina is past eighty, but as Oliver opens the door to the cabin, he notices for the first time that she is still an attractive woman. Keep in mind the observer is privy to the donor's thoughts and sensations. One is simultaneously observing and experiencing the memory.

. . .

The first sensation is overwhelming guilt and a sense of foreboding. As Karen peels off a heavy sweater, Oliver opens his mouth to begin his speech that their marriage is in name only, that she is free to take lovers as long as she is discreet. Karina takes her hair out of its knotted bun, and finding a brush, she sighs as she strokes the tangles from her hair. Then, she smiles shyly at him, asking if he is hungry and would he like to walk up to the casino. He stares at her as she realizes what is happening and without a word, her hand goes to her waist and her skirt falls to the floor.

. . .

I recommend you access "Mr. Jackson's Wedding Night." It was a memorable wedding night.

. . .

When she learned of Karina's sudden transition to Bali Hai after only four years of marriage to Oliver, Julie nearly burst with frustration. She was convinced that it would be only a matter of time before Oliver followed Karina into Bali Hai.

. . .

Surprisingly, Oliver continued his bio-life for another twenty-five years. During a final walk-through, Oliver slipped on the glossy top step of a grand staircase and broke his neck.

. . .

After Oliver's transition, the boys kept in touch for a while. The miracle was supposed to be that death didn't mean goodbye, but eventually, that's exactly what happens. Oliver had not been in Bali Hai a year when he and Julie fell into the Dreams.

. . .

I believe Oliver was unable to adjust to a life with no real estate. In Bali Hai, there are no gentrified neighborhoods for the upwardly mobile, no fixer-uppers to flip. Everything here is according to your memory allotment. Unfortunately for Oliver, his dream was an unending walk through before closing the deal.

Karina is still here and happily married to Sergei, a former dancer who toured with the Bolshoi Ballet. In an instant, Karina gained skills that Sergei spent a lifetime acquiring. It's a real love-match. I wonder how long it will last.

. . .

Gunter, Diego insists that it is important.
Miranda, I will meet with him when I am free. Tell him again.
Of course, Gunter.
Where was I?

. . .

Love and commitment, yes. Even those relationships based on the deepest, most unselfish love can disappoint. For example, the parent-child relationship. When it comes to virtual life, most post-bio companies offer programs that cater to child virtual developmental requirements and related family issues.

. . .

It's a sticky problem, the death of children. VEI spent time and resources developing "Candy Island Adventure" until I lost patience with parents and their countless demands. Many wanted to transition immediately to be with the child. Questions needed answers. Do we allow these new virtuals to remain children or design a program whose purpose is to create a virtual adult? What about the needs of bio-siblings?

. . .

I later recommended to the Board that VEI drop its plans to offer destinations to juveniles. Are you familiar with the post-bio company Evergreen Inc.?

. . .

I wondered after the reports of legal actions against Evergreen.

Salan vs. Salan

. . .

The most notable was the case of Salan versus Salan. The child, Jeremy Salan, transitioned three months before his ninth birthday. His father, Otis was a landscaper who designed environments for large corporate complexes.

. . .

You may have also heard of Jeremy's mother. She was a minor celebrity. Betsy Salan. She wrote cookbooks. Remember the "cooking from scratch" parties?

. . .

My simple-minded second wife, Therese insisted on cooking, and Betsy Salon's *The Holo-Chef* was Therese's bible. Everything must be fresh. Plus, the odd ritual of talking to each ingredient with positive energy was a must and for me, torture.

After two years of it, I divorced her. Her dream was that I give her the Hampton house. "The energy is perfect when I cook Betsy," was her plea. Gladly.

. . .

This story is true, but still a mystery. Despite their best efforts to solve the riddle of his behavior, Jeremy Salan is or was a mystery to his parents.

. . .

I know you like mysteries. I've read several of your efforts. Betsy and Otis Salan were both in their seventies when little Jeremy was born. By the time he was eight weeks along, Jeremy's genes were studied, and he was allowed to continue developing peacefully in Betsy's womb.

His intelligence was estimated as highly gifted. The Salans made reservations for schools. Otis planned a child's paradise of tree houses, winding paths and hedges. Nursery walls included dreamy seascapes. Jeremy would see a floating mermaid singing a soft lullaby at naptime and a "good morning sleepy head Jeremy" when it was time to wake.

The months passed blissfully. Betsy was radiant. The joy of motherhood seemed to overwhelm her. Otis was equally effusive in his enthusiasm. Do you have children, grandchildren, etcetera?

. . .

Why haven't you heard from them?

. . .

My sympathy. Ask any five people here if they communicate with family in the bio- world. Two out of the five will say no and at least one will tell a similar story of some misunderstanding.

The Salans' dream of a perfect life ended with Jeremy's birth. Jeremy was perfectly formed with a round head and with wisps of Otis' dark hair. Betsy, her eyes swimming with happy tears, noted her son's long fingers. "Just like his grandpa!"

Grandpa was a surgeon in Chicago at the time. In fact, he's now a Bali Hai resident. He occupies a penthouse in Paris where he paints. Prior to Jeremy's birth, he gave Betsy, his only offspring, a large check intended for higher education, hopefully med school and not "a goddamn cooking school."

The day his parents brought him home, Jeremy cried for hours, but Otis and Betsy were committed to caring for little Jeremy. No nurse or nanny was required.

. . .

Ha! How did you guess?

. . .

Of course, you went through this scenario yourself. After days of no sleep, they hired a professional nanny, a Venezuelan. Otis was Venezuelan and an aunt recommended the woman, a girlhood friend of hers. Plump and ninetyish, the nanny had no eyebrows and eyes like raisins. Her name was Isobel. Isobel inspected "Jeremy's house" and pronounced the nursery walls as the problem. "He doesn't like them—too much stimulation."

. . .

The boy went to specialists of all stripes. Isobel claimed that the parents were impatient and put their own needs ahead of their son's.

. . .

Yes, he was precocious. At fourteen months, Jeremy was a small, elf-like boy with light blue eyes and pale, reddish lashes.

. . .

I promise to finish Jeremy's story, however, there is the Board meeting, something important and I must consult with Diego, my bio-rep. Let's meet later and I promise I'll tell you the rest!

END RECORD

A Gift to say Goodbye

Byron— Feel free to skip if you aren't interested in what follows. These memory docs include the following: Gunter theorizes on why he remains friends with Thomas. Gunter reviews his first wife's (Marcia Evans) memory. Holden meets Tom in veranda environment and shares a memory of Jacob as a toddle and completes the Salan story.

GUNTER HOLDEN DOC.170

V-Loc: See 743.1, Chicago ELYSIUM penthouse PERSONAL, updated 6.28.2122. 19 detailed interiors include entry lobby, elevators 2 and 8, rotating 4 of 10 resident interiors and concierge. © 8.18.2120 by VEI Personal Options

Chicago Elysium Penthouse

Miranda, notify me when you have any news from the VEI Board. I don't trust my nephew. I feel cut off from VEI's operation, the company that I built. I suspect Diego is perfectly happy to keep me in the dark.

I understand your concern, Gunter. I will keep you informed concerning VEI.

Thank you for suggesting Tom as a confidant. I think my friendship with Thomas Bucklin has had a stabilizing effect on my files.

I agree. You have had fewer breaches.

Miranda, the messages sent to me while I was in the adjustment period. Somehow, I never found the right time to review them. I mean those I chose to . . . I know I avoided them.

Yes Gunter. Do you wish to delete them?

No, Miranda. I think it's time to review them. After that, perhaps I'll ask you to delete.

COMMAND, Miranda, RUN: Marcia Evans, Memory C2A

C2A RUNNING

She gazes at the holo-transmitter. Shimmering within its projection frame is an image of her and me on our honeymoon. "Continue," she whispers as her fingers touch the gold necklace she wears. It is a tiny bridge, a copy of San Francisco's Golden Gate, suspended by delicate links and my gift to her on our first anniversary.

The holo becomes a brief video. In it, I draw my new wife close as I tell her, "I love you Marcia, and I always will." She puts her hand on my chest and smiles as she pretends to believe me.

"The happy couple," she murmurs. "Cease." The holo-image freezes. Behind us is a panoramic vista, the Pacific Ocean as seen from "our" bridge. "Who gets the bridge now that our marriage is done? The new wife?" She wonders.

Miranda, COMMAND, PAUSE:

PAUSED.

I gave her the bridge holo. We knew that it was over, and I would be meeting someone else. I would never give away our bridge; how could she think . . .

Miranda: COMMAND, RESUME: C2A

RESUMED

"A gift to say goodbye," she thinks." I've lost him. He's meeting someone there." She blows a kiss to my image."

She's trembling. She feels waves of pain, sadness, pain; it's . . . pain—

Miranda, PAUSE:

PAUSED

Why does she—I rarely allow myself to feel sad . . . the indulgence . . . Why suffer when nothing can be done? Why did you allow yourself . . . never mind.

Miranda, RESUME: C2A

Marcia's memory RESUMED

"Is there a way to get him back?" She wonders. "What was I thinking? I knew what he was and still chose to be with him. Betrayal was inevitable. I want him to feel the pain I feel. He won't. How could he understand? I'm fifty-two, he's twenty-eight, still a child. It couldn't go on forever." She looks in the mirror. "The joke is on me." She starts to cry. "I had no eggs stored. How am I pregnant? Perhaps a side effect of the gene therapy." She sighs. "I won't keep it; he'd resent it." She caresses her abdomen. "Already, my belly swells. I'm so sorry, little one. It's best this way; I'm doing you a favor."

Miranda: END Memory C2A

ENDED

SHE WAS DOING ME A FAVOR? DAMN HER!

How could she think that? I HAD A RIGHT TO KNOW!

I wasn't a child despite what she thought! She kept me in the dark, her way of keeping some sense of control and . . . No.

She was right; I guess that I would have seen the baby as a trap. She knew me, after all . . . It might have helped if she had known that I still loved her.

She came to Bali Hai, her transition avatar glittering on the sand. I promised to make her happy. None of the past would matter, not the ex-wives, the long hours and all the pressure, even what happened with Joy Forever. I know she understood why I did it, even if she didn't . . . Why did she decide to leave so soon? Why did she follow Laura and fall into the Dreams?

She left no information on this. I'm sorry, Gunter.

The year we married we drove along the Coast whenever we could. The joy is like an old friend.

Yes, Gunter, I know.

END RECORD

THE HOLDEN ESTATE

G UNTER HOLDEN DOC. 735
V-Loc: Holden Estate (Connecticut) Day 18 of 46 days, selected from recorded days 2103-2112 CUSTOM, TACTILE/ VISUAL: NEW ENGLAND SUMMERS (VEI ENVIR0N- MENTS) © June 2117, non-event temperate, Sims: Animal 259 interactive level 5, Note Human-423 interactive level 5 available on request (connected New London site) AUDITORY- COUNTRY SOUNDS, INC. © August 2114

New England, Holden Estate, outdoor patio (veranda) early summer, mild temperature, birds and insects, sound of Thames River

. . .

I'm glad you could make it, Tom. Welcome to my father's veranda! I know I've been somewhat of a recluse.

. . .

Patel filled these surroundings with ants and centipedes, and worms, and snakes crawl through the grass. Butterflies drift, squirrels jump from branch to branch, and raccoons lumber in search of a meal. All rewind and replay the drama of their life cycles. Miranda recreates them like Genesis renewing Eden. There's a path leading to the Thames, which leads to the mouth of the Atlantic, where a new program waits.

. . .

I wonder how much the virtual life here differs from the biological. Life for a virtual ant could hardly be different, but what about the trees? Do they miss the end of winter and the return of spring?

. . .

The yellow-billed wrens remind me of Seattle. I remember the ducks quacking and fluttering their wings. By the way, forty-five is an excellent age for you. You move with confidence and the curve in your shoulders disappears.

. . .

So, Miranda told me you thoroughly enjoyed "Mr. Jackson's Wedding Night." What did you think of Jackson?

. . .

Exactly!

. . .

I promised to finish the Jeremy story, didn't I?

Evergreen

. . .

After Jeremy's birth, the Salans struggled to adjust. Otis continued his work at Evergreen; Betsy wrote cookbooks. Isobel became the diplomatic link between Jeremy and his bewildered parents. Worse, Jeremy adamantly refused to eat the food his mother prepared with such care. He thrived, Isobel testified, he thrived on cheese toast and tater tots.

. . .

I see that Jeremy's behavior doesn't surprise you. Sometimes, dear Thomas, you can be smug, but since you have experience raising children . . .

. . .

I think that Otis and Betsy came to see Jeremy as a project that would pay off sometime in the future, like a bond or a tree planted as a sapling. Life settled. Betsy and Otis were "mildly disappointed," in their words. Betsy claimed that Jeremy took after her father.

"We'll start planning for med-school soon."

. . .

Otis landscaped the Evergreen New Haven offices. You'll recall that Evergreen was the first company to offer a virtual post-bio destination tailored for the needs of families.

As part of his contract, Otis received Evergreen post-bio destinations for him, Betsy and, yes—Jeremy. On Jeremy's sixth birthday, Betsy mixed the Evergreen nano-transmitters into Jeremy's piece of "that monstrosity fudge cake" Isobel had made for him.

Evergreen included an early type of "projected development" software so that post bio children would continue to grow into "virtual adults."

. . .

The virtual Jeremy Salan

What happened was this: The morning of his bio-death, Jeremy and Betsy were at an impasse. It was summer vacation and Isobel was in Atlantic City. The boy had hidden rolls of food left for him by Isobel.

. . .

While Betsy was getting a massage, Jeremy, his pocket full of tater tots and cheese toast, went out to the pond. He had a fistful of food in his mouth while he dropped pebbles on the fish. When a crumb dropped into the water, a fish jumped up to get it and startled Jeremy, causing him to aspirate the tots and toast. In his struggle, the boy collapsed and fell into the pond.

. . .

Poor Betsy found him. As soon as arrangements could be made to protect their estate, the parents took the proverbial hemlock.

. . .

Now, here's where it gets interesting. The Evergreen program begins by reassuring the transitioned child, greeting him with something familiar. Jeremy transitioned to Betsy's virtual kitchen where an Isobel-sim offered him a plate of his favorite food. Records indicate that Jeremy was delighted with the change.

. . .

Falconcrest

Before they transitioned to virtual life, the parents made several attempts to contact Jeremy. Each time, he refused. He wasn't angry with them; he just didn't miss them. By the time Betsy and Otis joined the Evergreen family, Jeremy was living with the Isobel-sim and a few like-minded children whose parents, unlike Betsy and Otis, had decided to remain bios.

. . .

Unfortunately, what worked for Jeremy was unthinkable for his parents, who suffered desperate boredom at the droning pace of the Falconcrest Community, a small group of taciturn parents with self-contained offspring.

. . .

I—let me finish with Jeremy! He refused to live with his parents unless the Isobel-sim was included. Betsy couldn't abide the sim and so she poured her energy into her projects. And Otis? I have no idea how Otis made it through.

. . .

The maturity program was disappointing. Yes, physically, Jeremy changed, manifesting as five feet eleven in height, with Otis' slender build, but he remained a redhead with pale blue eyes.

. . .

The thing is, when you're a bio growing up, you never know what's going to be thrown at you or to you, so you learn to be flexible. But everything in virtual life is predictable. Jeremy remained a child by never having to adapt. Since all decisions are made by the new "adult," Jeremy announced he was marrying the Isobel-sim. The Salans sued Evergreen.

. . .

During the trial, Betsy let it slip that Jeremy resembled her mother's maternal uncle, Albert who was a reclusive entomologist. Uncle Albert spent his adult life studying the life cycle of the Hemlock wooly adelgid. This undermined the claim that the Evergreen program was defective. Genetics rather than software determined their son's choices.

Yes, there were other witnesses. During his "maturation" process, Jeremy had three roommates, fourteen-year-old Tupac and six-year-old twins, Wanda, and Sandra. All three supported Jeremy's decision to marry the Isobel-sim.

In his holo-deposition, the "adult" Jeremy smoked a pipe. The new "citizen" looked very content; his arm was around the nanny-sim.

. . .

Betsy prevailed upon her father to intervene, which he did by arranging the transfer of Betsy and Otis to Bali Hai. However, he refused to help them deal with Jeremy.

"I could've told you it wouldn't work out," he told poor Betsy. "The kid's just like Albert, as weird as they come."

They're still here, Betsy and Otis, though they're no longer married, their dream of a perfect life with their perfect child, long gone.

I need to know if you are willing to continue helping me.

. . .

Thank you. Your friendship means a lot to me.

. . .

Meaning there have been fewer breaches. I'm less distracted, which means that I'm better able to deal with glitches, rumors of mergers, Board issues and so on. I know I shouldn't disclose this. Bali Hai may be incompatible with the technology of newer holo-entertainment companies. My fear is that as we fall behind, our existence becomes more isolated, less relevant.

. . .

I have asked you here for a reason. Let me explain. There are files of private memories and messages left to me by certain people, friends and . . . I've known about these for a long time. I plan to review them and there's a chance that some may be upsetting. I might need advice. Can I count on your discretion?

. . .

A toast to big brothers

I—I'll tell you about them another time.

. . .

Let me tell you about one of my most memorable visits to Holden Estate. I was alone, watching the sailboats on the Thames. I had arrived to an empty house. It was quiet until I heard a scream coming from the trees near the river.

. . .

It was the scream of a small child, terrified and in pain.

. . .

I was startled for a moment, but then, I leaped out of my chair and as I neared the source, I saw Jacob, who was about three at the time. A large dog gripped Jacob's left arm in its jaws. Jacob's shirt was soaked with red, and he was crying, "No doggie, no, don't bite."

. . .

I looked around for something to use as a weapon. There was a rock about the size of my fist. Its sharp edges came in handy. I kept hitting the dog's nose and eyes until it let Jacob go. Then, it tore into me, which resulted in stitches in the palm of my left hand. When I managed to wedge the rock into the beast's eye, it yelped and took off.

. . .

Fortunately, they caught the thing and tested it for rabies, which proved negative. Anyway, Jacob sat and watched, blood dripping down his arm. He looked at me for a second as if he wasn't sure, then he said "Gunn . . .?"

Apparently, Celeste, like Marcia, realized the value of relationships and she would show Jacob my holo now and then. Unlike his gaunt drug-addict self, Jacob was a plump toddler with dark curly hair and Celeste's round eyes—very irritating. I noticed the dimples in his hands as he put his arms out. When I picked him up, he was shaking as I carried him back to the house.

. . .

Your reaction is understandable, coming from a parent. The nanny, who was fired promptly, had decided to take a nap. When they arrived separately, both Celeste and Dad made an event out of the incident—calling the local media, who wanted an interview.

. . .

No, I declined and left a day later, knowing that my relationship with my father needed no further maintenance. I had saved his son.

. . .

Shall we toast? There's something about a white porcelain cup that elevates my mood. I'd like to toast to . . . let's see . . . the River Thames, as it flows through the world of life and death and mean dogs and . . .what . . . uh . . . if you insist—a toast to big brothers.

. . .

I know that I said I invited you to discuss the old messages.

. . .

It seems that I'm still not ready to . . .

. . .

pause

THE SHUDDERING TREES

*V*ia messenger (confidential)

September 3, 2287

Desmond Webb

Archivist

Library of Congress

Des—

In reviewing the latest Holden memory records, I was startled to see an environment that I recognize from my childhood. Holden's Connecticut property, the one he said belonged to his father, was the place where I spent several childhood summers. The veranda was overrun by weeds one summer and I earned spending money clearing it. When I was sixteen, my cousin and I almost drowned in the Thames when our raft overturned.

How did my Uncle Andrew acquire this property from Holden's estate? Whatever the reason, it will have to wait. I need to focus on the business at hand.

If there are more veranda Connecticut memories, would you flag them for me?

Thank you,

Byron

****

Byron—the remainder of this memory takes place on the veranda. It includes a memory breach, also a veranda location.

Resume

'The Kidnapping of Jacob Holden

There was an incident . . . At the age of ten, Jacob was kidnapped.

. . .

By whom, I'm still not sure. It doesn't matter. I never bothered with the particulars. Ultimately, both Jacob and the ransom were recovered. Here's the thing. The kidnappers beat Jacob and broke both his legs to ensure that he did not try to run.

. . .

At the time, I was in South Africa. Unfortunately, Celeste made high drama of my refusal to leave pressing obligations to "rush" to my brother's side.

What happened to the wrens?

MEMORY BREACH!!

Just drink it, Dad. You won't regret it, I promise.

BREACH!!!

Just drink it, Dad. You won't regret it, I promise . . .drinkdrinkdrinkdrink

CACHE: BIO/ Holden Estate/Death of Eric Holden 67753982

Jacob sits in a wicker chair as he ruins my life. Dad is in a reclining chair on the far side. Dad keeps turning his head, as if looking for a reprieve. My father isn't ready for oblivion. The nanobots are ready. Bali Hai is up and running. I know my father. He will love Bali Hai! So why isn't he going?

Resting his hand on Dad's arm, Jacob says, "Dad, this is a big decision." I want to break that hand. "All I'm saying," my brother's voice oozes concern, "is that you might feel trapped."

I'm sitting here with the damn white cup, waiting to help my dying father. Dad's eyes dart back and forth between Jacob and the cup. Jacob sits stone-faced, holding his mother's hand.

Then Jacob says the word "trapped." I want to squeeze his neck.

"Dad, drink this." I beg him. "You'll wake up in Bali Hai!"

Oh God, Dad is beginning to cry.

"Jacob, tell him no . . . I can't . . . I didn't mean to . . . Nancy— I . . ."

Celeste gasps. I shoot her a warning look not to interfere.

Why did he say my mother's name?

Dad's eyes narrow. He twists his mouth in an ugly smile. He shakes his head as the shadow-leaves on his face continue their dance. Then he points a finger at me. "I'll be damned," my father says, "I'll be goddammed if I'll be judged. Eric Holden makes his own rules." He looks as if he hates me.

I try again . . . "Dad, it wasn't your fault—my leaving Mom, her death. I made the choice to go with you and it happened, an accident . . ."

But Dad won't look at me; he keeps staring at the trees and . . .

oh God he's beginning to sing . . . the croak and whine of an old man shaking his head, the sounds from deep in his throat until he flings them at the shuddering trees . . .

"I'll . . . see . . . you . . . soon . . . by . . . the . . . weep . . . willow . . . ummm . . . heart . . ." The dying man's head lolls.

END BREACH!!!

STOP!!!

I know . . . the rollercoaster . . . damn them both . . .

damn them . . . missing paint

MEMORY BREACH!!

STOP!!

CACHE: VIRTUAL (POST TRANSITION) V-Loc: Veranda, Holden Estate, "Summer Night" VEI 482-3

I'm waiting on the "virtual" veranda of the "Holden Estate." I marvel at the virtual fireflies that hover where the lights fade. I cradle a shot of bourbon in my left hand as I listen to the river. Tree branches bounce. I hear Laura, so full of sighs, her pleas spurned in the low hum of my brother's terse replies.

Jacob opens the French door. I remember that door. It's missing paint on the bottom edge.

"Where's Laura?" I ask him. He ignores my question.

The river and branches continue their serenade. Jacob looks the same. The "artist" sits in the same wicker chair that he occupied that day when Dad lay dying. Jacob stretches his legs out— God, he looks like . . . I can almost smell the ocean air and Dad's cigar . . .

"Where's Laura?" I ask again. 'What's next?" Don't ask.

"I didn't want this." Jacob says.

"Want what?"

Jacob trains those round blue eyes on me. "To be here."

I'm laughing. Delete yourself. I'll be glad to help you.

"Don't bother. I know about the Dreams." My brother stares at me.

"That's classified information. I'm curious. Who told you? Not Miranda, her program forbids it."

"Laura told me." Jacob studies his hands. "By the way, I'm here because she was afraid of you, of what you would do. She loves you and you pushed her away. Gunter, what is your problem? Work comes before everything! I was second choice, but I was her friend, and she tried to protect me by slipping nanobots into my food. I wish she had asked me if wanted it."

I give him a sympathetic smile and nod. "So, she was afraid in case I found out about what was going on you mean?"

Pathetic. He doesn't answer.

"The dog, it was behind those trees," Jacob tells me. *Does he think this earns him forgiveness?*

"I heard it barking. His bark sounded like he was hurt or something. I wanted a dog, but Dad said I wasn't old enough. I thought maybe if we found a hurt dog, Dad might feel sorry for it. Do you remember?"

I remember the scars on my hand, I tell him.

"You saved my life. All of my life I have I owed you."

"This is getting maudlin. It's time to cut the crap. So, you paid me back by stealing my wife. What's your point?"

"We're even. You saved my life once and then you took it. I owe you nothing." Ice in his voice. Good—the real Jacob.

I agree. I guess we are.

END BREACH!!

The scars. I guess we are.

What's your pointpointpoint . . . what's

STOP!!!

RESUME DOC 735

What happened? What do you think happened?

. . .

I'm sorry, Tom! I didn't mean to snap. It's . . . I'm fine. Yes, it happened again. I prefer not to talk about it. I wonder if we could meet later after I—I . . . it's kind of you to be concerned, but I simply want to shake it off. Thanks, Tom! I appreciate the kind words. I'll see you soon . . .

. . .

by the Weeping Willow . . . Oh God help me!

COMMAND: Miranda, RUN: sim sunbathing sequence aqua house . . . no

COMMAND, PAUSE: Sunbathing sequence . . . wait . . .

PAUSED.

COMMAND, Miranda, RUN: Seattle house sequence. Start the rain.

Beginning rain

END RECORD

THE HISTORY OF AFTER-DEATH

Via message (confidential)

October 12, 2287

To: Desmond Webb

c/o Library of Congress, VR Division

Des—

Let me thank you for your help. I'm afraid these memories do not yield clues to any weaknesses in the SEINI nondisclosure wall. Since you expressed concern that any further research might result in consequences, I am reluctant to ask for more Holden memories, solely for personal reasons.

If you can safely access more Holden memories, please let me know. I wish I was convinced he had nothing to do with SEINI.

Warmest regards

Bryon

***

Via message (confidential)

November 18, 2287

To: Byron Hernandez

c/o Trammell & O'Connell Law Offices

Byron—

The attached Gunter Holden memories include content that may be helpful in your research. Again, I am including less relevant docs. to avoid attention. Although some are solely Holden's thoughts and interactions with your grandfather, a few describe Infinite Bliss's hostile takeover of VEI, the Paris incident and the Everlasting Praise community. Jeremy Salan's replacing Gunter as virtual representative to the Infinite Bliss Board resulted in Gunter losing all his influence and ability to protect Bali Hai.

Let me know what you think. I'm aware that bio-relatives of Shemathra's Realm missing virtuals are demanding Congressional action. The focus of SEINI has shifted and is no longer on my department. I am now searching for the Holden memory docs that relate to SEINI and the early days of the Shemathra herds. Hopefully, they will document what happened during the SEINI takeover and your grandfather's short time as a secular virtual in the Shemathra Realm.

Since you are a direct descendent, you may be entitled to a copy of your grandfather's contract.

By the way, in terms of the veranda, I admit the childhood memories you shared are intriguing. Perhaps Holden willed it to your grandfather's estate.

Warmest regards,

Desmond

***

Via message (confidential)

November 24, 2287

Desmond Webb

c/o Library of Congress, VR Division

Des—

Infinite Bliss was involved with the Paris incident? I assumed that SEINI was responsible.

I am very interested in these files. Please send me all that you find.

Many thanks!

Byron

*Byron—there are several docs here. They cover your grandfather's friendship and disagreements with Holden, as well as Holden's personal memory docs. I suggest going through them for a clear picture of the events leading up to the Infinite Bliss merger and later, the SEINI takeover. I will flag certain topics ** for reference.*

From Bali Hai

GUNTER HOLDEN MEMORY FILES

FOLDER YEAR: 2204

GUNTER HOLDEN DOC. 764.

V-Loc: Oahu event IN THE PIPE COMPETITION OF 2142. South Pacific beach-2.74 k, ocean-2.6 k from shoreline, structures-1, vegetation-tropical no. 3347.1c, © 7.5.2124 by VEI Standard Environments. Audio: ocean surf (level 8) gulls 59 level 4, wildlife level 2, OCEANBASE INTERACTIVES © 4.23.2132, Tactile: Tropic Sun afternoon to evening light effect 4.7, Moonrise progression 3.5, breeze (level 3 fixed), Sand texture BEACHLIFE No. 6.8 © 6.2.2019, Sims: level 7 interactive, 47 participants interactive by HAWAII REMEMBERED, Olfactory: Ocean Sense © 5.19.2134,

Late summer, afternoon, Oahu Beach surfing competition. High surf and some wind. Assorted sims, including surfers and spectators.

Riding the turtle

Welcome to the Pipe Competition. Feel the breeze? Wonderful, isn't it?

. . .

I've missed our talks.

. . .

Thanks for coming.

. . .

I admit I ask for your help and then change the subject. It frustrates me too. I must confront the things in my past that press on me.

But there's a memory I can't access, and this feeling makes me erratic at times. I'm sure that you've noticed.

. . .

For now, let's enjoy something positive. This Hawaiian Pipe Master, the competition of 2142, includes sims of champion surfers, some of the year's best.

. . .

I know I haven't been easy to find. It's the memory breaches. I never know when one will occur. That you or anyone would be concerned about my welfare surprises me. I don't know what to say.

. . .

Wow! Did you see that barrel wave and how the surfer pulled into it? I've been busy putting together a list of programs, with Miranda's help. Bali Hai is due for some much-needed upgrading.

. . .

It has been too long since our last outing. I hear you are communicating with Pauline, your ex-wife. How is that progressing?

. . .

It's only been a short time since her bio-death and transition. I'm happy it's going so well.

My God! Did you see that? The Balinese champion just dropped into a pipe. The sims moving blankets close to the rock piles remind me of the sim-family-vacationers you encountered right after you transitioned.

. . .

These sims are more advanced. Watch the bored sim-mother, the one putting the hat on her son. The toddler is busy tasting the wet sand, licking it off the tip of his finger. Charming. The woman in her sixties handing out sandwiches to the twin girls often tosses them rather than handing them out directly.

. . .

Follow me. The rocks are wider here, but they are closer to the waves, so we'll get a little wet. All of this is only an echo. It's the romance of vacation, of escape, that I wish I could relive.

. . .

There's a tortoise crawling onto the shore. Do you see it?

. . .

Soon, a group of young sim-boys will gather. Here they come. Now, they're only laughing at the way it moves, but soon they'll start poking the animal with a stick. This same incident happens every time I'm here.

. . .

The interesting thing is the outcome varies. If one of us interferes, the boys will run away. If we stay out of it, the boys keep at it until tortoise bites one, causing him to cry and the others to flee. I never interfere. There he goes; see what happens?

. . .

Often, the tortoise locks its jaws on the thin arm of his tormenter, who has made the mistake of trying to ride on the beast's back.

you're seeing it . . . seeing . . .

be fierce . . .

BREACH!!!

CACHE: Post transition) VIRTUAL Kenya social occasion with Laura Holden (wife) and Jacob Holden (brother). Loc: Adventure Africa! @Wild Kingdom Environments VEI © 2235 see VEI 5667895 for sensory stats. Please note: JUMP to San Simeon 78896308

African environment, clear terrain, lion and other wild animal *sims.*

There is a lion bounding towards us

Laura grabs my arm. She doesn't scream. Good girl.

The lion stops several feet away and stares at us as if to consider which of us he will eat first. Jacob freezes and stares back. Even here, he acts like prey. Today's Jacob is in his late thirties. The scar on his face from the fire has disappeared. Today, I'm younger than Jacob. Laura, who today is twenty-eight, rests her hand on my shoulder.

"It's beautiful here," Jacob says. "I wish . . ."

"What do you wish," I ask him.

Jacob smiles as he answers. "I wish I had taken the time to see it when I was a bio. I could have done it, gone to Africa; we had the chance, the band I mean, and . . . but I didn't. Maybe if I had, things might have been different. You and I might have found some common ground."

"You're seeing it now."

I ignore my brother's regret. There's silence. I'm not surprised. The man is a cluster of weaknesses. The lion sim's memory makes it fierce. It roars, ready to pounce, and that's all it does until it spots the black-and-white zebras roaming near to where we're standing. The wind is against the beasts. Stalking its prey, the cat bounds toward it with the fluid stride of a killer. It brings the creature down with its powerful jaws clamped on the zebra's quivering throat.

The same zebra will graze tomorrow and perhaps escape while another member of the herd falls, the blood oozing and the eyes rolling back as it collapses. The program generates replacements, recasting the animal that becomes the lion's victim. I want to stay and watch. Laura and Jacob are jumping.

I follow them, follow them, keep it light . . .keep . . .

END BREACH!!

RESUME 764

V-Loc: Refer to Gunter Holden doc. 764. (Oahu Event)

. . .

No, I'm not bored. I've experienced another . . . never mind.

The sun is setting. We've seen what there is to see; all the best surfers are done. How about a change of pace? In fact, let's change oceans.

. . .

There's a program I'd love to show you. It starts near my father's veranda and from there, we'll sail a schooner on the Thames River to the mouth of the Atlantic. Follow my jump.

COMMAND, Miranda, JUMP TRANSFER: Gunter Holden, Thomas Bucklin

TRANSFER COMPLETE

V-Loc: Thames River 10.5 k with 1.2k New London (illusion only interactive) New London is another program, see New London 3.88 June 23, 2138, update NEW ENGLAND ENVIRONMENTS © 2136) non-event weather variations to pre-storm level 4, Atlantic 5.3 k Audio/visual/tactile by OCEANA © 2112, Olfactory is level 6 from OCEAN ENVIRONMENTS © 2111, Sims: 340 aquatic level 3, two sea turtles level 5.2 and whale level 5

Autumn, late morning, Thames River near Holden New England Estate, near mouth of Atlantic Ocean. High winds.

Ah, this is bracing. I think you'll appreciate the contrast.

Strange! I've never seen that species of fish in these waters. There have been so many anomalies that I imagine I'm seeing them everywhere.

. . .

In terms of designing oceans, Patel was careful. I often thought he was too careful. Monty knew Patel at Encore, where Patel oversaw the Environmental Sim Development for American Adventure.

Sounds primitive, doesn't it? At the time, American Adventure offered "an endless menu of excitement and the thrills of virtual adventure . . ." The real adventure was hoping that the mind-uploads were completed. Would "Aunt Millie" remember the names of everyone gathered for the virtual/bio-family reunion? They were happy if the new virtual remembered anything. Temporary amnesia was a problem and, occasionally, permanent memory-loss.

When we began VEI, we developed ways of stabilizing files and later, there were great leaps forwards in nanotechnology. When I created the Bali Hai platform, I was convinced that these platforms could become realities of exceptional beauty and opportunity. It frustrates me that there is no one here to help me protect VEI. Monty and Marcia came to Bali Hai but didn't stay. And Patel never came here at all.

It might have been different if Olaf Vanderbok had been involved. He created Encore. Vanderbok was a pioneer in virtual research. I studied his work at Stanford.

COMMAND: Miranda, RUN the whale migration sequence.

RUNNING: Whale migration

Fascinating creatures, aren't they? It was a challenge to include, not many were left, but Patel was determined.

You look perturbed. Am I boring you again or are you just "underwhelmed" by the Atlantic?

. . .

Vanderbok? Vanderbok was a visionary.

. . .

So, Vanderbok created Encore, but the investors were impatient and pushed to speed up the development of new destinations before Heavenly Horizons and Eternal Spring had their programs up and running. Then, someone funded a takeover of Encore and Vanderbok was out.

. . .

I don't know what happened to him after he pushed out. I think he moved back to Manitoba. I kept his lecture series on virtual city planning in my dorm room.

. . .

No, I never met him. I wish I had.

. . .

I did try. When I was at Stanford, I sent him a note saying I was involved in virtual environment research, and would he mind if I consulted him on certain ideas and questions. I never heard back. I heard he died not long after I sent the note. It was a traffic accident. What's wrong?

. . .

You keep looking as if you want to be somewhere else.

. . .

If you'd rather go, my feelings will not be wounded.

. . .

Are you sure?

. . .

So, Vanderbok. He rejected virtual existence for himself. It's hard to understand, considering. Several years later, VEI entered the equation and acquired Encore. My lawyers were careful. VEI became the new steward of Encore's virtuals.

. . .

You do look distracted. Shall we wait until after the storm sequence to continue or do you want to abort the entire experience?

I—oh, no—what the hell! The sun, it's in the wrong place!

Miranda!

You look upset.

. . .

I apologize for making too much of this. I have been in touch with the Board of Directors. We have an obligation to our residents, and I alert them whenever I encounter an irregularity. Sometimes, I feel like my finger is on the dike and the leaks are multiplying.

. . .

Randall Patel

Anyway, back to Patel. Monty came in and brought Patel with him. Ever meet someone that you can't imagine happy?

. . .

That was Patel. He never seemed comfortable unless he was immersed in a new virtual environment project. He might have been attractive to women. He was almost handsome, according to my third wife.

. . .

As a child, Randall Patel spent years moving from one military base to another. His dad was third generation Indian Michigan people, mostly doctors, but the dad was a disappointment, especially when he joined the military to avoid an arranged marriage.

. . .

Patel did open up a bit to Marcia. They worked closely together. Eventually, she filled me in on his background. Would you like to stop for a while? The storm clouds are speeding up.

. . .

His mother was a Las Vegas showgirl when she met the dad who was on leave. A hasty romance, a drunken proposal and a Vegas wedding resulting in pregnancy. When his response was less than enthusiastic, she filed for child support and then abandoned the two-month-old baby on the family doorstep. So, the dad was forced to take responsibility, something he deeply resented, and this resulted in years of child neglect.

. . .

It ended when someone saw ten-year-old Patel huddled against the rusted side of an old glide car surrounded by old tires, real antique Michelins, since before gliders. The kid was hugging his knees, trying to get warm. Whoever it was, called the police and the press covered it. Finally, the family in Michigan intervened. Patel was sent to Santa Barbara and into the household of a distant cousin. Feel the wind?

. . .

It's almost like being a bio again. I love this program . . . The way the boat skips on the waves and then dips up and down, what freedom! The only difference is there's no fear . . . sometimes I wish . . . never mind. The sun . . . why are we seeing sun on the water? What happened to the clouds?

. . .

Maybe another time when patches have been applied. Bali Hai seems to be experiencing more problems of late. Please don't worry.

I plan to meet with Diego, my bio rep on the Board. I'll stress the importance of updates, etc. Ah, there it is. The whale is surfacing again, about fifty yards out. Something I never tire of seeing.

END RECORD

MEMORIES OF LOVE AND LOSS

G UNTER HOLDEN DOC. 172
V-Loc: See 743.1, Chicago ELYSIUM penthouse PER-
SONAL, updated 6.28.2122. 19 detailed interiors include entry
lobby, elevators 2 and 8, rotating 4 of 10 resident interiors and concierge. © 8.18.2120 by VEI Personal Options

Chicago Elysium Penthouse

COMMAND, Miranda, SAVE: these activities in my confidential
files:

1. Review and reflect memories 23 A, B (Laura Holden-in early
relationship)

2. Review of post-transition (virtual) memory 827.1

*SAVED: Laura Holden 23 A, B, include TRANSFER to Bali Hai
TRANSITION site*

Activities information will be confidential

COMMAND, Miranda, RUN: penthouse environment.

RUNNING

COMMAND: Miranda, RUN: Laura Holden Bio-memory set 23 A and B.

Byron—During the review of these memories, (virtual) Gunter Holden was at the Chicago "Elysium" loc, however the two memories reviewed here took place in bio locations, which have been identified for your convenience.

RUNNING MEMORY 23 A

B-Loc 23A: Central Park, New York City on May 8, 2114

Laura's shaking her head, laughing at my silly jokes. They are simply to put her at ease, I tell her. It takes more than one lesson to get the hang of it.

"Laura, try to relax your hands," I advise.

Slightly out of breath, her voice shakes as her hands grip the reins. "Black and blue and God knows what other colors, I won't be sitting for a while."

"A little ice will help," I tell her.

A "get to know you" I had said when I invited her.

She was hesitant, saying, "I don't ride."

"Don't worry; I'll give you a lesson. We'll be spending quite a bit of time together in Costa Rica. We need to be a team."

Trees along our path are splendid in white and pink blossoms. The spring sun is kind today, welcoming like a mother's kiss.

I suggest, "Let's stop where the trail forks, just for a moment!"

"Good," she says. As we pause, the mare turns its head and looks at her. "Is it going to bite me?" Her question is only half a joke.

"No, but I might," I answer before I think. Her stillness says it all. "Sorry," I quickly say. "That was inappropriate; please forgive me."

Laura nods and I see the conflict and the fleeting thrill in her eyes.
COMMAND, END: 23A
23 A ENDED
COMMAND, RUN: 23 B
RUNNING 23 B

Costa Rican Friday

B-Loc of 23 B: Limon, Costa Rica August 23, 2114

We walk down the narrow hall and find her door. I know I won't be in my room tonight. My arm touches her breast as I reach around and turn the key.

It's Friday. Outside, the party's beginning as the sun goes down. The Limon streets fill with lovers and hustlers. Families stroll, children run, squealing, shouting, and pointing while old people shake their heads.

"Mijo—no!"

Vendors' carts are everywhere, two or three on each corner.

"Let's send a team down, solely for the vendor sims," I suggest as my arm lingers. She nods. We're at her door and she hesitates, then fumbles for her key, knowing what is sure to follow unless she says, "good night," as she opens it. Instead, she sighs and turns the key.

Laura flicks a switch, and a lamp goes on. The room is charming with bright reds, blues and tangerine orange on prints, courtesy of a local artist, Costa Rican Street life and the sea caught in the acrylic strokes of china red, aquamarine, and cerulean. Her bed is white; the chair beside it holds the gray jacket she left draped there. As she turns with a half-smile, I take the Do Not Disturb sign and hang it on the outer knob. Her eyes look elsewhere as she stands before me. I shut the door. It locks.

One step and I'm there. I take her face in my hands and kiss the tip of her nose, and then my lips hover until she offers hers. Her hands are at her side. I begin the kiss; oh, so sweet she is. Her lips part as my tongue caresses her mouth. The skirt is gone. We fall together on the bed. Oh, how I have waited for this!

END 23 B

23B ENDED

COMMAND, RUN: 827.1

Byron--re 827.1, this is a memory of a post-transition encounter with Laura Holden. It begins in Virtual Paris, however the loc changes to a Bali Hai TRANSITION STATION site.

RUNNING 827.1

V-Loc: Paris L'Affineur restaurant virtual Paris, France with 2.1 k by 1.4k accessible, 5.6 k environment illusion, Auditory/visuals PARIS ADVENTURE © 2122, Olfactory/dining by L'Affineur © 2123, Sim-animals 83 non-interactive pigeon, two poodles, 3 stray cats, Human 85 interactive level 5, 25 interactive level 6 patrons, 8 level 7 interactive wait-staff.

Interior of Virtual Paris restaurant, April, midday

Laura is eighteen today. We sit at a café in Paris, near the Louvre. It's glorious spring. The sim-waiter, an older man who acts as if he smells something unpleasant, is a copy of a waiter I once knew. Marcia and I encountered him in Paris during that triumphant year.

The baby fat of eighteen-year-old Laura confronts me as she sips her wine.

"Why are you so young today?" I am my forty-year-old self. No answer. My patience is paying off. I'll allow her to seduce me. She's eighteen because she is afraid of her more mature self. I know it. Do nothing; just wait. Keep it low-key, but, concerned.

"What's wrong? Why did you ask to meet here?"

She waits until waiter leaves. "Jacob wants to be alone for now."

"The waiter's a sim Laura. He has no opinion, only a role to play. You know the difference."

My God, she's struggling to stay eighteen. Now she's twelve! Damn! People are watching us—her. I see several talking behind their hands.

"Shall we go somewhere else?"

She nods.

"Follow me, madam. Let's find a more private place . . . There's a stretch of beach near the aqua house I told you about."

She smiles.

COMMAND, TRANSFER: Gunter Holden, Laura Holden

TRANSFER COMPLETE

CONTINUE MEMORY 827.1

V-Loc: TRANSITION STATION 46. UNIVERSAL ACCESS (See 136A for more details on this loc.) Visual: Standard daylight South Pacific beach-3.14 k, ocean-1.6 k from shoreline.

South Pacific, Island beach, standard day

We're sitting on the beach; I surprise her by becoming my eight-year-old self and the twelve-year-old Laura begins to cry.

"I made such a mess, didn't I? Poor Jacob, he doesn't say it, but I know he blames me . . ."

Don't frighten her. "So, where is my brother?"

"In the desert was all he would say. Which desert? I don't know."

I put my small hand on her face. I'm here; we're here and that's all I know.

I resist the urge to shift to my early twenties. Let her feel she's in control.

"This is what you were like as a little boy: adorable." She looks down and struggles with an impulse . . .

Laura's age shifts to thirty. For the time being, I stay eight. We sit and watch the tide's ghost.

Byron—The following is a memory contained within another memory, documented in the official record, 827.1

Childhood memory, Seattle Park

For some reason, I think of my mother and a day when we sat on the rocks near the duck pond. It was spring vacation. A bag of breadcrumbs sat between us. The ducks quacked loudly, vying for the wads of bread we tossed into the water. Mom insisted on making sure the females got their share.

"The eggs will be hatching soon, and they'll be busy, too busy," she laughed.

She had seemed excited all morning, even giving Mr. Donald a hug when he greeted us at the bakery, whispering something that made his face flush, and he said, "Nancy are you sure?"

Mom smiled at me and said yes. "Gunter will be getting a surprise."

I knew my ninth birthday wasn't until mid-October, so I thought it would be a welcome home surprise for when I came home from the summer's visit with Dad. I never did find out what the surprise was. I never went back to Seattle at summer's end.

END: Memory within memory (from childhood) within File 827.1

CONTINUE: 827.1

Laura squeezes my fingers, and my memory of the ducks and my mother's surprise fades.

"Gunter, there're some dolphins. Do you see?" She speaks to me as if I really were eight. Her voice has that gentle music that adults reserve for children. I shift my age. I am now the young man who celebrated with Marcia when VEI became a reality. I'm wearing a white tee shirt and jeans I favored that year. Marcia said they made me irresistible and that she would need to keep an eye on me. She was right.

Say nothing. Don't make a move.

The tide swells as the breeze caresses. Now, she looks at me. She reaches for my arm. I do nothing. She leans against me, her head on my shoulder. The blouse is unbuttoned. It's been so long since we made love, several weeks before the transition. She's made a few adjustments, just a few. The breasts are fuller and the freckles on her arms are gone. Her mouth is on my neck now. How long, I wonder, how long should I wait? I decide now is a good time and I whisper her name.

COMMAND: END 827.1

ENDED

Miranda, I had won her back; I know it. What happened? Why did she leave?

I don't know, Gunter. I am sorry. Would you like to review another memory?

No, thank you. That's all for now. I thought I'd won her back and instead she left for the Dreams. Marcia thought she was doing me a favor by not revealing her pregnancy. She said this to our unborn child. Was she? I had no say in the matter. Why do these things still haunt me?

I don't know.

END RECORD

Randall Patel memory records

GUNTER HOLDEN DOC. 182

V-Loc: TRANSITION STATION 46. UNIVERSAL ACCESS (See 136A for more details on this loc) Visual: Standard daylight South Pacific beach-3.14 k, ocean-1.6 k from shoreline.

Miranda, I've decided to clear some files. Also, I will be recording memories for a custom set of records and to gain insight into the past.

During this process I wish to be in my Chicago penthouse setting and unless I counter this choice, you will automatically provide it during these sessions. Do you understand?

Yes, Gunter.

Excellent. I'll begin with Randall Patel.

COMMAND SET and TRANSFER: Chicago CUSTOM
SET and TRANSFER are COMPLETE

V-Loc: See 743.1, Chicago ELYSIUM penthouse PERSONAL, updated 6.28.2122. 19 detailed interiors include entry lobby, elevators

2 and 8, rotating 4 of 10 resident interiors and concierge. © 8.18.2120 by VEI Personal Options

The penthouse

Good. COMMAND SET: the time of day at eight fifteen p.m. I want to see the Sunset that occurred on June 30th, 2085.

DAY AND TIME SET

Beautiful. The light kisses those rooftops. There are lovers on the one with the garden. They're holding hands . . . Thank you.

Gunter, as you requested, Randall Patel recorded memory—107.1. A word of caution: It's classified as personal, not research related. You are aware, am I correct?

Yes, of course. Why do you say caution? It's Patel. I've become curious . . .

COMMAND, Miranda, RUN: Patel memory 107.1 A and B

RUNNING PATEL MEMORIES 107.1 A, B

PATEL MEMORY 107.1A

"Nothing is wrong," she says as she greets me. I'm here for dinner and what else? Her hands shake a little as she lifts her glass. I put my arm around her. I know it's because of him. What time is it? Maybe . . . it is time . . . not enough. I haven't told her everything . . . even if she knew . . . One more, soon there will be another wife. Despite his claims, she will accept it.

COMMAND: Miranda, PAUSE Patel memory 171.1A.

PAUSED.

What was Marcia thinking? Patel was not her style. The man was a shell, no personality . . . Laura warned me, but I didn't think Marcia would ... after what we shared. Patel? How far did this go? Oh, my God!

COMMAND, Miranda, RESUME: Patel memory 171.1A.

PATEL 171.1A RESUMED

Light/dark/light/dark/light/dark. There's a breeze and the clouds move quickly across the afternoon sun. It's five-thirty. Such beauty here. I love the white stucco and the strips of woven coral-red that frame the open doors to the patio with its cushions of braided orange and brilliant blue. I wonder what it would be like to take her under a summer moon, my hands moving, caressing those secret places. I dream of them. They melt, enclosing, absorbing, granting me sanctuary.

Clouds slow down and block the sun, until it breaks free, bathing the ceramic chilies that she keeps, remembering her time with Holden. Why does she surround herself with his lies? Maybe I should put an end to him. I want to shake her.

COMMAND: Miranda, PAUSE: Patel 107.1 A.

107.1A PAUSED.

I see now. I get it. No need to finish this one. She must have frustrated the poor bastard but kept him in line. He was useful. Clearly, Patel was unstable. It's just as well I didn't know. Poor Marcia, she was walking a tightrope . . . Who would have guessed Patel was crazy and had a thing for Marcia? Where was I? Marcia must have been nearing sixty—still young, still beautiful.

I recognize the chilies. We got them in Cabo. Renee knew I was leaving, and she was getting greedy. Marcia met me in Cabo, and we discussed strategies, the coming divorce from Renee and our new project. Bali Hai was conceived on that trip. I still remember Marcia's eyes, guarded but amused. I decided I still wanted her, so we slipped away. I feel sorry for Patel.

COMMAND: Miranda, RUN: Randall Patel memory 107.1 B. I'm curious to see just how far he tried to go with her. Miranda?

COMMAND RUN: Patel 107.1 B . . . now please.

Patel 107.1 B RUNNING

"Sing to me, Patel."

"Chun Chun Karti Aayi." I whisper. "I don't know many songs."

"Ah, yes . . . what does it mean?" she asks.

"I don't know."

Her hands rest behind her head as she studies the moon. It's dark where we are, only the stars and the moon and the boat's dim lamps. Our small craft rocks us like children. "A lullaby. My cousin sang it to her children and to me when I first came to stay with them."

"Beautiful." She sighs.

My hand reaches for her breast, so pale as my fingertips map the contours. I have missed her. When he calls for her, I'm lost.

"I can't do this when he needs me."

Sobs hidden behind her door. Was she hurt?

"Are you all right?" I knock. She opens her door.

The only light is the glow of the computer monitor. My breath is quicker as I notice her dishevelment. "Are you hurt?"

"No, it's not that. Gunter's gone. He left me."

Her lip trembles as she regains her composure. There are faint echoes from those working in other offices a universe away. She caresses my face.

"No need for this," I protest.

"Don't worry," she says.

She embraces me, resting her head on my chest. I want more . . .

"He left me, Patel. He's in South Africa and meeting my replacement. I knew he would."

I don't know what to say. Maybe I could kill him for her. I wish it were that simple, but she would still love him.

COMMAND: Miranda, pause: Patel memory 107.1 B.

107.1 B PAUSED.

Incredible. If she was that upset, she could have come to me. Of course, she had a right to have other relationships. I just never thought that . . . At least I warned her when there was someone new. Okay, perhaps I didn't, but why Patel?

It doesn't matter. Patel knew he was second choice and always would be. Pathetic. I wish I'd . . . Perhaps that's why he refused the transition to Bali Hai. Oblivion was his only option. I never understood why she left. We could have—who cares. It's over . . .

COMMAND: Miranda, ERASE Patel personal memory records.

Gunter unfortunately, that is not permitted.

Not permitted? NOT PERMITTED?

COMMAND: Marcia, ERASE: the GODDAM MEMORIES!

Gunter, I am Miranda. The Board of Directors ruled against any deleted memories without the permission of the original bio or virtual, or the Board's review and approval. Do you wish to submit these memories for review?

No, Miranda. I apologize. Store them and make them inaccessible—no listing. Can you do that?

Of course, Gunter. I will store these memories in a cache of unlabeled memories. Is there anything else I can do?

No, thank you, Miranda. I had hoped for better from Marcia. And Patel, how dare he touch her?!

END RECORD

I OPEN MY EYES AND SEE THE SUN

Via message (confidential)

December 27, 2287

To: Byron Hernandez

c/o Trammell & O'Connell Law Offices

Bryon—

Recently, my assistant flagged these files for my attention. I urge you to review them as soon as possible. The attached memories contain events tied to major disturbances in the virtual life of Gunter Holden and evidence of his role, motive, and culpability in the Joy Forever tragedy. They show that he vigorously opposed the mergers that resulted in the death of VEI. In addition, there were appalling crimes against two virtual communities, including Bali Hai.

Rather than detail them in this note, I will let you review them, evaluate, and decide what steps you feel are appropriate concerning the criminal evidence in these files.

I will say that a major rift occurs in the relationship between your grandfather and Holden. Thomas finally tells Gunter that he was murdered and who did it.

After you go over this material, let me know what else you need. SEINI's influence on Congress continues. Whatever evidence we find may never be enough.

Des

***

Via message (confidential)

January 2, 2288

To: Desmond Webb, archivist

Library of Congress

Desmond—

Thank you for the heads up. I will immediately review these files and study the transcripts. Please know that I will get back to you as soon as I see what they reveal and how they change my case. Today, my assistant was in tears. Pleas for action flood the office daily. People want to know what has happened to their loved ones. Are they still in Shemathra? Have their files been erased?

You're telling me that Holden had a role in the Joy Forever mass erasures. And now you tell me there were other erasures that happened after he transitioned to Bali Hai. Was he involved with those? If not, who? Why can't we help to at least get a message sent to these virtuals? These families need answers.

Today, our office received a touching letter from a young woman about her father, who, due to an accident, had transitioned unexpectedly to Bali Hai just before the SEINI merger. Still a young man at eighty-five, her dad was her only family. Distraught at her father's transition, she and her father talked daily. Her dad had reassured her he was still part of her life until their communications ended when Shemathra went dark.

I intend to pursue this until I find out what has happened and why.

I'll let you know where this goes after I see what I can prove.

Again, thank you for everything you have done.

Byron

***

GUNTER HOLDEN MEMORY FILES
FOLDER YEAR: 2192

Byron-- while this record begins at Bucklin's CUSTOM Michigan environment, a JUMP TRANSFER occurs during the following encounter. Loc changes will be noted as they occur.

GUNTER HOLDEN DOC. 190
V-Loc: Thomas Bucklin personal environment Vandalia, Michigan Cottage, CUSTOM STRUCTURE, 1.5 k by 1.3k rural, pond, foliage level 5, TACTILE/AUDITORY/VISUAL by VEI Personal

Environments, Sims: ecosystem interactive includes 356 insects, 26 raccoons. 40 squirrels, 52 geese, brown bear cub level 4.

Tom's personal environment: Michigan Cottage, rural setting, pond, wildlife sims

. . .

Tom, it's Gunter. I haven't seen you for quite a while. I kept looking for you to turn up. Forgive me for knocking without an invitation. Please open the door!

. . .

You're my friend. Miranda suggested I might find you here. I've been here five times. Please talk to me.

. . .

I know you're upset. If I'm not welcome here, tell me.

. . .

Thank you, Tom. It's good to see your face. I've missed you. If you'd rather we go somewhere else . . .

. . .

I—I'm happy to go wherever you feel the most comfortable. I'll simply follow . . .

. . .

Can we please talk about what happened?

. . .

Don't leave . . . Fine, let's take a walk.

. . .

Why Africa? Well, the program has been scaled back and quite frankly, I find it depressing. I suggest a walk along the North Shore beach at Oahu . . . a quiet morning in March.

. . .

COMMAND, JUMP Gunter Holden and Thomas Bucklin

TRANSFER/JUMP COMPLETE

V-Loc: Oahu South Pacific beach-2.74 k, ocean-2.4 k from shore-line, structures-0, vegetation-tropical no. 3347.1c, © 7.5.2124 by VEI Standard Environments. Audio: ocean surf (standard level 8) gulls 59 level 4, wildlife level 2, OCEANBASE INTERACTIVES © 4.23.2132, Tactile: Tropic Sun afternoon light effect 4.7, mild breeze (level 2 fixed), Sand texture BEACHLIFE No. 6.8 © 6.2.2019, Sims: 2 level 4 interactive, , Olfactory: Ocean Scents © 5.19.2134

Oahu beach

I want to make it clear. I did not realize that Pauline was your ex-wife until our second encounter.

. . .

Don't turn away. Hear my account of things.

. . .

I did not seek her out, I swear. It was a dance. I never was interested as a bio, but . . . the pretense of seduction can be diverting. The program is relatively new, a 1950s New York nightclub. The women are in evening gowns; the men are in dark suits. Sims serve elaborate meals and drinks, popular in clubs of the 1950s.

. . .

I swear I had no idea who she was.

. . .

She sat at the bar with her legs crossed. Her dress was stunning. It was beaded with a white that shimmered.

. . .

No gloves. When she saw me, she seemed to stare.

. . .

I'm sorry.

. . .

You said you were finished with her, but I can see . . . Are you sure you want me to continue?

. . .

Okay, I didn't realize Pauline was your ex-wife. You've shared some of the pain and disappointment. I know that it wasn't over for you.

. . .

How can you say that? I've always been truthful with you.

. . .

It's different now; we're friends. Why are you laughing?

. . .

I will tell you all of it, but it's going to hurt you. That's why I kept quiet, out of consideration, but I guess Pauline didn't. So here we are, our friendship at risk.

. . .

She was staring at me. Even in the dim light, it was obvious. The band was playing *An Unforgettable Girl*. Soon after the first soulful "unforgettable girl," she moved toward my table.

. . .

I was alone. I never plan these things.

. . .

I don't care what Pauline told you; it wasn't planned. I was there because once in a great while, there will be a surprise, someone with news from the bio-world, unfiltered by Bali Hai's Board of Directors.

. . .

You weren't aware? News from the bio-world is rarely delivered unfiltered. When I was prominent on the Board, I received a full account. Sadly, that's no longer the case.

. . .

You told me that Pauline exploited your loneliness after Stephanie's loss. So, why isn't Stephanie here with you? Why did she reject virtual existence? She was dying and she must have known how her decision would impact you. And you had made it clear that Bali Hai was already purchased for both of you.

. . .

Okay, it's none of my business. But Pauline, apparently, without telling you, had Stephanie's plan transferred to herself. Why didn't she tell you? If she had told you, would you have agreed?

. . .

Rather than just "no," you're saying "hell no." What did this woman do? I don't mean to pry, but naturally, I'm curious.

. . .

I'm TRYING to understand why. Why did you get involved with someone like Pauline? You were in your cen-thirties, not young, but considerably well off. From what Pauline told me, you pursued her, a woman of fifty-five.

. . .

If you insist. I had no idea who she was when she looked me over, a real cat-and-mouse thing. I admit I was impressed—the perfect brown skin and her hair, hints of copper in the soft black, swept up with heavy combs. I can see you're upset.

. . .

She was obviously new at being virtual. Pauline's sultry goddess version of her virtual self-stopped short of caricature. I was in the mood for someone new.

"Gunter Holden?" She said it like she knew something I didn't. Did you ever mention me?

. . .

I see. She did know we were friends. I wondered if she did.

. . .

I thought about leaving—letting her play games with someone else. Instead, I shrugged and gave just a hint of a smile. "Guilty as charged. And why, might I ask, do I have the pleasure?"

"I know a friend of yours, someone named Martino," she said.

. . .

Martino? Um . . . probably some boyfriend. I had no idea. I shook my head and turned to move away, but she grabbed my arm, pulled me close and kissed me. As I said, I was in the mood for something or someone new.

. . .

Shall we stop?

. . .

Well, to put it politely, what do you think happened next?

. . .

I'll be brief. We danced. At times, I was a little put off by her aggression. I can see how she might have seemed to someone lonely . . . I'm not trying to patronize you, she . . .

. . .

DON'T YELL!

If you must know, we went somewhere private. The sex went on for hours.

. . .

We were here, on this beach. I don't know why I suggested this beach to tell you. I don't know . . . why I . . . sometimes I can't understand myself. Why does this woman have such a hold on you?

. . .

Are you serious? Your own wife?

. . .

So who left the metal spikes on the bottom stairs?

. . .

Incredible, she murdered you!

. . .

Ah, the boyfriend did it.

. . .

And you have no proof. What a monster.

. . .

All that Miranda revealed to me was the manner of your death; I had no idea.

. . .

Ha! The new husband murdered her—not a surprise. The inheritance. Are your grandchildren protected?

. . .

Ah good, now that the court case is settled, there's money enough to protect your interests. You might suggest that they can contribute to Bali Hai's "Support Your Virtual Family" Fund. It's tax deductible.

. . .

You're right! Again, I'm sorry. Now is not the time. Well . . . I . . . I hope that . . . Please don't let this bad judgment on my part and this woman, who clearly was unworthy of you . . . We're still friends?

. . .

Yes, I'll give it a little time.

END RECORD

***

GUNTER HOLDEN DOC. 194

V-Loc: Truckee River (California) non-event day 28 of 47, early morning to late afternoon, breeze variant 2 to 5.2, Site 1.8 k by 2.3 k (river), STRUCTURES 18 "log" cabins, Tactile WILDERNESS SENSATIONS © June 2134, Visual/Auditory GREAT RIVERS USA © June 2125, Olfactory PINE ENVIRONMENTS © April 2137, Sims-Insect /animal illusions level 6 ECO-KINGDOM © 2140, 230 native birds level 4, 180 "wildlife" raccoons, foxes, squirrels, deer, 2 brown bears, 3 bear cubs level 5.5, 508 fish including 169 salmon level 6 FRESHWATER AQUATICS © 2146.

California Truckee Riverbank, sim wildlife, virtual and sim tourists, salmon fishing simulation

Thanks for coming here. I know you're angry with me and rightly so. I looked for you and you seemed to have disappeared. Thanks for responding to Miranda's request.

. . .

Let's sit on the grass. If you watch the area near the one-story cabins, a bear comes strolling past those rocks.

. . .

I like to watch the sim-fishermen as they cast their lines into the Truckee River. Ever do any fly-fishing?

. . .

Me neither. Miranda varies the catch rate. Miranda suggested this river program. The required memory is lower than similar programs. We recently deleted the lake program and replaced it with this one.

. . .

I asked Miranda to find you. Tom, I need your help. I know there are others I might ask, but I have difficulty trusting them. There is information that some could use against me and I . . . have confidence in you, that you wouldn't betray me. Memories still plague me. I can't loosen the grip. It was easier at first. When everything was still new, but now . . . I keep trying . . . Look at that one! The trout, do you see it?

. . .

When it came to virtual wildlife, Patel was a genius. He—I didn't ask you here because of Patel. Forgive me for my cruelty concerning your wife, Pauline.

. . .

I heard she lives in Paris, not a place you are drawn to, I know. Tom, I need to talk to someone. Miranda can't help me. I must sort out things that happened and what I did.

. . .

Recently, I reviewed certain messages—memories left by colleagues. They have waited, unopened, for decades. So, I decided to review them. Now, I'm confronted with some unwelcome information.

. . .

I'm asking for your forbearance. You have no idea how difficult this is for me. I'm going to tell you what happened before I put that gun to my head and came here to Bali Hai.

. . .

It happened because Laura betrayed me with Jacob. As I told you, it started at "Burning Man." Laura was concerned that Jacob's feelings were hurt.

. . .

My brother saw an opportunity and took advantage of my wife's gullible nature. I'm sorry you don't see it. You can't seriously think that it was because of what happened with Joy Forever.

. . .

The truth about Joy Forever

I haven't been entirely forthcoming about what happened before my transition. The post-biological destination industry is extremely competitive. I was given some information. You're aware of the anti-virtual movement?

. . .

Most of them are wild-eyed fanatics who demand free access to after-death programs for everyone, free of charge. And they are ruthless.

. . .

All major companies employ spies to monitor the competition. Promoting itself as the next VEI, Joy Forever was new to the after-death field. I discovered that Joy Forever was stealing from us— mostly client profiles but also copies of VEI software.

. . .

At first, I wasn't worried. Joy Forever was too small to be a threat. Their programs hosted only two million residents. But when I learned that Joy Forever had acquired the contracts of over one hundred thousand future VEI virtual residents, I was alarmed. This was a major loss of revenue. My concern, as always, was to protect VEI.

. . .

Monty, my former mentor, and the head of operations at VEI, still saw LeRoi. Remember my high school graduation dinner? Besides

Marcia and Monty, LeRoi, Monty's lover was there. Sadly, LeRoi's idealism became an unhealthy fixation on the underprivileged and he joined the Anti-Virtual Society.

There was a brief marriage and then a messy divorce, where Monty agreed to a large settlement. I had assumed that Monty had moved on. I was wrong. Even though LeRoi was a dedicated anti-virtual, Monty couldn't break the tie.

. . .

There were rumors of a new software virus, something LeRoi's group had recently perfected. If introduced into a system, it would cause a mass deletion—every virtual. Assuming his ex-husband and cash-cow would want to protect himself financially, LeRoi confided his plans to Monty. Then, after some unnecessary angst over where his loyalties lie, Monty told me about LeRoi's plan to embed the virus in the new avatar software we were developing. Trials were being set up. The effect would be instant, too late to counter.

. . .

I knew I had to do something. Joy Forever was draining our resources. Clients were leaving; profits were down. We immediately installed an anti-viral program that protected Bali Hai and the rest of VEI products.

. . .

To put it bluntly, I allowed the theft of the tainted software. Joy Forever was done and all its residents, two million virtuals were deleted in one disastrous afternoon. Monty was horrified, but he understood I was looking out for VEI, for our survival.

. . .

If it hadn't been Joy Forever, eventually, it would have been VEI. And it wasn't my doing. Joy Forever made the choice to steal from us.

They were responsible for the welfare of their virtual residents, not me, not VEI. I take care of my own.

. . .

It took a shock like that to finally shut down the anti-virtual movement. My lobbyists took advantage of the mood in Washington to regulate. As a result, the anti-virtual movement was outlawed.

. . .

Don't look at me like that! Because of what happened, laws were passed, good laws that protect virtuals. I wish there had been some other way. I wish a lot of things.

. . .

Unfortunately, Monty told both Laura and Marcia what I had done. Laura became hysterical and much to my dismay, Marcia left the company. Then, Patel gave his notice. I could replace Patel some- how, but Marcia . . . her input was . . .

. . .

So, this is why, when I discovered Laura's betrayal with Jacob, my judgment was compromised. Otherwise, I would have found another way . . . There was all that pressure.

. . .

The Cloud Box

. . .

After the Joy Forever collapse, Laura became more secretive. I tried to let her know how much she meant to me by giving her a ring that belonged to my mother. What's wrong?

. . .

Yes, I see the bear. Watch, in a few seconds, he'll swoop his paw into the river. And there's the salmon!

. . .

Oh, the ring. It was the only thing I had that belonged to my mother. I wanted Laura to realize how much I loved her.

. . .

I remember that Mom kept the ring in her cloud box. I called it her cloud box because it had mother-of-pearl clouds on a blue sky. The blue was from abalone shells. I loved to touch it.

. . .

My mother rarely wore the ring. Twice, I saw her sitting alone, pressing it to her cheek. No, I didn't ask her why. Her crying always made me sad.

The setting was magical in my eight-year-old opinion. A small round diamond sat in the middle. Several tiny stones of varying colors formed a circle around the diamond.

. . .

Yes . . . that's what I called it. "The Solar System." How did you know? Have you researched my life?

. . .

You're right. It was a logical guess. I apologize.

. . .

It was Jasmine, Dad's second wife, who took the call when my mother was killed. The ring came later. Jasmine must have found it and sent it to me. I should have called and thanked her. The cloud box was gone, but I instantly recognized the ring.

I remember telling Mom that it looked like the solar system. I panicked because she began to cry.

"Your father's son," she said.

That summer, I told Dad about Mom crying and saying that I was like him. I guess I thought he might want to get back together with Mom. He was sitting under a palm, and I was building a castle. He pointed the burning end of the cigar in my direction.

"Oh really," he answered. Then, he smiled, "how would you like to get a better view of the real solar system?" And I left my mother's house for good.

. . .

I mean that I never went back to Seattle. Instead, Dad and I went for a week's stay at the New Hubble resort space station. I called Mom from there to tell her I was staying with Dad permanently.

. . .

Why do you ask? I didn't know that it was forever. I was eight. I thought that I would stay with Dad and visit Mom on vacations, but there were never any vacations.

. . .

She didn't cry. She was silent and for a moment, I thought the connection had been lost. "Okay, honey," she said to me. "Remember I love you and remember our clouds." Then, she smiled and waved, and then she was gone.

. . .

Dad was sitting right behind me, and he waved at Mom. I asked him what she meant by remembering the clouds? He only laughed. "Who knows? Nancy has always been a little odd."

That was the last time I spoke to my mother. I still wonder at how she slipped from my life without . . . I can see you're upset . . . Why?

. . .

I understand. It is sad. Shall I change the subject?

. . .

Then let's change the subject. After Joy Forever, I discovered that I could no longer trust Laura and—

Gunter?

Yes, Miranda, what is it?

There's an urgent call for you.

Alright. Please take a message. I'll return it as soon as I finish. Tom, I appreciate your help.

. . .

I'll tell you about Laura's deceit after I deal with this call. It may mean that despite my opposition, a merger is unavoidable.

. . .

Gunter, it's urgent.

We'll meet and I'll explain all that happened. I'm convinced you'll see how it was. Later then.

. . .

Infinite Bliss

V-Loc: VEI New York office

Yes, Miranda, I'm sorry for the delay.

COMMAND, Miranda, RUN the New York Office environment, please.

TRANFER New York VEI Office 2178 TRANSFER COMPLETE

Gunter Holden is available

Diego? I apologize; I wasn't sure at first. You look well and considerably younger.

Diego: *"Thank you, Uncle."*

I can appreciate the importance of staying current. I didn't realize pointed chins were back in fashion. The "Ming" Look?

Diego: "*It's called The Sage.*"

Really! It suits you, especially with the fan collar and the algae modifier robe. You must be doing well.

Diego: "*I try to keep current.*"

And please convey my compliments to your gene therapist. Your face is devoid of furrows, very enigmatic.

Diego: '*I will.*"

So, what is the situation?

Diego: "*Uncle, VEI has been sold to and absorbed by another company.*"

What do you mean sold?

Diego: "*VEI as a separate company is gone.*"

I trusted you to represent my interests and . . .

Diego: "*Do you want me to continue to call and keep you informed? If not, I can have my AI secretary notify you of any future developments.*"

No, of course. It's just that the focus in virtual society is a bit different. There is no stock market, and we trust our lobbyists to . . . I mean CHRIST where does all that money go?

Diego: "*I object to your tone.*"

I didn't mean to yell. I can understand that fees negotiated seventy years ago might fail to allow for current inflation, but we did allow for quite a lot. What's the bottom line? Who controls VEI?

Diego: "*VEI is now part of Infinite Bliss.*"

INFINITE BLISS!! Ridiculous. A fifth-rate operation, offering destinations that would drive most virtuals to choose oblivion controls VEI and the fate of over five million virtuals?

Diego: "*I understand your disappointment. However, I was offered double the price for our shares and an important role on the new board. I had no choice.*"

I see . . . I . . . uh . . .understand. You had an incredible opportunity. But you are a Holden. I know that you'll do right by the VEI family. How is this going to affect Bali Hai residents?

Diego: "*The plan is to reapportion one half of Bali Hai's memory, including that in current use to include new communities. Infinite Bliss will decide what Bali Hai programs will be eliminated. I'm told losing only one or two major cities should free up enough memory.*"

Wait! If you do that, there won't be enough memory to . . . I don't understand. Which major cities? You can't. At least give us the opportunity to coordinate personal environment options and relocate them. If not, I predict major legal actions on behalf of residents affected by—

Diego: "*Uncle, be very careful in what you say next.*"

Does loyalty mean anything to you? I have friends in Washington. There's a world of hurt in what they can do. I have only to ask.

Diego: "*I'm sorry, Uncle. I want you to know that what's going to happen next is not what I want. It's on you.*"

Let me warn you, Diego, and your bosses at Infinite Bliss. I would hate for HOLO-COM, which I might remind you is followed by more bios and virtuals than any other news entity, to learn what Infinite Bliss is about to do. Forgive me Diego, but Miranda has recorded and transmitted this call.

Diego: "*Uncle, you leave me no choice. The penalty process has already begun. Let me know if I have your support.*"

NO! You CAN'T! PLEASE, don't do that! I'll make a statement. I'll say it was a misunderstanding.

REBOOTREBOOTREBOOTREBOOT!!!

BREACH!!!

CACHE: VIRTUAL (post TRANSITION 44 SEC after bio-shut down) TRANSITION SITE 46

I open my eyes and see the sun

Amazing. I can look at the sun, and for as long as I like. I know this sun. Oh, God, I'm in Bali Hai. I'm virtual! I see my avatar arm. Interesting, as if everything is in focus but me. The sand, oh the sand—I can dig my fingers into it. It feels wonderful! It sticks to my fingers. What's different? What's different?

END BREACH

Gunter, Gunter?

Miranda, what happened? I feel as if I have jumped to another setting, but I'm still here.

The system has been rebooted. Also, the city of Paris has been deleted.

NO! It was just a threat; they weren't serious, they wouldn't . . .

Gunter, Diego is waiting for an answer.

Of course.

COMMAND, RECONNECT: holo to incoming call

RECONNECTED

Diego, did you do this or was it those who are pulling your strings?

Diego: "*Does it matter? I didn't foresee the mass erasure, however, it's done and we must go forward and accept the coming changes.*"

It does matter. What just happened was a massacre. You won't be able to hide it. There will be an accounting.

Diego: "*Perhaps someday, Uncle, but you won't be a part of it. Be careful. I've been advised that the fate of virtual Chicago is in your hands.*"

You've made your point. What do you want?

Diego: "*I want your legal consent to the merger.*"

All right, I'll go on record giving my consent to the merger. Anything else, Diego?

Diego: "*My AI will contact Miranda.*"

Anything you want. Notify me when you're ready.

CALL ENDED

Oh, God.

COMMAND, Miranda, TRANSMIT: The following message to the legal department of Infinite Bliss:

After careful consideration of what will benefit the residents of Bali Hai and protect their rights now and in the future, I am ceding control of my stock in VEI to my grandnephew and heir, Diego Putman. I look forward to working with Infinite Bliss and coordinating the resettlement of IB virtual communities into VEI destinations to avoid future tragedies, such as the recent accidental deletion of Bali-Hai's Paris and its virtual residents.

Sincerely,

Gunter Holden

TRANSMITTED. Will there be anything else?

Yes. Access my Federal Star Account 2865. Scan available files for interests and preferences for all Infinite Bliss Level B Board members. Send category six gifts to all. Include the following message: Welcome to our new bio-family. Gunter Holden.

Done.

Wonderful. Send Diego Putman a category two. In Diego's case, sign it Uncle Gunter.

Done. Anything else?

Yes, I'd like to know who was in Paris, I mean any virtuals, people who were friends of mine. Those lost that I might miss.

Of course, Gunter, I can give you those names now if you wish.

No, thanks! I'll let you know when I'm ready.

END RECORD

"THE DEVIL HAS TAKEN RESIDENCE HERE"

Via message (confidential)

January 22, 2288

To: Desmond Webb, Archivist

c/o Library of Congress, VR Division

Desmond—

While studying the recent Gunter Holden memories you provided, the following facts emerged:

As a bio, Gunter Holden knowingly allowed tainted VEI software to be stolen by a rival (after-death) company, Joy Forever. Prior to the theft, members of an anti-virtual group had infected this software with a destructive virus. This resulted in the unintended deletion of millions of innocent virtuals. For this crime, individual members of this anti-virtual group were convicted. Holden was never charged.

Several decades after Holden's bio-death and transition to Bali Hai, Infinite Bliss, an after-death company, controlled by the Christian religious group, Everlasting Praise absorbed VEI, including the Bali Hai platform. Using questionable legal rights of inheritance, Holden's bio-grand-nephew, Diego Putnam, abetted in this merger.

Further, when notified of the impending merger by Putnam, Holden opposed and threatened to contest it. As a show of force, members of the Infinite Bliss Board, without warning, deleted Virtual Paris, a major Bali Hai city. Residents of Virtual Paris, thousands of innocent virtuals, were illegally erased. Each erasure was a felony.

The Infinite Bliss Board was responsible for the erasures, although technical difficulties were cited as the cause.

Desmond, this is very helpful. We know that SEINI claims that all residents (including human virtuals) of Shemathra's Realm have agreed to sever ties to the bio-world and all cult members have ceded their remaining assets to the Shemathra group. Bio-family members are heartsick.

I have uncovered several unverified documents, after-death contracts from before the mergers, but SEINI claims they are counterfeit. The virtuals who signed them are unable to verify these contracts because they are trapped in Shemathra. What has happened to them? How long before they "self-delete?" Donovan Hosseini, the "llama god/conman" will answer for what he has done.

Please send remaining Holden docs on Infinite Bliss and SEINI.

Many thanks,

Byron

***

Via message (confidential)

February 2, 2288

Byron Hernandez

Trammel & O'Connell Law Offices

Byron—

I am glad that your investigation is progressing. I have attached the requested Holden docs, including personal memories, breaches, and messages. Some show the growing friendship between your great grandfather and Holden.

In addition, they demonstrate Holden's increasing alarm as he dealt with Everlasting Praise, the evangelical Christian faction that held controlling shares in Infinite Bliss. Recently, I located the files leading to Holden's and your grandfather's self-deletion. After I review and format, I'll send them. As usual, I have flagged ** certain topics for easier navigation.

Also, in his talks with Reverend Bardot, leader of the Everlasting Praise religious group, Gunter discusses Shemathra and its followers and he jokes about the cult's belief system. In response, Bardot's remark, "the Devil has taken residence here," is sadly accurate.

As soon as I locate the remaining files leading to Holden's (and your grandfather's) self-deletion, I will make them available to you.

Regards,

Desmond

From: Bali Hai

GUNTER HOLDEN DOC. 195

V-Loc: See 743.1, Chicago ELYSIUM penthouse PERSONAL, updated 6.28.2122. 19 detailed interiors include entry lobby, elevators 2 and 8, rotating 4 of 10 resident interiors and concierge. © 8.18.2120 by VEI Personal Options.

I'm going to tell you about the Dreams

. . .

I appreciate your support more than you know. Paris is gone—a loss of one of Bali Hai's most beautiful cities. I'll miss . . . I'm sorry about Pauline. Despite what she did, I know you still cared. Remember Betsy Salan's father, the surgeon?

. . .

Yes, he was also Jeremy Salan's grandfather.

. . .

Betsy's dad was one of my many friends who were in Paris when it happened, and yes, there were too many others. Infinite Bliss announced it was a reboot mishap and that most residents had already relocated. A lie. There were over ten thousand virtuals there—all gone. The Anti-Virtual Society has crowed about it being a matter of time before this happens again. They're right.

. . .

This has been hard on all of us. But I don't know what I feel. Maybe shame, considering what I recently confided about the Joy Forever deletions. I didn't comprehend the impact and I . . . There's nothing I can do.

. . .

That won't change what happened.

. . .

What do you WANT? I CAN'T CHANGE IT!

. . .

Let's change the subject. I said I would keep my promise. I'm going to tell you about the Dreams.

. . .

Self-Deleting Protocol

It's about deletions. After what happened to Paris, I can see that no one is safe now. We were supposed to be safe from the outside, meaning bios can't legally delete a virtual without a court hearing and it is rarely granted. It's why I couldn't touch Jacob after his bio-death. But we all have impulses, good and bad. Some of us self-delete because of lost dreams, like Oliver Jackson in a world without real estate. Denise destroyed Pam's dream of unending celebrity. Pam faded in the reality of her daughter's hate. I think Laura left because . . . If I had known she was . . . I could have stopped her.

. . .

My dreams now? Without Laura, I don't know, other than to save Bali Hai at all costs and restore it to its original perfection. I take pleasure in the details.

. . .

I . . . Sorry, self-deletion is a difficult subject for me. I am subject to occasional mood swings, and I lose sight of my own dreams.

. . .

I worry that a bad breach experience or feeling overwhelmed an impulse might lead me to self-delete.

. . .

Let me answer your question. Self-deletion protocols vary, depending on the platform. The deletion itself comes in different forms, from stepping through a door, jumping into a pool, or taking a "sleeping" pill. Most companies don't advertise their methods.

The thing is, a strong desire, free of any survival instinct, can trigger the erasure process. During the game, Laura's eyes changed. She was beginning to fade. I didn't recognize it, although I knew that she was stressed.

. . .

I was startled because I saw my reflection in her eyes. I don't know why; perhaps it was because of the clarity—my image, I mean. Before I knew what was happening, she and Jacob climbed that damn ramp. I know I could have stopped her if it hadn't been for him.

. . .

I'M TELLING YOU WHAT IT IS. You're not listening. If I hadn't been afraid . . . I didn't want people to know my business.

Babylon Dreams

When we were creating the Bali Hai platform, Marcia and I discussed the problem of self-deletion and my moods. They're erratic on occasion, though God knows that's understandable with losing Laura and then Marcia, and now, this damned merger.

When I expressed my concern regarding my moods, all Marcia would say was, "Don't worry, Holden! I'll think of something." And she did. When programming Miranda's personality, Marcia allowed Miranda to scan her memories for a solution to my fear of deleting myself on impulse. The result is Babylon Dreams.

. . .

The Dreams is a roller coaster, and not just any roller coaster. It's the Thunder Coaster, the one that terrified me, the one that made me humiliate myself . . . I . . . I . . . wet my pants. You're laughing. Please, don't.

. . .

The thought of the Dreams, the rails rising into the dark clouds and the sound of those slow clicks would terrify—upset me. If I hadn't been . . . I might have followed Laura and stopped her.

I—I'll record some memories, things that happened after my transition. Her betrayal continues to haunt me. I want to lay the matter to rest. I have more important matters that demand my attention.

. . .

Yes, as I have told you, Miranda could adjust my memory, but it might create significant gaps in my timeline. Given my personality profile, my file could destabilize. I need my wits to negotiate with the new Infinite Bliss communities.

. . .

Let's jump to the Summit! The perfect white of the Everest snow helps my focus.

COMMAND, Miranda, JUMP/TRANSFER Gunter Holden, Thomas Bucklin

TRANSFER COMPLETE

The virtual dead

V-Loc: Everest Summit 4.5 k by 5.8 k, non-event day 27 of 58, Tactile MOUNTAIN RISE © 2188, Visual/ audio EVEREST EXPERIENCE by VEI Adventures © 2187, Olfactory DREAM HIGH © 2145, Sims 18 gray geese level 4, Human 5 climbers' level 2.

What do you think of this environment?

. . .

The bio-Summit is not only beautiful, but also quite deadly. I often reflect on its challenge. In case the Summit must go, I wanted the time to . . .

. . .

This ice dome sits near the South Summit, 28,700 feet above the coastline. The entire experience is derived from a collection of memories gathered from the best climbers, including many locals.

Bettina Bradley, Laura's Sherpa, was dedicated to the "Sainted Mother" as she called the Summit. "When Mother calls me," she smiled, "I'll see her in your 'virtual world." Bettina had rejected London. She went home to Nepal and her "Mother," only to fall into the rocks and ice of the Cornice traverse. She woke up on the sand, and instead of Mother's icy winds, she felt the warm breath of the ocean on her face.

. . .

Sadly, we had offered "The Summit" package only to Bettina. None of her friends transitioned here and there was no one who could understand her outrage at the sight of so many inexperienced virtuals violating "Mother." Do you see those small, dark shapes, the ones a few hundred feet down from the ridge?

. . .

They are the virtual dead. Technically, they are only illusions, images taken from the memories of climbers who survived, but glimpsed the collection of Mother's rejects. Like a spider, Mother shrouds her victims in ice, keeping them from the arms of friends, who risk joining them in death by attempting to retrieve the bodies of their fallen comrades.

. . .

Okay, we can change the subject.

. . .

I'm not avoiding anything.

. . .

Why do you continue to ask questions about my brother? I don't miss him, nor do I have regrets. Whatever memories that are responsible for these breaches, none involve Jacob.

. . .

You think that I never gave my brother a chance?! His parents gave him EVERYTHING!

. . .

Please don't leave.

. . .

Let me try again to be objective when I talk of Jacob. I've come to value our friendship. I admit that people have different points of view. Something is obvious to one person, but less so to another.

. . .

Let's agree to discuss Jacob another time. However, there is something that greatly concerns me.

. . .

It involves my nitwit nephew, Diego and the religious community, Everlasting Praise. Have I mentioned them or our newest addition, Eternal Classics?

. . .

External memory is the issue. Classics residents access a relatively small space compared to other communities like Everlasting Praise. Are you familiar with the Classics group? They use the narratives of over three hundred works of literature. Sims play the smaller roles with residents portraying the pivotal characters. When the narrative ends and the performance is over, the group gathers to discuss insights and venture opinions.

. . .

You mentioned you wrote fiction in bio life. Murder mystery short stories, correct?

. . .

I thought so. You might like this group.

. . .

I see, just a thought. Anyway, occasionally, the residents request additional memory. For example, *The Lord of the Rings* trilogy requires considerably more, several times more than the average novel. The only comparable demands would be some of the war novels like *War and Peace*, *Pioneers of Mars*, etc.

Everlasting Praise

Recently, under the guise of hospitality, welcoming the newest community to our Bali Hai family, several representatives of Everlasting Praise jumped unannounced into the middle of a wizard fight during one of the *Harry Potters*. This disrupted the entire re-enactment.

. . .

Then, Everlasting Praise filed a protest, claiming preferential treatment was being accorded to the Classics Community. Contractually, Classics is entitled to this extra memory. They pay a premium, and their right to access additional memory was in place under the Infinite Bliss agreement; but the merger has clouded the issue. Of course, for Everlasting Praise, the point is to exert power and prevent as many "undesirable" narratives to play near their Everlasting doorstep.

. . .

Recently, I participated in one of Classics' stories. My performance was widely applauded, and many citizens commented I was compelling. Why are you laughing?

. . .

The Everlasting Praise's Savior City folk flooded the board with protests. To placate them, Diego granted them all the Kenyan Adventure territory, most of the African Way, plus what used to be Oslo/Valhalla. It's insane. Many of our Bali Hai people are requesting transfers out of Bali Hai to other programs offered by competitors. Capitals USA and Pan Asian residents are looking for other options.

play fair... play fair. play fair.

They need to understand. They don't play fair.

Two million . . .

No I didn't . . .did not did not did . . .

BREACH!!!!

CACHE: BIO-memory 34778950 VEI Chicago office May 8, 2121

The future was a fantasy

Laura trembles. Marcia stares in disbelief. Christ! *Did anyone overhear Monty's sobs?* Monty has collapsed on the small couch near the window.

"Do you know? Do you know what you did?" Monty points his finger at me.

I don't answer. What good would it do?

Monty sighs and, oh my God, he's going to faint! Looks so fragile with his short thin legs and his arms with the delicate wrists, the shirtsleeves always rolled.

Marcia avoids looking at me while she comforts Monty. Why won't she look at me?

"I'm sorry," I tell her, "These companies don't intend to play fair, and they would destroy VEI as surely as the virus destroyed Joy Forever. I had to protect us."

Laura turns her back, but she doesn't leave. Marcia's busy with Monty. I hope she can quiet him. No one else can know about this. She puts her arms around Monty. Laura shuts the door. Monty cries deep sobs, and the tears fall on Marcia's breast.

My mentor is rocking back and forth. I remember him standing in the California sun, urging us to imagine our futures. The future was a fantasy, something that would never touch us.

Marcia holds Monty's hand as she sits in a chair. His body is splayed against the couch's soft leather, the tufts of white hair floating on the couch arm. Monty's eyes are naked with grief, but I feel nothing. What did he expect?

"Two million," Monty's voice cracks in disbelief. "You deleted two million?!"

"I didn't," I say. "LeRoi deleted them."

Marcia is finally looking at me. What is it? It's pity.

END BREACH!!!

Pity me pity me pity . . . no no no no no no no no no no

END BREACH!!!!

RESUME 195

A fresh perspective

. . .

I'm fine. It was another . . . intrusion. Miranda removed some duplicate files—memories—and they're happening less frequently. Tom, what really troubles me is what's happening to Bali Hai. This merger threatens all of us. I can't afford these interruptions in my timeline.

. . .

I struggle to stay focused, to come up with a strategy. Who do I know? What lawyer, what person of means, who in the outside bio-world can help? I've tried reaching out, but no one returns my calls. There must be some way to fight. I don't know. What happened with Laura and Jacob continues to haunt me. I need a fresh perspective to help me move on.

. . .

I hope so as well. After Laura self-deleted, I was devastated until Marcia transitioned here. When Marcia was here in Bali Hai, it was beyond wonderful; the pain of losing Laura was gone. Then, inexplicably, Marcia decided to delete herself. Nothing I said convinced her to stay. She just shook her head and said goodbye.

. . .

You'll never know how much your help means to me! I'll make a point of completing the memory records. Miranda will notify you.

. . .

Oh my God.

checking on you, checking on you, checking
Checking on you checking on you you you you the bridge the bridge
BREACH!!
checking on you
Breach!!
CACHE: BIO-memory 4778930 Loc VEI Chicago office May 19, 2122 (Marcia Evans meeting)

My head is swimming. Why can't they understand? There's a muffled knocking. I believe I said no... The door's opening. Marcia . . . my friend, my love . . .

"Holden, I'm checking on you. You don't look good."

Why might that be? Perhaps because you're deserting me, abandoning the man you swore you'd love.

"I'm a little tired," I sigh. She's sitting across from me. I see that Marcia has neglected her anti-aging protocol. Time is making progress on its claims. Her jaw line has softened and there are new creases around her eyes. Maybe I'll treat her to some catchall gene therapy. "Your birthday is coming up. Shall we get together? You could use a little spoiling."

"No, Holden, I'll be out of town by then. Perhaps later." She smiles. Is there someone else? The thought goes through my mind.

I won't ask. She sits and studies my face as if she'll never see it again. "I love you Holden. I'll always . . . love you." She whispers one more "love you" as if it were the last time.

"Why so sad, Marcia? We've made it through tougher times than this."

"Remember that bridge, the one on the Pacific Coast?" she asks. "You were so young. I knew I couldn't protect you. I wish . . ." She dabs her nose with a tissue and tears are falling onto her hands like they did that day on the bridge.

Is there anything to say to let her know that I've loved her all these years? I know I disappointed her . . . I . . . "We'll get together when you're back," I whisper.

"Yes." She nods.

I hug her goodbye. It occurs to me I don't want to let her go. She kisses my cheek and turns.

"Don't be too long," I tell her. "We have an offer from a new company. Infinite Bliss wants to be a subsidiary, and it has a proposal. Frankly, I don't think much of it, but I know I'll need your help."

"Don't you remember? I'm retired now," she reminds me. How long before she changes her mind?

I nod and say, "We'll discuss it after your trip."

"Goodbye, Holden. Take care of yourself while I'm gone." The door shuts. I am alone.

Alone alone alone . . .

END BEACH!!

END RECORD

Another Flock of Gray Geese

Byron—you'll see the first mentions of Shemathra's Realm in these records.

GUNTER HOLDEN MEMORY FILES

FOLDER YEAR: 2193

From Bali Hai

GUNTER HOLDEN DOC. 210

V-Loc: Everest Summit 4.5 k by 5.8 k, non-event day 27 of 58, Tactile MOUNTAIN RISE © 2188, Visual/ audio EVEREST EXPERIENCE by VEI Adventures © 2187, Olfactory DREAM HIGH © 2145, Sims 18 gray geese level 4, Human 5 climbers' level 2.

Mount Everest Summit, virtual climbers, geese

Gunter, Diego wants to know when you are going to address the problems in Savior City. Reverend Bardot is irate and threatening to go to the Infinite Bliss Board. What should I tell him?

Tell him that I'll take care of it when I'm ready. I'm still adjusting to the reality of the merger and . . . Tell him I need a little more time.

I will tell him, Gunter. Is there anything else?

Yes, I'd like to see another flock of gray geese.

Of course.

END RECORD

***

Via message (confidential)

March 22, 2288

Byron Hernandez

Trammel & O'Connell Law Offices

Dear Byron—

The following memory records and transcripts reflect Holden's loss of authority and his relationship with the Infinite Bliss Board. At the time, members of the religious sect, Everlasting Praise controlled the allotment of memory and resources. Holden was forced to manage petty disputes and to do trouble shooting.

This situation signaled a significant erosion of Holden's influence over decision-making. I feel it is unlikely that Holden stood to benefit from the eventual SEINI takeover.

After reviewing them, let me know what you think.

Desmond

***

GUNTER HOLDEN DOC. 211

Savior City

V-Loc. "New Amsterdam" (renamed "Savior City") 3.8k by 4.9k, non-event day 32 of 180 days, 10 event days available (check schedule) 12 concentric canals/terrains, Structures 25 "cabin" prayer rooms, 40 historic residences, one "Oude Kerk," 10 canal bridges, 62 "business" structures (restaurants, clubs, café's, art museums. Sim-animal/insect eco systems level 7 EUROPEAN TERRAINS © 2140, 43 dogs (rotating breeds), 53 cats, Human sims—320 levels 5 to 7 service personnel including 45 prostitutes (30 females, 15 males) ages 24 to 76, 32 erotic performers, TACTILE by EUROFAIRWEATHER (limited temp span and scheduled event weather © August 2141, AUDIO/VISUAL by NETHERLANDIA © 2141, OLFACTORY by CANALWORKS © 2143, DINING by FLAVORSINTERNA-TIONAL © 2134.

Amsterdam (renamed Savior City) urban area, historic art centers, churches, window prostitutes

Reverend, welcome to Bali Hai's Amsterdam.

Bardot: *"I assume you are unaware that this is no longer Amsterdam."*

I stand corrected, Reverend Bardot. Savior City. I am Gunter Holden, and I'm here to address your complaint.

Bardot: *"This program is ungodly. Certain changes must be made. I'm told you're the one to make them."*

New Amsterdam was programmed for more secular activities and we're in the process of making the changes that you requested. I must say, the long black coat with the white collar is striking, especially with your silver hair.

Bardot: *"Process? How are we to pray? This program's hellish sounds are relentless. Several of our women parishioners came to me, distraught, begging me to make all of them stop."*

Please, I understand that several of your prayer circles were interrupted. I agree that it must be a vexing experience.

Bardot: *"Thank you."*

You are welcome. I'm curious, as a non-believer, might I ask why you chose to transition to a virtual program rather than go straight to heaven?

Bardot: *"Is this the first time you've wondered about our purpose here?"*

It's not the first time I've wondered. I've spoken with several leaders of religious communities. It seems that religion-oriented post-bio destinations are a specialty of Infinite Bliss.

Bardot: *"I see. And what did you discover?"*

I'll share their answers, but if you please, Reverend Bardot, what is your reason and as far as you can determine?

Window whores: *whistles, groans, and invitations.*

Oh, dear! Yes, I see what you mean. Excuse me for just a moment.

COMMAND: Miranda, SCAN: Amster—Savior City and DELETE all window whores and all sims engaged in drug activity.

DELETION complete. What about the strip clubs and those hosting sim-sexual performances? Should I DELETE all—hetero, homo and bestial?

Yes, please, immediately.

DELETION complete.

Ah, much better.

Bardot: "*We are grateful and profoundly relieved.*"

You're entirely welcome. Miranda has informed me of your "reformation" plans for New—Savior City. I'm told that you refer to members of your community as "New Pilgrims."

Bardot: "*Yes, we came here as pilgrims seeking grace and to spread the good news. There's still time to escape the eternal fires of Hell. Fulfilling the godly destiny of the Amsterdam of John Calvin, Savior City welcomes all sinners. Now is the time to repent!*"

How descriptive! Yes, I do remember the early history of the city. I can see why you chose it.

Bardot: "*I am grateful for your help. You have an invitation, Mr. Holden. Soon, there will be a celebration at the Kerk. We hope to see you there!*"

I will certainly attempt to attend your celebratory service at the "Kerk." We at Bali Hai want our new citizens to feel at home. I'll give you the command that will enable you to reach me at any time.

Bardot: "*Mr. Holden, we never did discuss what answers you received from other "religious" officers. I'm curious. What did they say?*"

Yes, we were talking about the "why." I'll share just a couple. The Catholic clergy virtuals are all residents of one destination The Sacred Heart Penitents is a retreat. There weren't enough Catholics residents to populate a colony, especially since the focus of this group is prayer and penance.

Regardless, I have seen several of them in our territories. Even the most dedicated need a break. When I asked one of these solitary-minded folks, a nun, why she decided to transition to a virtual community, she answered, "God will call me when I have completed my task. In the meantime, I will pray for your soul to be released from its prison." This was a woman who had died prematurely at the age of seventy-three.

Bardot: *"I'm curious. Do you know the manner of her death or why she came here?"*

The why, she wouldn't share. From the looks of her, her death wasn't pleasant. Her skin . . . I could barely look at her. She was covered in hideous boils and . . . You're nodding? Why? She could have chosen perfect health, an end to physical pain and yet . . .

Bardot: *"Did you ask her?"*

Yes, I did ask. And she said the strangest thing. "My pain is nothing; I suffer it gladly. Trust in God and he will deliver you from your painful burden." I stood there, in perfect health, though a bit uncomfortable. Then, she lifted her eyes and turned her gaze to a tree.

Bardot: *"The woman is suffering God's wrath for refusing to follow the righteous path."*

I see, interesting. You think God punishes her for rejecting the true path to the Savior.

Bardot: *"Exactly. We hope to guide others along the true path. If she begins to follow God's path, I know He would ease her pain. We plan to reach out and spread the word. I'd like to know what other communities share this platform."*

Our new religious communities are all a form of Christianity or Judaism. There are no Eastern religions. As you already know, Infinite Bliss' market was strictly western religions, so no Muslims,

Buddhists or Hindu groups are part of the Bali Hai Family. There is one exception.

Bardot: "*What? What exception? I was unaware.*"

They are our most recent addition. They follow Shemathra, Goddess of the Universe, and are a cult of nature worshipers.

Bardot: "*Pagans? Are you sure?*"

Yes, pagans. They call themselves "Children of the Mother of All." For the Shemathra, cyberspace is merely a new dimension. The cult is dedicated to the worship of their goddess, Shemathra who will send the most faithful to the planet Shemath. On Shemath, they will become corporeal again. Interesting to visit them. Each follower chooses to manifest as a herd animal. I felt as if I were in the middle of some fairy tale with all the talking goats and cows.

Bardot: "*I see. The Devil has taken residence in this program.*"

I can understand why you believe they follow the Devil. I'll issue a warning for Shemathra followers to avoid Savior City and to confine their "artificial" manifestations to their own colony, Of course, they may decide to repent.

Bardot: "*Mr. Holden, again, I appreciate your help. Please consider joining us for the glorious opening of the new Kerk. I hope you will seek God's light. If so, you are most welcome here.*"

Absolutely, Reverend! If I feel the need to find the true path, I'll not hesitate.

END RECORD

***

GUNTER HOLDEN DOC. 765A

V-Loc: See 743.1, Chicago ELYSIUM penthouse PERSONAL, updated 6.28.2122. 19 detailed interiors include entry lobby, elevators 2 and 8, rotating 4 of 10 resident interiors and concierge. © 8.18.2120 by VEI Personal Options, Non-event day.

Gunter?

Yes, Miranda?

A formal complaint has been lodged. Diego asks that you represent the Board and investigate.

I'd like the specifics.

This is a joint complaint filed by members of three of the four communities now occupying what was formerly Northern Europe's Valhalla against the fourth community, Everlasting Praise.

Christ, Bardot is an ass. What is it this time?

The complaint is in two parts:

Part A:

Section one. Privacy violations, including jump intrusion. Unnamed individuals, identifying themselves as Everlasting Praise citizens, coordinated their jump patterns, uninvited by the complainants, while continuing the promotion of their religious beliefs.

Section two, (a). Interruption of age-shifting. During the 1994 Spring Formal, one of the most popular proms of High School Town, members disrupted the scheduled sim rap and break-dance performance, appropriating the sound system to condemn "the impersonation of teenagers" as an offense to God's plan.

How interesting. When I visited Savior City, only a few who looked more than fifty.

Section two, (b) which concerns the High School Town's Spring Formal, was seen as particularly offensive. The program was a gift to one of Yesteryear's citizens, Trudy Valentine, by a family member. This resulted in participants, including Trudy, to age shift back to a much older version of themselves. The timing was unfortunate. Trudy had arranged for digitals to be transmitted to family as she entered the gym.

Trudy had perfected her younger self. The space between her eyes was wider, and she opted for a more defined jaw line. In the confusion, Trudy did not cancel the digitals and her family saw her in the prom dress as she was at the transition age of one hundred and sixty-two. As a courtesy, I have erased most of this incident from her memory and advised her family of the erasure.

The Falconcrest Avatar

Part B:

Section one: A complaint filed by the Falconcrest Colony claims that recently, citizens from Everlasting Praise interrupted the Falconcrest Annual Avatar Festival by publicly denouncing the practice of manifesting as an avatar. This Avatars Celebration event is an important part of the culture of the Falconcrest Colony, one of the two Evergreen Communities.

I'm familiar with Falconcrest from the Salan vs. Salan court case. Miranda, before you elaborate, what is Section B?

Section B: This was a single complaint filed by Jeremy Salan, a prominent resident of Falconcrest, on his own behalf and on behalf of his "wife," the sim Isobel.

Pain and suffering. "These bullies upset me and I want them punished." Several individuals identifying as Everlasting Praise representatives held up signs outside the Salan home, while shouting the printed message "abomination."

They were referring to Jeremy's "marriage" to the sim, saying that it was unnatural, and God never intended a virtual to marry a sim. The fact that our new residents are not bound by the Bali Hai Ethics Code makes this more difficult.

I understand. Tell Diego, Uncle Gunter has it covered.

In those words?

Yes, Miranda, in those exact words.

END RECORD

***

GUNTER HOLDEN DOC. 215A

V-Loc: See 743.1, Chicago ELYSIUM penthouse PERSONAL, updated 6.28.2122. 19 detailed interiors include entry lobby, elevators 2 and 8, rotating 4 of 10 resident interiors and concierge. © 8.18.2120 by VEI Personal Options, non-event day.

COMMAND, Miranda, please SEND: The following message to Diego Putman, CEO of Infinite Bliss.

Yes, Gunter.

Diego:

After meeting with Reverend Mark Bardot, revered leader of the Everlasting

Praise community, I am pleased to inform you that we were able to negotiate a solution and resolve the complaints lodged by those communities sharing the program location formerly known as Northern Europe's Valhalla. Until a consensus can be reached to rename it, I will refer to it as Valhalla. Reverend Bardot has graciously agreed to confine his flock to Savior City and adjacent Everlasting Praise territory. In exchange, members of the Shemathra Goddess of the

Universe community will refrain from visiting Savior City and appearing as herd animals.

Further, Jeremy Salan has agreed not to visit Savior City while manifesting as the custom avatar he was awarded in the Infinite Bliss settlement for his pain and suffering. This avatar is patterned after the fabled Greek centaurs and possesses an enormous phallus, which Jeremy realizes might result in the discomfort of the citizens in Savior City. Mr. Salan assures me that should he need to clarify his position his avatar will be prominent in any subsequent face-to-face with Reverend Bardot.

Sincerely,

Gunter

END RECORD

***

GUNTER HOLDEN DOC 215 B

COMMAND, Miranda, TRANSFER: Gunter Holden CUSTOM Chicago office VEI Oct 2121

V-Loc: The Chicago VEI, small boardroom

TRANSFERED

Gunter?

Yes?

Diego is holding for you.

Tell him to give me a moment.

Yes, he'll wait.

COMMAND Miranda, SET: The Chicago VEI small boardroom—the maroon wingback chair and mahogany desk.

Environment SET

Greetings Diego!

Diego: "*Hello Uncle.*"

You're looking well.

Diego: "*I need you to hear me out. There's a problem concerning the Classics Group.*"

Yes, of course I'll hear you out.

Diego: "*I'm afraid that Classics will need prior approval from the Board for any title of any book they plan to enact.*"

I thought the matter was settled now that Everlasting Praise has the new territory. But, but Classics . . . they have a contract.

Diego: "*Uncle, please understand, Everlasting Praise will determine what titles are suitable and Classics must accept their decision. If you like, I'll inform you of any changes to this situation.*"

Well, with so many Board members being bio "New Pilgrims" I guess they will decide. When did they—

Diego: "*Does it matter?*"

You're right! It doesn't matter.

Diego: "*Uncle, there's something else. Jeremy Salan will be replacing you as representative to the Board. The Board wishes me to thank you for your help.*"

WHO? Jeremy Salan? I see . . . well . . . Yes, of course I'll step down.

Diego: "*Thank you, Uncle. I know this is difficult for you.*"

You are welcome. I know you appreciated my efforts. I wish Jeremy the best of luck as the new virtual representative to the Board. I'd be happy to help him in any way I can.

Diego: "*I appreciate your understanding. I'll be in touch.*"

You as well, Diego. We'll catch up on family news soon.

Diego: "*I'll keep that in mind. Goodbye, Uncle.*"

Call ended

Idiot—the fucking idiot!

COMMAND Miranda, ACCESS: My Federal Star Virtual Account 2865. Send Jeremy Salan a pond. Place it in his compound, near the entrance. Fill it with virtual carp from the Tokyo Eternal Horizons collection. Include the following message: Congratulations to our new board representative, Gunter Holden.

Done—anything else?

No. Thank you, Miranda!

COMMAND: Miranda, ENTER the next—

Excuse me, Gunter, it's Diego and he says it's urgent.

All right.

COMMAND: INTERFACE

INTERFACED

The real Isobel

Diego, Miranda said it was urgent . . .

Diego: "*Jeremy Salan is to be married and we need your help.*"

But Jeremy Salan is already married. You lost me. Although she is a sim, some might . . . I don't understand.

Diego: "*That abomination, as Reverend Bardot puts it, is irrelevant. It seems that Jeremy has an unnatural concern for the well-being of this Isobel-sim creature. He wants his "wife" to be happy by providing her with a companion sim. After praying for a solution, Bardot has decided to create a Jeremy "sim" to reassure Mr. Salan that his sim companion won't be alone.*"

We need you to locate Jeremy's parents, Betsy and Otis, as well as his former Falconcrest roommates and persuade them to allow access to their Jeremy memories. These memories will help create a "rounded" Jeremy-sim which will placate the current "Mrs. Salan." Then Mr. Salan will agree to marry the real Isobel."

What do you mean, the real Isobel? You mean the bio? When did she transition?

Diego: *"I don't know. This task was thrust upon me today. She, I mean the bio-Isobel, is currently a guest of Reverend Bardot in Savior City. Can I count on you, Uncle Gunter?"*

This is unexpected. The new Isobel is a resident of Savior City. Fascinating.

Diego: *"Apparently, this version is younger and more attractive."*

Well yes, it stands to reason the virtual Isobel would choose to be a younger and more attractive version. It seems that Jeremy's maturation program wasn't entirely without an effect. What can I do to help? I don't follow. She's a sim. How could she have anything to say about his decision?

Diego: *"The aim is to reassure Mr. Salan. I believe guilt is a factor. He feels guilty, a sort of separation anxiety. We have already approached Jeremy's mother, Betsy. It seems that she is unwilling to allow access to her Jeremy memories. I cannot stress how important this is, Uncle."*

Poor Betsy. How did he track her down?

Diego: *"Reverend Bardot called upon the Everlasting Praise bio-Board members for help."*

I suppose Reverend Bardot would have an interest in settling this. I'll talk to Betsy and let you know what she decides.

Diego: *"I would greatly appreciate your assistance. I know you won't let me down."*

You're welcome, Diego! Glad to be of help.

END CALL

Call ended

Everlasting idiots.

END RECORD

***

GUNTER HOLDEN DOC. 408

V-Loc: See 743.1, Chicago ELYSIUM Penthouse PERSONAL, updated 6.28.2122. 19 detailed interiors include entry lobby, elevators 2 and 8, rotating 4 of 10 resident interiors and concierge. © 8.18.2120 by VEI Personal Options, Non-event day.

Tom, thanks for being available. I want you to know that our talks are helping. I've had fewer breaches, but I still feel that I'm losing my mind.

. . .

I've been tasked with the assignment of creating a sim.

. . .

You're right. Denise would be an ideal person to tackle it, however, she's not "approved" by the Board as "desirable." Believe me, nothing would make me happier than to have Denise take care of it. Besides, Diego assured the new Board that I would see to it personally.

. . .

My nephew takes great pleasure in offering my services. I'd like you to look at my report to the board.

. . .

Fine, here it is:

A sim's sim

Diego,

As you requested, I have met with Betsy Salan. At present, she is reluctant to have her memories of her son, Jeremy, accessed for the purpose of placating the sim "Isobel" who refers to herself as "Mrs. Jeremy Salan." I explained the situation, and I must be candid. Part of her reluctance stems from an unfortunate accident, namely the deletion of a major Bali Hai city, Paris, resulting in the erasure of Betsy's father.

Now, Betsy controls her father's estate. She has advised me that her attorneys are prepared to assert her rights as stated in Article 6 of the Virtuals' Bill of Rights, namely that her memories are her property and may only be accessed at her discretion. She has refused.

To move forward, I have taken the following steps:

One: I contacted Otis Salan, Jeremy's father, who has graciously agreed to have Miranda scan him for memories of Jeremy. However, many of them are corrupted and unusable. In addition, Otis has far fewer of these memories than Betsy, as he was often away during Jeremy's short bio life.

Two: I located Jeremy's former roommates. The two girls elected to remain children. Unfortunately, neither girl felt she could spare the time.

Tupac Dean, Jeremy's third roommate is currently a member of the Shemathra Goddess of the Universe community. Tupac is part of a flock of mountain sheep and the dominant ram in this group. I conveyed my request via the appropriate Shemathra communications. After he has fulfilled his obligations to the ewes, he will be happy to help.

Tupac cautioned, "Everyone here, those who choose the life of the herd, is counting on me." Tupac will be glad to record his Jeremy memories, saying, again, in his words, "Anything for the Jer."

It will be four weeks and two days in bio-time before mating season ends.

If there are other steps you wish me to take or if there are other individuals to contact, let Miranda know. I am aware of no other sources of Jeremy memories. I have instructed Miranda to notify me.

Sincerely,

Gunter Holden.

End report.

Any suggestions?

. . .

I agree, it is ridiculous. I wish I could opt out and leave my idiot nephew to deal with the whole mess. But I must remain informed of anything that could threaten Bali Hai. Do you understand?

. . .

Tom, I'm going to record some memories that you may find shocking. After you review them, let Miranda know if you want to continue helping me. I hope so.

. . .

Miranda, send my new report to Diego Putnam.

SENT

END RECORD

BAD NEWS, MR. HOLDEN

G UNTER HOLDEN DOC. 410A

V-Loc: See 743.1, Chicago ELYSIUM Penthouse PER-
SONAL, updated 6.28.2122. 19 detailed interiors include entry
lobby, elevators 2 and 8, rotating 4 of 10 resident interiors and concierge. © 8.18.2120 by VEI Personal Options, Non-event Day.

COMMAND, Miranda, RESTRICT: access to this memory.
I, Gunter Holden, and Thomas Bucklin are the only ones, virtual
or bio.

Yes, Gunter. I will restrict access.

GUNTER HOLDEN Memory File 410 A

RECORD: Gunter Holden Memory 410 A.

RECORDING 410 A

B-Loc: Chicago VEI Building, Gunter Holden's office

I'm staring at the monitor. *Find something . . . something . . . distract . . .* God, what time is it? Shouldn't he be here? It's almost one
thirty-three. My hands are cold! He won't want to shake hands. Good
. . . that's good, because . . .

"Mr. Holden?"

"Yes?"

"Your one-thirty appointment is here."

"Send him in. I don't wish to be disturbed for the rest of the afternoon. Take messages."

"Will do, Mr. Holden."

My heart's pounding. I can't get a good breath . . . *hold it together* . . . Martino must respect me. Men like him need to respect you or you can't trust them.

"Hello! Have a seat."

Martino sits in the green chair and inspects his fingernails. I can see it isn't good.

Martino: "Bad news, Mr. Holden—I'm sorry to say . . . yes, very bad, I'm afraid, sir. Your wife is seeing someone else . . . I'm awfully sorry, but it is your brother Jacob. He's Laura's lover."

Don't react . . . stay calm . . . cover your reaction, shade your eyes with fingers laced—don't clasp your face in your hands; he'll see it as weakness. *Breathe . . . breathe . . . He's* waiting for me. I must tell him how to fix it.

Martino's relaxed and his arms hang loose, draped over the sides like he's ready for a nap, but his fingers tap the leather as he waits for me.

Lincoln, he looks like Lincoln. Dear Jacob, the Great Emancipator is fixing to set you free from this world. The last face you'll see won't be my wife's, but a sad worn face, mournful eyes and the dark hair coiled from the widow's peak. Such a gentle voice, regretful . . . Maybe the resemblance will catch you or you'll hear the soft voice of your liberator, just before the bullet rips through your sensitive skull.

"The antique, the laser pistol you mentioned, I'm interested in buying it. You say it's old, and it's untraceable. It is untraceable, no record?"

He doesn't move. My voice sounds like it's coming from somewhere else, another dimension where sound is muffled.

"I'd prefer that you test it out, the target, only the one target we discussed. I require this to be sure it's an effective weapon. Let me know how accurate it is. I'm positive that if this is done to my satisfaction, I'll double the original asking price."

"So, Mr. Holden, are you sure? You want to do this? He is your brother and taking care of this situation won't guarantee your wife's coming home."

"I only ask once, Mr. Martino. There are other dealers with more extensive collections."

He nods his head. "I'll be in touch."

Oh, Laura! God damn you both.

COMMAND, END: 410 A

410 A ENDED. Shall I notify Tom that it's available for review?

No, Miranda. I'll let him know. What will he think of me after he knows?

END RECORD

***

GUNTER HOLDEN DOC. 236

V-Loc: See 743.1, Chicago ELYSIUM Penthouse PERSONAL, updated 6.28.2122. 19 detailed interiors include entry lobby, elevators 2 and 8, rotating 4 of 10 resident interiors and concierge. © 8.18.2120 by VEI Personal Options, Non-event Day.

. . .

Your suggestions have been very helpful. I reviewed the facts as you advised and began to realize my part in creating what happened. Laura needed attention. I was overwhelmed and couldn't be there when she—

. . .

Why, what are you getting at?

. . .

You keep bringing up Jacob. Tom, I keep telling you that there are no conflicts, no mixed feelings when it comes to my brother. None.

. . .

I've told you how grateful I am for your counsel. The unwelcome memories are less of a problem now. Miranda has been running scans on me, and she says that my psych profile has improved. You have no idea what a relief it is. Why keep talking about Jacob? I don't see the point.

. . .

I have closed the sad chapter of my brother. If it will help convince you, I'll record the events that followed my first virtual showdown with Jacob in Bali Hai.

. . .

It's the last of my demons, I'm sure. I can give our current Bali Hai crisis my full attention.

. . .

I doubt their significance, but Miranda has mentioned that two files still wait for my review. One of them is Monty's before he deleted himself. Ironic, isn't it? Some people are not cut out for this life. It seems Monty was one of them. Nothing I said made a difference. He fell into the Dreams soon after he came here.

. . .

The other file is stored under Marcia's name. She left several messages, but I'm not sure what they contain. The pain of her leaving
resulted in my reluctance to review them, but now I feel ready.

. . .

I hope that she recorded some of the early days of Bali Hai. For
example, places she visited. I plan to access Marcia's collection after
I finish with my last memory record and after I look at Monty's
message.

. . .

END RECORD

Sacred Ecstasy, Infinite Nirvana Inc.

Via message (confidential)

April 10, 2288

Byron Hernandez

Trammel & O'Connell Law Offices

Byron –

These next files occur during the SEINI take over before another mass erasure. Be careful. Technically, they're Holden's property, but that's only because Hosseini's lawyers are unaware that they exist.

Let me know if you have questions.

Regards,

Des

Byron—the first memory of this group of records reveals the early days of SEINI's takeover of the Bali Hai platform and the growing dominance of the Shemathra herds. The second one involves the exploitation of Holden and the hapless Jeremy Salan. This exploitation continues as Holden records and reviews memories.

GUNTER HOLDEN DOC. 245

V-Loc: See 743.1, Chicago ELYSIUM Penthouse PERSONAL, updated 6.28.2122. 19 detailed interiors include entry lobby, elevators 2 and 8, rotating 4 of 10 resident interiors and concierge. © 8.18.2120 by VEI Personal Options, Non-event Day.

Gunter, Diego Putman is waiting to speak with you.

I'd prefer to go on to the next memory. Tell him I am in the middle of a scanning and ask him if I can return his call.

He says it's quite urgent and requests that you be interrupted.

I see. SET: The Chicago office with the usual preferences.

COMMAND, TRANSFER: Gunter Holden CUSTOM Chicago office VEI Oct 2121

TRANSFER COMPLETE

SETTING in place.

Gunter Holden here. Diego, please accept my apologies for the delay. Miranda said it was urgent.

Diego: "*Yes, Uncle, it is. Do you know who Donovan Hosseini Is?*"

Of course, I know who Hosseini is. The man dominated the holo-porn world at the time of my transition, and I hear he's big in the off-world habitats industry. The eco-system kits on Mars are all from Hosseini Interplanetary Products.

Diego: "*I'm impressed. You seem to know more than I do about Mr. Hosseini.*"

Be careful! Hosseini is dangerous.

Diego: *"We all need to be careful, Uncle."*

We virtuals know what's in our best interests.

Diego: *"I'm to inform you that SEINI has acquired controlling interest in Infinite Bliss."*

I'm sorry; I don't understand. Please repeat what you just said. So, what is the company's new name?

Diego: *"Sacred Ecstasy, Infinite Nirvana Inc."*

SEINI? That was sudden. How much of a controlling interest did Hosseini acquire?

Diego: *"I believe that it is about seventy-five to eighty per cent. Apparently, Hosseini is a bio-member and sponsor of the Shemathra group. I am to aid in the redistribution of memory. The Shemathra group requires additional memory for grazing areas."*

You must be joking. Hosseini is a member of the Shemathra? So, if you implement Hosseini's new design, you will retain your position. What about the rest of the Board?

Diego: *"There will be a new Board."*

Ah, of course, they'll all be Hosseini's people. What else?

Diego: *"Hosseini wants no bad press. Everlasting Praise will retain what is necessary."*

Okay. Everlasting Praise will keep its territory. Where are these new mountains, tundra and plains going to be? Hopefully, Bardot realizes the wisdom of not contesting the new Board's decision.

Diego: *"Uncle, I urge you to be careful. Hosseini frightens even me. He can make people disappear. Both virtual and bio."*

I'll be discreet. Convey my regards to your family. Did they enjoy the Christmas gifts?

Diego: *"Yes, thank you for thinking of us. I hope you found my gift helpful."*

Yes, thank you. I plan to use my stay at The Pilgrim's Hotel when I attend the Salan wedding.

Diego: *"Your visit will be helpful in building a good relationship with Reverend Bardot."*

I agree. We must look out for one another in this. Goodbye, Diego.

Diego: *"Remember to be careful. Hosseini has plans and things may change soon. Goodbye, Uncle."*

Communication ended.

Christ. What next?

END RECORD

Jeremy Salan's wedding

GUNTER HOLDEN DOC. 242

V-Loc: Venice Beach /Strand environ, RICKS BEACH CAFÉ, 2.7k beach-4.14k, .4k ocean-1.6 k from Strand. See 141 B, Day 5 of 20 Events Volleyball West Coast Competition 2186 Venice, California.

Venice Beach, Strand Environment, virtual tourists, sim-traffic, summer, mid-day, volleyball competition, Rick's Café

I know I haven't finished recording the last of my memories. I appreciate your patience. It was good of you to spare the time. I'm told you're making memory records. When will I have the privilege of reviewing them?

. . .

I've been to a wedding. Be grateful I didn't drag you along. I did consider it.

. . .

It was Jeremy Salan's marriage to the virtual Isobel. Unforgettable.
I would have been free sooner, however, I was forced to do damage
control. Tupac Dean, currently a member of the Shemathra community, was best man.

. . .

Tupac and Jeremy were roommates in the early Evergreen days.

. . .

Unexpected. Reverend Bardot bade the trembling Jeremy to kiss
his bride. This prompted Tupac to shift into his Shemathra manifes-
tation, a large ram, who, to put it delicately, was in rutting mode. This
triggered the unfortunate mounting of the bride by the best man.

. . .

My guess is that Tupac's recent servicing of the ewes resulted in
his confusion. If he had been in his human form, he would never have
committed such a faux pas.

. . .

It is funny now, but then it was a disaster.

. . .

The idea was to entice Jeremy into the fold. This was to be a major
coup because of Jeremy's new role as mediator in disputes. When
Isobel saw a chance to transition to a high-end post-bio program,
embracing Reverend Bardot's brand of Christianity was an easy decision. She stood to gain a lot when she downed the pills with a fifth of
Chivas Regal.

. . .

Bardot found her in San Diego. She was living over a grandniece's
auto-glide port.

. . .

She's changed, though I'm not sure it's an improvement. Let's just say she has a certain crude charm. When I saw her at the wedding, she manifested in her early thirties.

. . .

It could have been the dress. It was a white satin. The train was ten feet of white satin. Sim-flower-girls threw pink rose petals onto it, causing a polka dot effect. My eyes were drawn to the dots, so I might have missed the signs that all was not well with Tupac.

. . .

Jeremy reminded me of a mouse cornered by a cat. Miranda confided Isobel had manifested as a younger, more attractive version of her "nanny" days. On the day of the wedding, Isobel went for a different, sexier look.

. . .

The day before the wedding, Reverend Bardot asked that I meet with Jeremy and go over his "husbandly" duties. Stop laughing if you want to know the rest.

. . .

That's better. Let's stop walking. I want to sit at a table and watch the passersby. Venice Beach is alive with color today.

. . .

Anyway, yes, the "talk." Jeremy and I sat at a table, much like this one. There's a small café in Savior City located on the edge of "Come All Ye Sinners Rebirthing Pool and Waterfall Center."

. . .

The Splash-o-rama Waterpark is for residents who want to revisit their childhood. Jeremy was very attractive to Isobel. The bank funds he acquired when his lawsuit finally settled were impressive. By the way, Jeremy is now Reverend Jeremy.

. . .

He seemed quite confident when we met. In Jeremy's mind, the sim-marriage was a dry run for the real thing, a concept introduced by Bardot. He mentioned his new status as a minister and how "proud" of him, Isobel, his fiancé was.

. . .

I admit, I was at a loss as to how to bring the subject of sex into the conversation subtly, and so I decided to just dive in. Pretend you're Jeremy.

. . .

"Jeremy, what kind of relationship skills did you "practice" with the sim Isobel?" Now you nod and say, "We practiced many meaningful exchanges."

. . .

Now it's my turn to clarify. "I'm glad you are such an experienced communicator, but Jeremy, what about sex?"

Now you look puzzled and say "Sex?"

. . .

I sat, waiting for the concept to sink in. Now, you look like you just ate a dinner of raw cockroaches, antennas, and all, and you say, "You . . . you—mean like . . . what they do in holozine-porn?"

. . .

Good! You are a talented actor! Too bad you became an engineer and too bad the Classics colony is off-limits now to outsiders. I see you in a period classic.

. . .

The wedding? Officially, they're married, though the bride disappeared a day after the wedding. Unofficially, the story I heard from my sources in Savior City was that the bride wasn't happy the morning after the wedding. She was overheard expressing her dismay at the wedding breakfast, saying, "The boy don't know what to do and I deserve a man, not a goddam baby boy."

. . .

I agree. Jeremy is still a child, one better off being with the nanny-sim. The good reverend must know this. He saw Jeremy as an opportunity. A child is easier to manipulate. Isobel vanished later that day. After a short time in seclusion, Jeremy returned to baptizing.

. . .

I hear the Isobel-sim is back. Everyone is pretending she's the virtual. Ah, I do love Venice Beach . . .

END RECORD

***

Byron—Gunter records a memory involving post-bio activity using Jump TRANSFER effect. Gunter Holden, Laura Holden "fly" over Bandon, Oregon.

GUNTER HOLDEN DOCS. 413A, 255, 413B, 414

V-Loc: See 743.1, Chicago ELYSIUM Penthouse PERSONAL, updated 6.28.2122. 19 detailed interiors include entry lobby, elevators 2 and 8, rotating 4 of 10 resident interiors and concierge. © 8.18.2120 by VEI Personal Options, Non-event day.

COMMAND, Miranda, RECORD: The following as Gunter Holden . . . Holden . . .

Yes, Gunter?

MEMORY 413A.

RECORDING 413A. (post-transition encounter with Laura Holden)

Gray clouds surround us as we dance. It's a trick of the mind. I'm no longer bound by physics.

Laura spreads her arms and legs and dives into the gray below, then floats up like a flower in a pond. She's turning around and faces up as she laughs. Oh God, I've wanted this.

There's Bandon below us, a small town on the Oregon coast. I point downward and motion for Laura to follow. She smiles giddily as we drift down to the sand. Gray clouds are now above us.

"Shall we be hungry?" I ask her. "I can arrange for a candlelit dinner in Madrid, like our wedding night." Her face changes in an instant, as if some of the sky's gloom fell with her. We're sitting on a grassy area near the sand. She hugs her knees and stares at the restless waves.

Marcia insisted on bringing Bandon to Bali Hai. Why do women choose dreariness instead of joy? My giddy wife looks troubled, an unexpected response to my offer. What now?

"I never told you about what I saw on the day of your dad's funeral." She says it in one virtual breath.

Oh Christ, what nonsense will I have to endure? Let her get it out of her system.

"Okay, Laura, tell me what you saw."

She turns away and lays her head on her knees.

I'm still waiting. I hope this is fast.

"Your dad had just died." She sighs, her arms now crossed, as she looks at me as if I were a stranger. "I heard you were back from the funeral, so I stayed late at the office. I just wanted to be near you, so I hid in my office, the lights turned low."

"Nice, but what's your point?"

"I heard you tell Marcia about what you did to Jacob. You described the pleasure you felt when you tried to kill Jacob after your dad's funeral."

So that's it! I can deal with whatever misconception she has about her sensitive musician-lover.

"Do you know, Laura, what my brother did? How he paid Dad back for the honor of being the favorite?"

She's shaking her head. "No, it was what I saw when you returned. Marcia mentioned Jacob, and you exploded. You told her that you had always hated him, even when Jacob was ten and he was kidnapped, his legs broken. After they found him, he begged for you, his big brother, to come. You said, 'I wouldn't have interrupted a trip to the dentist for that little bastard.'" She shrugs. "Then, you laughed. Your eyes were flat, Gunter, dead calm, like my father's eyes before he'd yank my mother's head back and bloody her nose. I told myself that it was grief and that I'd never see that look again. I was wrong."

Maybe sympathy will change her mood.

"Laura, you should have told me about how bad it was with your father. I could have helped. You could have seen someone." *Where did all these seagulls suddenly come from?*

"Gunter, what kind of man are you?"

"Did Jacob come crying to you about THAT? All you have is his story. Why didn't you ask ME?" *I can't believe she's been chewing on this!* "Laura, you knew how upset and if I had known you could hear us, I would have been more . . . Can we talk about this?"

She won't look at me as she pronounces judgment. "I thought it was the stress of losing your father until I met Jacob at Burning Man. I knew how much you hated him. What I didn't know was how much he loved you. Who do you love, Gunter? Have you ever really loved anyone? Me? Marcia? Maybe only yourself." She studies her palm. Is she looking for her lifeline? "I couldn't go on pretending after the Joy Forever deletions. What about now? Why am I still with you?"

Oh Christ, how do I fix this? She's leaving!

"Laura, please! I wish I had known. I know you're upset, but you never let me defend myself!"

Thank God, she's stopped her jump! I want to keep this private. Her age shifting is out of control! She's forty, eighteen and now she's twelve! *Control it, Laura . . .*

She stares at me like I'm something alien, not human. "Defend, Gunter?! You murdered your own brother; you murdered me. Did you allow us to defend ourselves before you pronounced sentence?"

Oh God, what do I say? The goddamn gulls are landing six feet from here, the tide is coming in. I want it all to go away.

"Okay, Laura. You're right. I'm a snake, a rat, and a bastard. In a heated moment, I was crazy because I thought I'd lost you forever. I did something unforgiveable."

She's jumping now, probably back to Jacob. I won't follow her. The whole thing's out and she'll cool down. These birds must go. Miranda should delete them. No, delete this whole environment. It's a mistake to trust the judgment of others when it comes to pleasure. We can use the extra memory.

COMMAND: END recording memory 413 A

ENDING 413A.

Gunter—Diego wishes to speak with you—are you available?

Yes, COMMAND, SET: Chicago office, please.

TRANSFER COMPLETE, Gunter Holden CUSTOM Chicago office VEI Oct 2121

SETTING in place.

Diego! Greetings.

Diego: *"Hello Uncle. I need a favor. It might not be easy, and I must have your total discretion."*

I'm happy to do you a favor.

Diego: *"I want you to find the virtual Isobel Salan."*

I can't say that I know Isobel's current location. All the information I have is that the new Mrs. Salan is a member of the Shemathra community. Are you sure you don't want Miranda to—

Diego: *"Please, no AI. This search must be untraceable!"*

Of course, I understand. I'll take care of it personally. I agree. This needs to be discreet. When I locate Mrs. Salan, what steps should I take?

Diego: *"Send me a note, something casual about how you 'happened' to run into Mrs. Salan or... I'll leave it to your judgment. I know you won't let me down."*

Yes, Miranda will contact you and it will be a "family" discussion. Anything else?

Diego: *"Nothing else. Thank you, Uncle."*

You're more than welcome.

COMMAND, END: holo-communication.

Communication ENDED.

THE TRUTH WAS NEVER EASY

COMMAND, Miranda, RECORD: The following memory as Gunter Holden memory record 413 B.

COMMAND: Miranda, CLASSIFY: Gunter Holden memory record 413 B as available only by my approval.

Memory 413B CLASSIFIED as by approval only.

Byron--This memory record is of a post-transition encounter and conflict resolution with Jacob Holden. Given your interest in the Connecticut estate and specifically, "the veranda," this recording might hold particular interest. The location of the encounter was Bali Hai: Holden Estate (Connecticut) veranda eve-night. See Doc. 735.

RECORDING memory 413B

"What now, Jacob? I'm here because Laura persists with her peace and love fantasy, a sentimental reconciliation and the crowning achievement of Laura, the peacemaker."

Jacob sits across from me on Dad's veranda. I occupy the chair I always do, the one with the best view of the river. The birches and the sweet gums frame the Thames. Boats close to shore disappear sooner than more distant sails.

It's evening as we listen to crickets chirping and the click of sweet gum leaves. Purple and orange leaf-stars shudder and the river sloshes. I still wonder how Laura managed to retrieve this setting. It was archived after Dad's death, but Jacob called it up anyway. And I keep coming back.

Jacob swings his chubby legs. Neither of us can tap the floor planks. I am eight years old today. I decided to be eight when I saw Jacob waiting for me as his three-year-old self.

Does he think he'll trigger some dormant filial love? There is a plus. Because Jacob is three, I won't see those daddy long legs . . . ha.

"You're better at this than I am," my brother says in his toddler voice.

I stifle an urge to laugh. "Well, Jacob, Bali Hai was my dream, not yours."

"My dream was to be like you." He turns his face towards me. I see the fat toddler cheeks and the innocence.

"That's clever, Jacob!"

"Mom tried to shield me from the truth," he says. "You hated me because you thought I took Dad's love away from you. I couldn't accept it until I was ten and you didn't come to see me when I in the hospital."

Don't take the bait. Don't get angry. Let him think you've seen the light. I slip off my chair and walk to the edge of the veranda. Dried and lifeless, spiked spheres of sweet gum fruit lay in the grass. I pick them up and throw them through the tree frame as we talk. The wicker chair squeaks as Jacob scoots off. Now, he sits on the edge of the planks behind me. *Don't look back. Just pick up the sticky balls and keep throwing them.*

"Do you believe in fate?" Jacob asks.

I suppress a laugh. What a ridiculous question, especially when the voice belongs to a three-year-old.

"Oh God, please don't make me listen to superstitious artist musings."

"Gunter, I know that you're angry that I urged Dad not to come here." His voice has changed; it's deeper now. I glance back and see that Jacob is ten, the babyish curls gone. Lank brown strands of hair obscure his round blue eyes.

"I remember you making up his mind for him," I snap.

I'm eighteen again, the last year of my normal life. I turn back to the trees and the river.

"This is pointless. Laura should choose either joy or despair, whatever it is she wants, but choose." I'm ready to leave. "Goodbye, little brother!"

As I throw the last sticky ball, I see Jacob change. He's still ten, but he's different. His eyes are blackened. A purple bruise puffs his cheek, distorting his jaw line. He wears a striped shirt and some athletic prep-school shorts. He has no shoes or socks. Bright red oozes from a gash on his forehead. Rusty smears of old blood and black grime cover his shirt. His wiry arms are landscapes of welts and cuts.

But it's his legs that are the most difficult. They accuse me. They're swollen and the bones are clearly broken; I can see the sharp edges pressing against the skin. His bare feet are caked with dried mud, and they fold, tilting up from the ankle joints like Jacob was a forgotten doll. How dare he show me this pathetic child!

"Bastard! You can't force me to be responsible for what happened. It was not my fault!"

"No Gunter, this wasn't your doing," he whispers through cracked lips.

What does he want me to say?

"Shift your age you bastard. It doesn't change anything."

"This is who I was when I finally accepted that you didn't love me."

"Oh, please!"

"You were my hero. Whenever I knew you were coming home, I'd count the days until your visit. I'd make lists of things I wanted to tell you and try to think of ways to impress you."

This is getting out of hand. Obviously, he wasn't and still isn't stable.

"What do you want me to say?" I'm forty-three now. I sigh.

Jacob doesn't change. "My point is that you didn't know me, and Gunter, you didn't know Dad."

I scream at him. "I don't give a crap about your opinion of my relationship with my father!"

"Yes, Gunter, I know." Jacob nods and then hesitates, as if debating whether to continue. "My mother urged me to stay out of it. 'Let him do it,' she said. 'Let Gunter deal with the big man and see for himself what Eric is, because he'll never accept it if it comes from you or me.'"

Is there nothing Jacob won't try to destroy, nothing sacred, even my father's memory?

"Oh, little brother, this is a new low. You try to take all I have left of him. The man gave you EVERYTHING. Thanks to you, all I have of him are my memories. There's nothing more to say."

The ten-year-old is gone and the wasted musician stands on the planks where my father spent his last hours.

Jacob's shaking his head and his mother's eyes stare at me.

"I'm sorry, Gunter. I'm so sorry about what I knew and couldn't tell you. You thought you knew Dad, but believe me, dear brother, you didn't. I'm finished here".

"Then go, Jacob."

He's staring at the trees, then he goes to the door. It still needs paint. Maybe I'll have Miranda change it.

"It's Laura's decision. It's you she loves. Laura and I are friends; we understand each other. There's comfort in knowing what you cannot have and accepting it," he says softly.

I can still hear the gifted tenor in that voice, the one my father gave him.

"I'll make sure she knows I'm leaving," he tells me. "And then I'll go. She can go with me or stay with you. I'll tell her you did your best and I know how much she loves you. I know you don't believe it, but I still love you. Dad loved you in his way. Mom tried hard to protect you and so did I."

"What are you saying? *Still playing games, are we?* Your mother tried to what? I KNOW what she did. She tried to 'protect' me by turning my father against me. She succeeded when she had you."

"The truth, Gunter, was never easy. Take care of yourself," he says as he leaves.

Let him go.

COMMAND: END RECORDING Memory record 413B

413B ENDED.

Laura is gone. Let's finish it. I want to leave it all behind.

COMMAND, Miranda, RECORD: The following as Gunter Holden memory record 414C.

Do the same access restrictions stipulated for 413 A and B apply to 414C?

Yes, Miranda, please make available only through my approval.

COMMAND RUN 414C as available only with my approval.

414C is only available with your approval.

Byron-- The following is a review of the last post transition encounter with Laura Holden. Laura Holden self-deleted 1.2 hours after she exited this game (GAME DOC. 288653729.3). In addition, within this post bio-memory record (414C) is another, earlier Gunter Holden bio-childhood memory.

V-Loc: "The Hunt" Game Program- Baltimore Disaster Level TWO SET TWO, © Sun Discovery, Inc. May 2127, update Sept. 2128.
RECORDING MEMORY 414C

Cherry Hill

We hear explosions, a chain reaction of old-fashioned gas-fueled appliances, triggered by the initial blast that leveled the structures of over sixty percent of Baltimore's Inner Harbor.

This is Cherry Hill, a high poverty area with people hanging on to what they have and slum landlords going about their indifferent business. There's another BOOM, and Laura jumps a little. Her skittishness should make the sex more interesting. It would be more believable if she were eighteen, minus a little of the baby fat.

Regardless, Laura's forty-year-old self will have to do. Today, Laura is Peggy.

I feel invincible. My nineteen-year-old body is lithe. My face retains its boyishness. The sex, scheduled for after our first "Suspects Report," should be excellent. What does fear do to the body? A racing heart and what else?

She still seems troubled. I wonder if Jacob's leaving is the problem. I expect her to put the whole situation behind her. I admit I was surprised when she appeared at the Chicago penthouse. Incredible. She offered no explanation.

"I want to be with you, Gunter," she said. So humble that I almost sympathize with her sadness over Jacob's inevitable deletion.

Sirens are blaring several miles in the distance as our helo-glide rises. Thousands of "casualties" are strewn over several blocks. What a change. Yesterday, the parks and apartment stoops, the corner markets and the outdoor bins of produce were swarming with life. It's eerily quiet. Where was the location of the first "big" explosion? It's an important clue, something that might help us establish a motive. Was it political, religious or extortion?

"Let's keep going, Peggy," I tell her. "We have a job to do." There are more pops as the helo-glide drifts up and down the piles of steel and concrete. Sheets of jagged window glass separate parts of unfortunate citizens. Exciting! I want to win this game and so I order the sim pilot to fly lower over the park.

The dark green of a bench, where a sim couple in their cen-fifty-plus years sat

watching the children playing, now rests on the melted remnants of the white "sand" that held the monkey bars and swings. What's left of the monkey bars lies a hundred yards from the bench. A snarl of bicycle wheels and body parts teeter on the detached door of a red auto-glide.

The helo lands.

"It's time to role-play, Peggy." I remind her. Peggy seems transfixed, looking at the pile of twisted metal and severed limbs. "Peggy, remember, you're Peggy Ryan and I'm Seth Crandall. You're a detective and I'm a summer intern." She looks at me as if she doesn't see me.

I turn back to the scene. For the next level of this game, perhaps we should attempt a more authentic experience, not just the role-playing, but deeper into the drama. We'll come up with a new approach, something original. She won't be able to resist the idea. She's staring at a severed arm hanging on a stop sign. What's going on?

Yesterday, we spent several pleasant hours here, walking, holding hands as we sat on the grass. I felt closer to Laura than I had since months before our transitions.

***

Mom and I spent several hours in a park much like this one, walking and singing and Mom carrying our picnic basket while I searched for a spot near the ducks . . .

Byron—The following bio memory occurred during 414C and is included as part of that record.

Bio-Location: Seattle Park

It's our day to celebrate the end of school. Tomorrow, I will leave Mom for my ten weeks with Dad. I see Mr. Donald—he's sitting at a picnic table.

"Fancy meeting you here, Gunter," he says.

"Hello, Donald," Mom smiles, and she puts her hands on her hips. "What a surprise! Gunter, let's spread the blanket under the oak."

Mom climbed the oak tree with me once. I asked her if Dad knew she climbed trees. "No, Gunnie, your dad was very busy when we were married, and the subject never came up."

I pictured them together; Dad, with his arm around her as they traveled and then, while he negotiated prices and managed his properties. Maybe she didn't kiss back enough, and that's why he left her, or Mom missed her own mom and dad and was sad. I remember them a little. I was just a kid, only three when they drowned in the Puget Sound. I called it the Poogit Sow then. I remember Grandma Tomlin always said I was her best boy.

Mom opens the picnic keep-sack and offers Mr. Donald one of our extra sandwiches. "I made more just in case," she tells me, "I thought you might get extra hungry."

We sit on the blanket, and I tell Mr. Donald about Dad's Island, and about the aqua house and my sand cities. He listens while Mom sits across from him. And then, they sit on a bench and watch me as I climb and swing until the light changes and clouds started to collect.

END 414C bio-memory segment

Resume: The Hunt, Baltimore disaster

The scream of distant sirens

Mr. Donald's in the past; leave him there! Laura's mired in her own grievances. "Peggy" is ignoring my game cues. Maybe we should exit the game. She's clearly not ready to move on.

I hear the scream of distant sirens and the groans of the injured and the dying. How do I get through to her? Do I tell her to let Jacob go or she'll never be happy?

I never saw Mr. Donald again after our picnic lunch. I shook his hand goodbye and he hugged me. The next morning, I left my mother behind for what became forever. But that's all in the past.

Move forward. Laura and I are together. We'll erase the past together now that Jacob is gone.

"Detective Ryan," I say. "There's a possible blast site. See how the rubble is spread?"

SHE'S CRYING! Oh God, WHY?

"Rubble?" She sobs. "Gunter, don't you see them? All those people, the old couple we saw holding hands in the park and the three kids on their bikes—their legs are gone."

She's covering her face with her hands. Being more in the "game" is obviously not good for Laura.

"They're sims; they're just sims! What's wrong with you? Can't you see what's real and what's a fantasy?" Did she hear me? I'd better have Miranda do an evaluation. My wife's behavior is concerning me.

Ah yes, she's responding at last. Her hands and arms fold and rest under her breasts as she looks over my shoulder. "I know the difference. I always have, do you?" she asks.

We'll see. I'm tired of this. "Let's get back to the game, Peggy." But no, she just stands there. "Come on Peggy Ryan, if we want to win, we have to play."

Laura's tears

What's going on? Her eyes . . . They're changing; the dark brown is shifting to dots of gray, like smoke. An ash-white light surrounds us now. Her tears are collecting, covering her eyes with my image. I can see my reflection shimmering in her pool of tears. Beautiful. Her tears have captured a moment. I'm still nineteen in her tears.

This isn't real. Where were we? We were looking for clues.

"Detective, I see a crater near the park's edge where the clinic stood. Let's check it out . . . Peggy?"

"Where is my wife? Miranda, tell me her location."

I'm sorry, Gunter. By her request, Laura Holden's location is private.

COMMAND: END: Memory record 414.

414C ENDED.

Miranda, these memory records are done. I hope Tom can help me put them behind me. I can't seem to free myself.

Gunter, I can only give you a probability. With your extended interactions, compatibility factors and your personality traits as individuals, there is a sixty percent chance of at least a minor improvement in your anxiety level—minor is defined as ten to twenty-five percent.

God help me.

END RECORD

***

GUNTER HOLDEN MEMORY FILES
   FOLDER YEAR: 2194
   GUNTER HOLDEN DOCS. 265, 601A, 601B.

V-Loc: See 743.1, Chicago ELYSIUM Penthouse PERSONAL, updated 6.28.2122. 19 detailed interiors include entry lobby, elevators 2 and 8, rotating 4 of 10 resident interiors and concierge. © 8.18.2120 by VEI Personal Options, Non-event day.

Miranda, I can't seem to get comfortable.

I'm sorry, Gunter. Can I be of help?

Tom still hasn't contacted me. I know he's accessed all my memory records. I worry that I'll lose his friendship and I need . . . It's difficult to focus. Now, Diego wants an answer on Isobel Salan's location. I suspect Bardot plans to arrange for her to "transfer" to another platform. Then everyone can accept the sim Isobel as the real one and things will go back to "normal."

Diego wants an update. The Shemathra Group program prevents any unauthorized search. Your request for Isobel's location has been denied. Shall I prepare a status report?

Diego can wait. I have my Classics friends touring the Shemathra territories open to tourists. They're promoting a possible collaboration.

Shemathra, together with Classics, could perform *Animal Farm* and *Black Beauty* for bio and virtual audiences. I'm not sure if the idea will catch on with the Shemathra herds or if the bio-distribution idea is practical, but it will give the Classics team an excuse to look for Isobel in Shemathra territory. If they find her, you can give Diego the information and, perhaps, he'll stop calling.

END RECORD

***

GUNTER HOLDEN DOC. 266 A

V-Loc: See 743.1, Chicago ELYSIUM Penthouse PERSONAL, updated 6.28.2122. 19 detailed interiors include entry lobby, elevators 2 and 8, rotating 4 of 10 resident interiors and concierge. © 8.18.2120 by VEI Personal Options, Non-event day.

. . .

Tom, thanks for coming. I was afraid you wouldn't. Have you reviewed the memories that I gave you?

. . .

You're right. I am all those things, including a murderer.

. . .

I know I've been difficult, but I have responsibilities to the virtuals here.

. . .

Your advice has been a great help.

. . .

Don't leave, please!

. . .

Because this memory, the one I can't access, keeps pressing. I've decided to confront some of those messages I mentioned, the ones sent here shortly after my transition. Maybe clearing them will help me relieve the pressure.

. . .

I know that; you're not at my beck and call. More breaches might destabilize me, but that's not why I asked you here. There's danger coming.

. . .

I mean more mergers, new territories and another city that is no longer there. It overwhelms me. I'm not myself and I need to be.

. . .

To prevent the destruction of Bali Hai.

. . .

Thank you, Tom, for understanding and for your support. It means a great deal to me.

As soon as I see a path forward, I'll have Miranda contact you.

. . .

END RECORD

***

GUNTER HOLDEN DOC. 266 B

V-Loc: See 743.1, Chicago ELYSIUM Penthouse PERSONAL, updated 6.28.2122. 19 detailed interiors include entry lobby, elevators 2 and 8, rotating 4 of 10 resident interiors and concierge. © 8.18.2120 by VEI Personal Options, Non-event day.

Monty Delgado

I want to escape this situation as soon as I can. In the meantime, I'm ready to review and clear old messages.

COMMAND: Miranda, ACCESS Monty Delgado Files 601A, B.

Monty Delgado files Accessed.

Ah, my old friend, seeing your face, I realize how much I miss you!

Running Monty Delgado messages, Files 601 A, B

Audio message from Monty:

Hi, Miranda!

Please title this message and my files 601A, B, "Messages to Gunter Holden" and the following Dream record available according to and consistent with the designated conditions stipulated in my will—no sooner than thirty years after my self-deletion.

Label FILE 601A "To Gunter from Monty."

Thanks, Miranda!

COMMAND, Miranda, RUN: Holo-message-file 601A

601A RUNNING.

Monty sits on a stool. There's only one light. It settles on his face. He doesn't look well. The well-cropped fringe of white hair that formed a semi-circle is now an uneven mop, the jagged edges spilling over the collar of his frayed shirt, an ancient synthetic weave. There's enough light on the shirt to see where holes were mended. He's wearing old-fashioned San Francisco tight jeans. They emphasize his short legs, plus brown sandals and white socks, part of his uniform during the Stanford research days.

Monty taps his fingers on his chest. "The shirt," he says, his voice fading as he struggles not to cry.

"The shirt was a gift from my baby, my LeRoi, who just hung himself in his cell and now I'll never see . . ." Heaving a sob, Monty shakes himself and swallows. "Down to business, eh Gunter? You understand that business goes on even when people don't, like your old man. But I'm not the one to tell you about Eric. I'll leave that gem to someone else, though maybe I should cut you a little slack considering."

COMMAND, PAUSE: 601 A

PAUSED.

Do I really want to continue? Fuck him. I make no apologies. This holo must have been done shortly before his transition to Bali Hai. Ah, Monty, I miss you. After Marcia went into the Dreams, I had hoped that you and I could share the wonders of this place, so many experiences . . . but your stay was even shorter than Marcia's and now this.

COMMAND: RESUME 601A

601A RESUMED

The room lights up. I see concentric circles of desktops and dozens of holo- receivers and transmitters. It's a presentation room. Monty's face is twisted with rage as he delivers his message:

What people think of you

"Gunter, you're an asshole and a bastard. If you're viewing this, I've been gone for quite a while. Someone needs to tell you what people think of you, especially the people who work for you. Heartless comes to mind, soulless maybe, but none of those terms would insult you because you pride yourself on that 'cold' efficiency, doing what's necessary."

COMMAND, PAUSE: 601 A

PAUSED

You're wrong, Monty. I thought, I assumed we were friends and that you understood I did what I had to do to protect what we built.

COMMAND: RESUME 601A

601A RESUMED

"So let me offer up some new ones for you to chew on."

Oh Monty—please . . . no.

Monty is pacing. He's in the large presentation holo-communications room, that magical place where the holo-world rotated, the Eiffel Tower twinkled, and Rio danced.

He's talking to no one in particular, ranting as he gestures. It reminds me of my high school days when I sat outside on a wrought-iron bench and listened to his lectures. From a sagging shirt pocket, Monty produces a control. Holding the control close to his nose, he stares at it, nods, and his thumb finishes the search.

I see myself at age forty-five

The room is restless as investors wait to see the results of VEI's newest nanotechnology. Marcia is leaning forward, gripping the glossy rail. Her hands tremble and her smile is radiant. We have shared so much, she and I. I wonder how much longer it will last. Monty and Patel stay in the shadows. They will study the crowd's reactions to what comes next.

COMMAND, Miranda: PAUSE

PAUSED

I remember how wonderful I felt. My dream had come true.

COMMAND, Miranda: RESUME

RESUMED

As I activate the presentation, potential investors, those present and holo-attendees, gasp when we witness a traffic accident. This event, I tell them, took place in Des Moines several weeks ago. We watch an incident, captured by a traffic holo-recorder document-ing the last moment in the bio-life of a middle-aged man who walks absent-mindedly in front of a public transpo-glide and is crushed.

His brains burst out of his skull and onto the shoes of horrified bystanders. Several women scream and a little boy who points to his mother's bloody sneaker.

I'm smiling as I freeze the holo.

"The women in the holo, the witnesses, I say as I see the same hor-ror on the faces of many in the audience, express what we all feel when the unthinkable happens. Ronald David, the unfortunate victim, did have a post-biological plan, VEI's Great Cities USA package. A year before his death, Mr. David agreed to participate in testing a new product, VEI's patented nanotransbots."

Excitement races through the audience. Like a master teacher, I wait until the murmuring quiets.

"The standard practice," I say, "is to update your file on a regular basis. We all do it. We have our brains scanned and copied to update memories as often as we can, at least twice a year. Some people do it several times a year, and why? Because the sum of who we are, our experiences—good and bad, is right here."

I point to my head.

"How many of you are being scanned more than twice a year?"

As I look around the room, those present and those on holo-receivers, most hands go up.

"Ladies and gentlemen, meet Ronald David." There's a pause. A full sixty seconds go by as I stall, making jokes about "The late Mr. David."

COMMAND, Miranda: PAUSE

PAUSED

It's been ninety plus years or is it more than a hundred years ago? Holo-communications between virtual and bio environments were difficult. I had forgotten this part. How far science has come from those pioneer days!

COMMAND, Miranda: RESUME

RESUMED

"Finally, there he is! Oops, he's manifesting in his early twenties and sits, surrounded by beautiful women, sims of course, but not the appropriate scene to showcase the 'new life.' Ah good, there he is as we saw him at the point of death." Ronald David sits at a desk in an office environment copied from his memories.

"Mr. David, what do you remember about the accident that ended your bio-life?"

David grimaces. It's clear the accident is an uncomfortable topic. "I remember I was thinking about my wife's sixty-seventh birthday. It was a month and a half away and I was wondering whether to make a dinner reservation."

"Before the accident, when was the last time you updated your memories?"

He taps his temple and shrugs. "My wife was always getting on me to do that." He imitates a woman's voice. "Update your file; update your file. What if you forget something important, like where you put something? Uh, truthfully, Mr. Holden . . . uh, it was when I took the experimental nano a year ago."

The audience chuckles.

"Yet, you remember the accident."

David smiles sheepishly and nods.

"So, Ronald, did you talk to your wife recently?"

"Well, of course, it was on her birthday." This response results in an outburst of laughing and applause.

"Glad you didn't forget! Does your wife think you are missing any memories?"

"No more than usual," he says, "but Nadine will think of something."

I cut him off; he's served his purpose. "Thank you, Mr. David! Enjoy your VEI package."

"Will do," David says. We see him change back to his twenties self before the holo-connection ends.

"Ronald David remembers everything," I say, "including the accident and Nadine's birthday because of these." Reaching into a coat pocket, I point to a small vial and introduce the VEI nano-transbots. The vial is sealed in a pliable, clear case, protecting it from accidents and degradation.

COMMAND, Miranda: PAUSE

PAUSED

It was less than a year after our introduction that VEI's nano-transbots became the standard for the entire post-bio industry. Thieves, I never did discover who they were. If I had, I would have made them regret it.

COMMAND, Miranda: RESUME

RESUMED

The presentation fades as Monty's holo interrupts. "So, Gunter, memories. I'm sure you enjoyed reliving this one. We all had to listen to it enough. So, yes, now it's time for new information: First, guess who is responsible for VEI's success? Who oversaw nanobot tech development? Here's the answer:

NOT YOU

Monty's smile is vicious. Do I continue listening to this?

"I discovered the prototype," he says. His eyes glisten with hate. "I decided to review the mysterious Mr. Vanderbok's files, NOT YOU! You remember, don't you Gun? Vanderbok founded Encore, and people like YOU took it all away."

Oh please, Monty! This is beneath you. He's sitting on the stool again and he turns out all but that first light, and now he's wondering how long I'll listen. *I'll hear it all, dear friend. I wish you'd had the guts to say it to my face. Who's the coward, Monty; which one of us?*

Monty leans forward on the stool. The harsh light drains his face of all kindness. He purses his lips.

"Pea Cock, yeah, peacock, you were a dick after all. That's what they called you in the operations department. One of the guys would say, 'Here he comes boys and girls, make sure all those looks are admiring ones—we wouldn't want to ruin Mr. Holden's day.'"

Is that the best you can do?

The blond rooster. Monty nods emphatically. "That's what LeRoi called you."

What is your point? Monty points his finger like he was still teaching. I don't need a lecture from you.

"The thing is, Gunter . . . the thing is, everyone would have forgiven your fucking vanity, your insecurity, but besides not contributing a damn thing to VEI's success—other than your money, of course, which you didn't earn, let's face it, Daddy gave it to you—you damaged everyone who cared about you and never gave it a thought.

Poor Marcia might have been happy with someone else, rather than waiting around for the honor of your convenient access when you were in trouble. Together with yours truly and Patel, Marcia made VEI an industry phenomenon a thousand times more than you did, my friend. If there had been any justice, you would have been 'Mr. Evans' and not the other way around, and you would have hung on to her for dear life. Patel adored her, and he was several of you in terms of value."

A moot point now.

"As for that brother of yours, Jacob, do you have any idea how wrong you were about him? He worshipped you. More than once, people tried to use him to get to you, challenging your stock ownership. You did use some of the estate money that was rightfully his."

Monty says as shakes his head. "Let's talk about little Laura. She was way out of her league, cohabiting with a snake, but she never caught on until . . ."

Monty shakes his head again. "This isn't going to help. Gunter. People loved you and gave you so much. What did you give in return, but pain? I plan to transition to Bali Hai and check out the results of all that effort, and in your case, all that ego. While I'm there, I'll enjoy myself. I see no need to deal with you there. I already gave in that department. When is it your turn to give back? I'll let you discover this message when some time's gone by. Maybe by then, you'll get what I'm saying, and who knows, maybe you'll understand.

"Seriously dear friend, I don't know what will become of you when you're forced to face the truth. It will hurt like hell. For what it's worth, I'm tossing some of my hope to you. When it's time for the Dreams, I'll be with my LeRoi." Monty turns out the light.

END message

Ended

I'm done with Mr. Delgado and his opinions. Afterwards, don't bother to hide them. Make them available but reclassify and store in the "Failed Adjustment/Self-Delete Memory Records."

Shall I file it now?

Yes, Miranda, file it.

Filed

END RECORD

***

GUNTER HOLDEN Doc. 270

V-Loc: Truckee River (California) non-event day 28 of 47, early morning to late afternoon, breeze variant 2 to 5.2, Site 1.8 k by 2.3 k (river), See 194.

Truckee River fishing program, Sierra program, virtual and sim anglers, wildlife sims

Thanks for coming, Tom. I prefer quiet locations where I'm unlikely to run into people.

. . .

Why here? Because it's perfect in terms of being out-of-the way. Fly-fishing lacks glamour. Diego keeps calling me and I've been avoiding him. I wasn't avoiding you. I've needed some time. Lately, I have experienced disappointments involving people I thought I knew, and yes, I know you've reviewed my memory files.

Miranda gave me your messages. You want to go over some things but I— I've had to address several issues on behalf of the Board. The Isobel Salan problem is getting out of hand. Reverend Bardot has lodged a fraud complaint against her. We finally located Isobel. She's manifesting as a llama. We found her in one of the Shemathra grazing areas.

Recently, Tupac decided to manifest as a llama and join her.

. . .

I'm glad you think it's funny. I suppose it is. Some of my Classics friends discovered the pair during a "talent scout" foray, looking for Shemathra folk to play the sheep in the proposed joint production of Animal Farm.

. . .

Yes, you heard right. Isobel and Tupac are llamas acting as "protectors of the flock." Llamas are known to bond with sheep in this way and shortly after she disappeared, a llama was rumored to be part of

Tupac's group, a flock of Shemathra "sheep." Tupac became a llama to avail himself of Isobel's "charms." This meant giving up the ewes, much to the dismay of the ewes, but the delight of the rams. Now the llama pair guards the flock.

. . .

When one of the Classics scouts, the librarian I mentioned a while back—you know, the Jane Eyre to my Mr. Rochester—approached a ewe, she encountered the guardians, as the llamas refer to themselves. I'll share with you her report.

COMMAND, Miranda: Run Isobel Salan location report.

Running:

The new llama

Jane's report on finding Isobel Salan (confidential):

I was just introducing myself to one of the larger females when I heard what sounded like someone gargling like when, as a bio, you'd gargle after brushing your teeth. When I turned around, a wad of llama saliva hit me. The bio 'me' would have been nauseated, but I shook it off. Two large llamas were glaring at me. One of them, the one with the small mean eyes asked me just what did I think I was doing?

The other llama nudged the mean one and said, "Don't worry, honey, she's one of the Classics people. They're looking for actors.'

Then the mean one said, "Tupac, honey, you don't know these people! I do. She says she's looking for the actors, but that Reverend guy has spies." Then, she turned to me and said, "Look, if you know what's good for you, you never saw us." I don't doubt for a minute that it was a threat.

End report.

. . .

Tom, the pressure on me has been intense. I'm reluctant to share this information with Bardot. These two communities, the Everlasting Praise people and the Shemathra group are natural enemies. The Shemathra philosophy, officially, is to "live and let others live the way they like," but I'm wary of the power they wield through Donovan Hosseini, their bio-leader.

. . .

He made billions in the portable eco-systems market and before that, billions as the "Holo-Porn King." Hosseini essentially controls Infinite Bliss, having bought out most of the Everlasting Praise stockholders. If provoked, the peaceful herds might rampage.

Thanks for listening and for your support. I'll let you know if there's a way you can help.

. . .

Okay, I know that we should continue working on my timeline, however, I'm puzzled. I'm perfectly willing to consider your point of view when it comes to my brother, but why do you want to change locations?

. . .

I'm not sure that I'll be comfortable . . . Fine, we'll jump to the Connecticut estate.

COMMAND, TRANSFER:

V-Loc: Veranda Connecticut estate, Gunter Holden, Thomas Bucklin

TRANSFER COMPLETE

V-Loc: Bali Hai loc: Holden Estate (Connecticut) (Day) See Doc. 735

Connecticut, the Holden Estate, the veranda, day

Now what, Tom? By the way, this morning in August was recorded soon after the day my father died.

. . .

Sorry, right now, I'm not comfortable including a sim of my father. Tom, I value your insight and advice, but you're not a psychologist. I know I asked you, but still . . . I can't . . . no sim, please.

. . .

All right, I'll sit where my brother sat. His chair was turned, like this, so that the river was to Jacob's right . . . and mine?

. . .

I always faced the river. Are you going to sit facing the river? Take my chair. And what now?

. . .

What do you mean what do I see? I see you sitting in my seat and . . . what? You're looking at the river and . . . not . . . looking at me.

. . .

Yes, I avoided looking at Jacob. I am aware that he said that I didn't know him, but he also said I didn't know Dad.

. . .

I KNEW MY FATHER!

BETTER than—okay, okay, OKAY, I'll calm down. What's your point? My father and I rarely had lengthy discussions. We didn't need them. It went without saying that we loved each other. Saying, "I love you" just wasn't Dad's style, but I knew he loved me. I knew because of those summers and the trips. They ended, but just take my word for it, HE LOVED ME until Jacob was born.

. . .

You're quite the therapist, getting to the bottom of my problems. "Daddy didn't love me." I'm all better now. My mother loved me, and I loved her, but she died.

. . .

Can we talk about something else? I understand what you're saying. I made judgments about people and things that happened based on a limited amount of information. It might have helped if I had been more open to other points of view. Recently, I became aware of this very thing. Someone who misjudged me and belittled my contributions and—it doesn't matter. I'm not comfortable discussing it now.

. . .

The thing is, lately I've been plagued with images, bits, and pieces of something that may have happened, but they could be pieces of a dream. I'm so young in them that I don't know the words to process. Perhaps it's pieces of a corrupted memory file, but more likely, they're parts of an old dream, a nightmare. I can't make sense of it.

. . .

Thank you for your friendship. Miranda tells me you rarely participate in any social events, other than on the occasions when we're together. I hope you've found some enjoyment. I'd hate to think that you might . . . Then I won't worry about it. Shall we have our coffee now? You remembered. It always tastes best in a white cup.

END RECORD

***

GUNTER HOLDEN DOC. 415

V-Loc: See 743.1, Chicago ELYSIUM Penthouse PERSONAL, updated 6.28.2122. 19 detailed interiors include entry lobby, elevators

2 and 8, rotating 4 of 10 resident interiors and concierge. © 8.18.2120 by VEI Personal Options, Non-event day.

This truly frightens me. I don't know why. You'd think with all these skeletons popping out lately, I'd be immune. So . . . the scan, Miranda . . . what did you discover?

They're from a very early memory. I recovered enough for you to review. How shall I classify it?

It is private, by my approval only, and as Gunter Holden Memory Record 415.

Record 415 is by approval only.
COMMAND: Miranda, RUN 415
415 RUNNING: Infant Dream

Mama

I'm sitting on the floor sucking my thumb and watching a bored teenager. "Mama? I want my mama!" I'm crying and beginning to hiccup.

"Shut up ya little brat, or I'll give you mama." Someone (who?) looks up from . . . the . . . an old-fashioned portable holo-device, a game of some kind. The door opens and the face, where do I know it? The beard . . . it's Ron Martino, Dad's Martino. The kid playing the game has a long face and a mop of black hair with widow's peak. Who do I remember? He's Fred, Martino's son, the rat Abe Lincoln! Oh my God, HE was babysitting me? Asshole!

I see Mama! I put up my arms. How old am I? She picks me up and holds me close. Mama's crying, shaking . . . why? THEY TOOK ME! Oh my God, they TOOK ME when I was playing in the sand. They hit Grandpa and Grandma screamed and . . . Oh Mama! I bury my head in her shoulder and she's singing softly, "I'll see you soon . . ."

Someone else is in the room now . . . It's a man with a mean face.

"Okay Nancy, you've seen him. It's time for your end of things."

I scream and struggle and kick at Martino when he tries to take me from Mom.

My mother yells, "Eric, don't be a jerk! Let me settle him down!"

Oh my God! He slaps her, and she falls to the floor!

I produce broken sobs. Mom is doing her best to not react. I know she's trying to reassure me that she's alright. She stands up and says, "Eric, please! I'm sorry. I thought you were done with me. You were gone over two years. We had harsh words. You don't love me . . . why are you doing this?"

"Mean man," I yell in my toddler voice, "you made Mama cry!"

The man is smiling, but it's a mean smile. "Fred, take him out. Nancy and I have some business. Remember this, Nancy; he's mine now as well as yours and no one else's, if you know what I mean. In the eyes of the law, I'm his father. If your boyfriend knows what's good for him and you, he'll go back to Canada. Tell him I'll make you a deal. He stays out of our business, and he continues to breathe. "

The man squeezes my mother's face, his broad thumb pushing into her cheek. I whimper, "Momma?"

"You be a good girl and do as I say." The man tells my mother, "Now, what was that song you sang to the boyfriend, *I'll see you soon by the willow*? I want you to sing it to me, because Nancy, I have ways of being around and sometimes you'll see me and sometimes you won't. Fred, take Gunter out. Buy him some ice cream."

Fred tries to take me, and I start screaming as I reach for . . . NO—MAMA! She's crying and now the man's got her arm. He starts hugging her and trying to kiss her, but Mama turns her face away; she thinks he's yucky. He's talking to her like she's a little kid. "If you want to see him again, dear, start singing."

Mama's trying not to cry, and she starts singing the *I'll see you* song. I reach out for her, "Mamamama!" I'm crying.

Martino slams the door and tells Fred to get going. Fred is laughing and making a circle with one hand, and he pokes a finger through the circle. Then, he grabs me and swings me up as I kick and try to get free. Fred pinches my leg.

Martino yells at Fred, "Get the kid ice cream." I'm still kicking, and Fred decides to carry me under one arm. I hear Mama crying. Fred's father goes and sits down. He grabs Fred's holo-game, and points at Fred. "Don't be too long. Get the ice cream and get your ass back." Then he says, "That son-of-a bitch better pay up this time."

MIRANDA—END: 415!

415 ENDED.

The mean man was Eric Holden . . . who is, was . . . not my father. I don't understand. Oh, God, my whole life was a lie—what he did to my mother and I never—I can't . . . What other lies? Jacob wasn't my brother and what else? What else did Eric hide from me? Were our island vacations only to punish my mother?

I'm sorry, Gunter, I have no answers for you.

I wish not to be disturbed. Make it rain.

RAIN

END RECORD

SERENE VISTAS

GUNTER HOLDEN DOC. 280
V-Loc: See 743.1, Chicago ELYSIUM Penthouse PERSONAL, updated 6.28.2122. 19 detailed interiors include entry lobby, elevators 2 and 8, rotating 4 of 10 resident interiors and concierge. © 8.18.2120 by VEI Personal Options, Non-event day.

Gunter, are you available? It's Diego.

Yes. COMMAND, Miranda, TRANFER me, SET: Chicago office, mahogany desk

TRANSFER to Chicago VEI office, mahogany desk.

INTERFACE

Oh God

Diego! Sorry I haven't been available of late. I know you kept saying it was urgent, but—I . . .

Diego: *"Uncle, there's no excuse for your negligence. When I say something's urgent, I mean it!"*

You'll just have to accept my apology. I was preoccupied with an internal matter that impacted my ability to be effective.

Diego: *"I'm sorry, but at present, your excuses are irrelevant."*

Fine. I'll do my best; so, what is the disaster?

Diego: *"Do you recall a man named Fred Martino? He was in your employ when you were a bio."*

Martino . . . yes, the name is familiar. There was a Martino who worked for my father. I don't recall his first name. What about this person concerns you?

Diego: *"Mr. Martino's bio-life was recently terminated when he was caught assaulting one of his ex-wives. An off-duty police officer heard the screams and shot Mr. Martino who was repeatedly stabbing the victim. Apparently, Martino had nanobots in place and would have been uploaded to Fantasy Valley. Instead, his file was transferred to The Vistas. Uncle, Martino wants to go back to Fantasy Valley. He says he has a story to tell, one about you."*

I . . . I . . . yes, The Vistas, his rehabilitation, this Martino's . . . oh God.

Diego: *"Fortunately, Mr. Hosseini has friends in law enforcement. The story will go no further."*

What will happen now? Yes, I—I guess it could appear that. . . I might be transferred to the Vistas program.

Diego: *"We need a guarantee. Changes are coming; we require your cooperation."*

What deal? I'll try, but if I fail, the Everlasting Praise community will have to . . .

Diego: *"There will be some transfers soon."*

Transfers to where? All right. I'll try again to reason with Bardot. I'll tell him he must cooperate with the Shemathras and withdraw the fraud suit against Isobel, uh . . . Isobel Salan-Llama-Dean.

Diego: *"Or his entire community will be transferred to a more basic program."*

How will the discovery of my past . . . bio-indiscretion impact you? I know you must tread lightly, and so will I. Diego, I want you to know that what I did, I've come to deeply regret.

Diego: *"We all make mistakes, but now, Uncle, you and I must be very careful. There have been riots. The anti-virtual mob is demanding low cost after-death plans. Several hundred of them have been picketing SEINI Corporate offices in downtown Milwaukee. Our security team was forced to act. Some rioters were injured. A few died. SEINI denies all responsibility, claiming it has no idea what happened."*

Thank you, I can understand your concern, and I appreciate your confidence. I'll try not to let you down.

END holo-communication.

Communication ENDED.

God help me.

END RECORD

MAMA, I CAN'T BELIEVE THE PAIN

G UNTER HOLDEN MEMORY FILES
FOLDER YEAR: 2195
GUNTER HOLDEN DOC. 516
V-Loc: Holden Estate (Connecticut) Day 21 of 46 days, selected from recorded days 2103-2112 CUSTOM See 735 PERSONAL ENVIRONMENT Veranda.

V-Loc: Connecticut, Holden Estate, veranda

. . .

I created Bali Hai to . . . There should be no pain here and now pain is everywhere I am.

. . .

Thank you for meeting me. I need and greatly appreciate your support.

. . .

When I reviewed a memory from Marcia's file, one of three she left me, I learned something, a devastating truth. The memory wasn't Marcia's. It was Celeste's.

. . .

Tom, you were right about everything, about Jacob. God, what did I do?

. . .

The idea was to clear everything. Let's sit on the edge of the veranda. We can watch the river as we talk.

This day was recorded in early May, ten years after Dad had died and Celeste was gone. As a gift, Monty arranged to record dozens of "veranda" days. He didn't know that, for me, there are too many painful memories here. Or maybe he did.

. . .

The memory that I'm asking you to review with me is shattering. It shows how wrong I was about Jacob. It's too late now. I wish I could tell him, ask Jacob and his mother to forgive me.

. . .

Yes, the memory file, it's one of the files Marcia left. When I began to clear everything in my past, I became aware of these files. I decided to start with what I thought would be the easiest to . . .

Celeste Holden

Miranda told me that Celeste recorded it the day after Jacob's murder. When Celeste heard I had shot myself, she sent it to Marcia as well as a copy to Bali Hai for Jacob to keep. I suspect my brother already knew most of what it reveals. Before Marcia self-deleted, she left it for me. I knew there were several messages—memories waiting for me to review. I had just murdered two people and followed them here. I wasn't ready to face them.

. . .

I wish Marcia was here now. Oh, God! I miss her! I thought that I could handle whatever truth Celeste's memory might tell me. I was wrong.

. . .

My life, everything I thought I was, what I believed in, has been a lie. I don't know what to feel, other than pain.

. . .

Thank you! You'll never know how much . . . I asked Miranda to locate Celeste, to see where she transitioned. I didn't know that like Jacob, Celeste rejected virtual existence. She died in Italy twenty years ago. Other than natural causes, I don't know the circumstances. I had hoped to tell her how sorry I—

. . .

We'll talk about regrets later. I must accept that Celeste is gone. I've arranged for us to review her memory together. Although it's not common, now and then people do want to experience a particular memory record together. Do you mind?

. . .

Perhaps you could help me. I must find a way to make sense of this. The memory that Celeste left for me occurred after Jacob's rescue from his kidnappers. He was in the hospital and under sedation.

. . .

Yes, I know I belittled Jacob's pain. I deeply regret that. I have discovered that Eric controlled women by kidnapping their children. He kidnapped me to punish my mother. You look shaken.

. . .

Fine. Let's go forward! Celeste came home to change and found Dad, I mean Eric, who ordered her not to leave. She sat where I'm sitting, and Eric faced her with his chair near the door, so let's sit with our chairs, facing the door.

Miranda, COMMAND, RUN: Celeste Holden Memory Record 825.

pause

Byron–This memory is of particular importance to these records. Reviewed by both Gunter Holden and Thomas Bucklin as a shared experience, this (bio) memory documents what took place at the Holden estate after the kidnapping and rescue of ten-year-old Jacob Holden. The information it revealed was unknown to Holden before he accessed it. It details his subsequent re-experiencing of Celeste's memory while in the process of allowing Thomas Bucklin to experience it.

resume

Celeste Holden 825 RUNNING

Celeste's Memory

Do what he says. Just do it. There's nothing else. Oh God, they almost killed him—killed my baby—his poor legs . . . oh . . . keep control. Let him calm down. Stay still . . . don't draw attention!

Eric's hand is trembling and the ice clinks as he finishes his bourbon. His face is even redder now and swollen with too much sun. It's his fourth bourbon in an hour. Should I get him another? Maybe he'll pass out.

"It's your fault, you know." His voice is flat, dangerous.

Don't react; he's waiting to see, even if he's not looking at me.

He's rubbing his forehead with the glass as he slumps in the rattan chair. His boots are caked with so much mud, you can't tell that they're boots, and the khakis have blood spatters on the thighs and blood dripping down to the cuffs. *The blood of Jacob's kidnappers, I hope.* The older Martino, not his delinquent son, the sheriff said. Fred, the son, is in prison now. A nephew was part of it. Both are dead. Eric says he's the one who killed them. Who knows for sure; Eric is a liar!

"Things got out of hand, Celessh ..." My drunkard husband is shaking his head as if he's sadly disappointed. "Things got way out of hand and because I had to act fast and trust some people, who had a grudge I hadn't counted on, Jacob was almost killed. I have to say, YOU are sneakier than the other one, Nyancy."

He slurs her name. Poor Nancy. "She decided not to honor her obligations, had a kid by another man, and she didn't even TRY to hide it. She got pregnant and had the little bastard while I was gone. Still, I wanted her back."

Eric's eyes are dead as nods his head and rants, "I was patient. I said the blame was mine. I was gone too long and even though we were having differences of opinion on a wife's role, I should have taken her with me. It was a misunderstanding, a mistake. The other woman was nothing. I regretted the time we weren't together."

He smiles sadly. His self-pity is nauseating. He curls his lip and stares at me. *Is he going to hit me? Can I reach the door before he ...*

"HOWEVER, ..." Eric chuckles through his clenched smile. *I hate this man.*

"Nancy," he spits her name, "decided to betray me, her husband." He sighs and shakes his head. "I wasted two years on gifts and patient humility. You see Nancy was an exceptional woman, a journalist when I met her, the daughter of a biologist. She was smart, educated, witty, not a social-climbing parasite like you. And the other man?" He stares at me. His glass tilts and threatens to spill. If it does, will he kill me?

"Be thankful that I didn't find one in your case. Nancy knew enough to tell him to keep away. I saw she wasn't going to listen to reason despite my patience, so I decided we had to play by my rules. It was the only solution, don't you agree, dear?"

I nod humbly. *Poor Nancy, poor Gunter. Eric could kill me like he killed Nancy.*

Eric shrugs, continuing his singsong litany of grievances. "What's mine is mine, and you're MY wife as long as I want you to be. I DECIDE, NOT YOU." He leans towards me; the faded blue in his eyes overwhelmed by bleary red. "Now, are we clear?" he whispers. I nod again. There's no hope, now . . . "Excellent. See what happens when you don't play it straight with me?" Why is he pointing at me?

Oh God, I think he's going to hit me! Instead, he smiles and hisses, "Jacob's MY boy, MY BOY, and YOU almost got him killed!"

You hired them but you didn't count on how much they HATED YOU, enough to hurt your son. It's easier to blame me. Our son is suffering now. He's a little boy all alone. Eric, for God's sake, let me go to him!

COMMAND: PAUSE: Celeste Holden 825

825 PAUSED

Now, do you understand, Tom, why it's so difficult? The man I thought— my father—the man I loved, idolized my whole life, everything I ever . . . oh God . . . he . . . he . . . killed my . . . This is almost more than I can . . .

. . .

There's more.

. . .

Yes, I'm sure. I want to see things . . . people as they are, were . . . Let's finish it.

COMMAND: RUN Celeste Holden 825B

825B RUNNING.

Stay still and listen . . . *He's drunk.* You can't let Jacob down by staying home, waiting for bruises to heal. Be very still.

My husband's hands shake as he lights his cigar. He waves it at me, using it to emphasize his point. "You know Gunter might not be mine," he pauses, as if to stress his insight. "But I see a lot of myself in the lad. He's focused."

Eric blows the smoke in my face.

"He's ambitious and look what he's doing! Building his own company. He's charming the right people and making all the right connections. People are talking about Gunter Holden, the son of Eric Holden. It's too bad he's not a real Holden like my boy Jacob." He shakes his head and laughs to himself.

I can see he's tiring as he staggers to the chair. Maybe I can . . . there's the holo-signal. *It's the hospital!* I put it on audio.

As Eric collapses in the chair, I answer the call.

"This is Hallenoak Hospital calling. It's about Jacob Holden. Is this Celeste Holden?"

"Yes, this is Celeste Holden—how's my son?

The medic's holo appears as she answers, "Jacob's awake and asking for his brother."

What do I tell them? "I'm sure his brother will want to be here." *Oh God, but Gunter's in South Africa.* "Of course, I'll notify Gunter;

and I'm positive he'll come as soon as he can. Tell Jacob his mom is getting in touch with Gunter. I'm leaving and I'll see my baby right away. Tell him his mom loves him and I'll be there."

"I will let him know."

"Thank you, goodbye."

"Sit down ... SIT DOWN!" Eric growls. He knows what scares me.

I thought he passed out. Shit!

"But Eric, Jacob's in pain and— "

"And whose fault might that be?"

Oh, God! Please let him pass out!

He points a shaking finger at me. "You decided that you were tired of being my wife. I didn't pay enough attention. I had the audacity to do what men do and look at attractive women." He's trying to rise from the chair, but I can see it won't be long before he collapses.

He begins to shriek, "You . . . dee-cided that YOU were going to take MY SON out of school and disappear until I 'cooled down,' (is he drooling?) AND THEN, there would be a divorce. Little Celeste," he sneers in a little girl voice, "the trailer trash from New London, would have a townhouse in Old London. How sweet a dream . . ."

I move away from him. I can't do this anymore. Shit he's getting up again. Should I run? I . . . Oh God, I forgot how fast he can move when he's angry!

"Eric—please don't—my arm...don't break it. Jacob has suffered enough."

"So, sit down, Celeste." He forces me into the chair next to his. Then he takes his seat like a presiding judge. "Thank you. Let me tell you a story" (he's a liar) "about what happens when people don't learn. I decided to keep Gunter, but I let Nancy go. That would have been the end of it except Nancy decides to have another baby with the same boyfriend and dear Nancy thinks it's vital that Gunter meets his 'real' brother. She was determined."

Raising his eyes to remember, my husband points his index finger at me. "Her exact words were," he tells me, "Nancy says, 'I won't let this go on. Gunter's my son, he deserves to meet his brother and yes, his father.' I already had someone fix this."

This brutish man, this thug, giggles as he tells me how he stole Nancy's child.

"A government friend made a little change in Gunter's records. I believe in being careful. The birth certificate says Gunter's mine. Then, Nancy has an unfortunate accident and," he sighs, "no more Nancy. Her folks are already gone, not my doing but convenient."

Eric waits to see how this information affects me. I return his stare. "Now the sad thing is the boyfriend. Years later, there was a chance that he might cross paths with Gunter and so the boyfriend is . . . no longer with us. Don't look at me that way."

Ha—even Eric knows how despicable he is as he struggles to justify what he's done to Gunter.

"I've given Gunter a good life, a better deal than I got as a kid. There was no pharmacist, no Midwest house with a fence. My world was two drunks sleeping in the back seat of a sedan. I woke up alone one bright morning to find my dear mother dead, her head bashed in and my father gone. I was eight when Social Services placed me in a group home, the first of many.

I thought it would be different there, I could live in a place where no one would beat me. I was wrong. Even worse, some of the older ones . . . never mind. You make your own rules if you want to survive. Yes, I'd say Gunter had it easy and now look at him."

As he sits and studies my face, waiting for an excuse to hit me. Eric nods. Poor Gunter, I wish I could tell you the truth, but Eric would kill me. He would call me a liar. I doubt you would believe me. I wish . . . He's letting go . . . thank God! He's passing out. Jacob, hold on, Mama's coming!

COMMAND: END: Celeste Holden 825B.

END 825B.

I can see how upset you are by this sorry revelation, but I would appre—

What's that? What just happened? It felt like we jumped and yet . . .

Gunter?

Miranda, what happened?

The system rebooted. Gunter.

The Everlasting Praise Territories have been lost.

Savior City is deleted

. . .

We'll talk later . . . I—

. . .

Yes, we will.

END RECORD

HOSSEINI WILL BE COMING HERE AS A GOD.

G UNTER HOLDEN DOCS. 290, 291
V-Loc: See 743.1, Chicago ELYSIUM Penthouse PER-SONAL, updated 6.28.2122. 19 detailed interiors include entry lobby, elevators 2 and 8, rotating 4 of 10 resident interiors and concierge. © 8.18.2120 by VEI Personal Options, Non-event day.

Gunter, are you available? It's Diego.

Yes. Miranda, SET Chicago office, mahogany desk

TRANSFER Chicago VEI office, mahogany desk. END TRANSFER

COMMAND: SET: Chicago VEI, mahogany desk.

Chicago office SET.

Hello, Diego.

Diego: *"There's been a terrible accident. Tragically, we have lost Savior City as well as many members of our Everlasting Praise community.*

I understand. It must have been an accident.

Diego: *"There's to be a press conference—both bio and virtual report-ers. Mr. Hosseini wants you to talk to them. There may be questions about Isobel Salan-llama. She and Mr. Hosseini knew each other years ago. He has plans for her to help him lead the Shemathra herds. Of course, none of this sad event is related to Isobel and her dispute with Reverend Bardot."*

I am to stress that this "unfortunate mass erasure incident" was a terrible accident, totally unrelated to Reverend Bardot's disagree-ment with Isobel Salan, sorry, Isobel Salan-llama.

Diego: *"I'm relying on you to protect my—our interests, Uncle."*

You can count on me to represent Holden . . . interests . . . but how do you . . .?

Diego: *"You will represent Mr. Hosseini for the upcoming press conference."*

I see . . . And when will this occur?

Diego: *"You'll be notified. In the meantime, this tragedy must never happen again. Mr. Hosseini has hired world class programmers to install safeguards. Plus, he is demanding that Congress revise the tax laws revisions that make virtual file backups difficult."*

I see . . . I'll wait for your alert. I'm glad to hear that your teams are working on a solution. Backups would certainly help. Hosseini's right. I . . . I'm not sure. It's been so long since I have had a press conference.

Diego: *"I've just been informed that the press conference is to take place immediately. Please, Uncle. You know what to say. Another thing, don't mention Jeremy Salan."*

Now? Diego . . . I . . . couldn't . . .

Diego: *"Uncle, please don't mention Jeremy! I wish it hadn't hap-pened, but there's nothing I can do."*

Yes, I know Jeremy Salan's deletion puts you in an awkward . . . All right. Give me a moment, please.

Miranda, Diego asks that I talk to the reporters of Associated Worlds about the Everlasting Praise accident. Hosseini wants damage control because the Shemathra Community is expanding its properties. Has anyone notified you of the new configuration?

I have been alerted, Gunter, I'll summarize it briefly but Gunter, it's not official:

The Everlasting Praise Community and the New Savior City will occupy approximately seven percent of the space they formerly controlled. The Classics community will recover thirty percent of what they lost, which was fifteen percent of deleted Everlasting Praise territories. The Shemathra Community will use the remaining space to expand and most of this will be varied grazing areas, tundra, prairies, meadows, et cetera. That's all I know for now, except—

Yes?

Donovan Hosseini, noted entrepreneur, philanthropist and spiritual leader of the Shemathra Community is planning to transition to Bali Hai within the next few weeks, depending on how much time it will take him to set up a structure for retaining control of his assets in the bio-world, namely his wealth, influence, et cetera.

I understand.

And one more thing: Hosseini will be coming here as a god.

Oh, my God

COMMAND, SET: New York VEI Office—no—CANCEL. Miranda MODIFY: The New York office setting by removing any visible VEI reference or logo/image.

New York Office SET

SET MODIFIED

TRANSFER: New York VEI office

TRANSFERRED to MODIFIED New York office

SET: Holo-Link for Press Communications

Holo-Link for Press Communications SET

Good afternoon, members of the news media. Welcome to the Bali Hai Bio Hospitality Center. My name is Gunter Holden. I represent the Virtual Communities of Sacred Ecstasy Infinite Nirvana, Inc. We, in the virtual community, grieve the loss of our Everlasting Praise family.

I have been informed that due to this sad experience, new procedures will soon be in place. Donovan Hosseini, Esteemed Leader of those who follow the goddess Shemathra, has appealed to Congress to amend the tax law preventing post-bio companies from retaining copies of their virtual citizens. In the future, should unplanned erasures occur, such copies would prevent the tragic, irreversible loss of our virtual loved ones. Mr. Hosseini urges Congress to act quickly to allow these copies to be available for upload without the burden of a significant tax increase.

This tax, which was created in response to lawsuits dealing with inheritance and identity, all but prevented backup files as insurance against unintentional deletions. But times change and so should laws. Mr. Hosseini asks that the Virtual Bill of Rights be amended to protect the virtual community and the right to protected existence. In the interim, SEINI will create a backup file of any SEINI resident virtual who requests it. I am confident that my community and those in the bio-world with virtual loved ones here need never again fear accidental deletion.

Questions?

"Helga Udall, Universe News:

Mr. Holden, a mass deletion occurred shortly after Infinite Bliss merged with VEI. At the time, Everlasting Praise members held the majority on seats on the Infinite Bliss Board. Can you comment on any problems that may have led to the deletion?"

I can't speak for Everlasting Praise. Yes, sadly, VEI's Paris was deleted on their watch. I lost many good friends. It is my understanding that the same rebooting problem was the cause.

Next question.

"Evan Chang, I'm with Bio-Virtual Reports:

How will this erasure affect bio-Everlasting Praise members who have purchased after-death plans in Bali Hai? Can they expect their contracts to be honored?"

Reverend Bardot's bio-followers who have purchased transitions will find their contractual rights protected. Savior City and Everlasting Praise territory will be reinstalled. This is a sad event for all of us here. I wish to express personal condolences to the bio-loved ones of those deleted. After spending time with Reverend Bardot, I know the importance of prayer in their lives. I'm sure their faith must be a comfort.

At this time, I have no further information.

"Mr. Holden, Sadie Love, Virtual Post Network:

You spoke of a plan to make backup copies of virtual residents. How soon will these backups take place?"

I'm sorry. I don't know the schedule in terms of the backups.

"Mr. Holden, Evan Chang here: Do you have a backup?"

My own backup? That decision is private. Thank you, I have nothing further.

"Mr. Holden, Clarissa Hayes, Singularity Express:

Sir, aren't you THE Gunter Holden, former CEO of VEI and creator of Bali Hai? And second, wasn't it you who oversaw the introduction of nano-transbots, enabling instant uploads?"

I am Gunter Holden, CEO of VEI. I was the person who was responsible for what you call "instant transitions" by using nanobots. But I was only part of it. It was my team, Marcia Evans and—uh—Monty Delgado . . . and . . . Olaf Vanderbok.

"Clarissa Hayes again:

Was Olaf Vanderbok part of VEI? If so, what role did he play? Also, was the bio- murder of your wife and brother ever solved? Is the case closed?"

Vanderbok, yes. He wasn't a part of my company, VEI, but there wouldn't have been a VEI if it hadn't been for Vanderbok. He was a pioneer and a brilliant inventor. The murders were never—all I can say is that I miss my wife and brother and would give anything to tell them how much I—no more questions for now. I'm sure a SEINI representative will be available when the backup copy program is operational.

COMMAND: END holo-communication.

Holo-communication ENDED.

END RECORD

SHEMATHRA'S REALM

Via message (confidential)

May 5, 2288,

Desmond Webb

Archivist

Library of Congress, VR Division

Desmond—

Another mass erasure! This time, members of Everlasting Praise were deleted, allowing SEINI full control of the platform and memory allotment. I suspect that Hosseini's association with Isobel was incidental. The real motive was more memory for the herds and their pastures, paid for by Everlasting Praise.

I have added this event and probable crime to my account.

Most likely, Mr. Hosseini, virtual though he may be, will be called before Congress to explain his actions.

I see at last Mr. Holden was confronted with evidence of one of his crimes—the bio-murders of his brother and wife. As a result, he was forced to aid in covering up another crime of mass erasure. It seems that rather than protecting himself, he focused on protecting Bali Hai and its residents.

If possible, would you send the files of Gunter Holden that followed this confrontation? I am interested in whatever you have, including the beginning of Shemathra's Realm and Holden's self-deletion, along with my great-grandfather, Thomas Bucklin's.

Thank you, Desmond.

Byron

You are entering Shemathra's Realm

The Herds

GUNTER HOLDEN DOCS. 290A, 290B

V-Loc: Thomas Bucklin personal environment Vandalia, Michigan Cottage, CUSTOM STRUCTURE, 1.5 k by 1.3k rural, pond, foliage level 5, TACTILE/AUDITORY/VISUAL by VEI Personal Environments includes seven weather variants (mild to extreme) Sims: ecosystem level 6 interactive includes 356 insects, 26 raccoons. 40 squirrels, 52 geese, plus brown bear cub level 4.

They're asking that I "welcome" the new god.

. . .

I know it's ridiculous, but be careful who you talk to. Donovan Hosseini plans to transition within the week to rule the Shemathra Group. He's been a member for years. I asked Miranda about his history with Shemathra or "The Herd People," the name the press has given them. Hosseini helped found the group about fifty years ago.

. . .

He described it as a conversion. "The Goddess Shemathra, a dazzling creature with the head of a beautiful woman and the body of a magnificent white wolf, came to me in a dream. Reaching out her left forepaw, the goddess said: 'You must bring my people home. Let them come as one.'"

. . .

Let's take a drive. Miranda has a vintage car waiting. We can drive along the California Coast, and I'll tell you the rest.

The California Coast

DOC 290B

JUMP (Gunter Holden Thomas Bucklin): V- Loc: "California Coast Drive" by PACIFIC DREAMS © 2132

I must thank Miranda. I asked for something special, and a 1966 GTO is a special driving experience. When I drive the Pacific Coast, nothing but a muscle car will do. Beautiful, isn't it?

. . .

Back to Shemathra. Hosseini was so "shaken" by his "dream" that he assigned his second assistant the task of researching the name Shemathra and interpreting the dream's meaning. Information pointed to the Goddess "Shimatre," a deity whose image was a woman's head on the body of sled dog.

. . .

The Sacred Narrative

The dogma came from the dreams of several people reported and cross-referenced via an old, internet-style website devoted to dreams. The result was a "Sacred Narrative." These dreams all contained some version of a story where a goddess who refers to herself as "Shimatre" hears the cries of Earth's children.

She enters our universe from another dimension. In her parallel universe, she and other gods and goddesses reign benevolently over "creatures of many worlds." Touched by our misery, she decides to investigate and manifests as a sled dog, a servant of "Man." She urges her worshipers to roam and share the bounty of "Mother Earth" until "The Call" when "Mother Earth" releases them to the care of Shimatre. The goddess will take them to another galaxy where the "Chosen" will become deities and rule our universe.

. . .

The idea is to live virtually as herd animals until Shemathra transports the faithful to their new home on another world, where they will become corporeal beings possessing godlike powers.

. . .

No one can tell who the chosen. Hosseini claims to have "influence" with Shemathra. In Shemathra, he will be "second in command," deity-wise.

. . .

You'd be amazed at the number of people who believe these lies. Lies have more power than the truth because lies need no boundaries. All this was started with private funds donated by Hosseini.

Do you mind if we stop for a while?

. . .

I'd like to think about something else. It's peaceful here. I asked Miranda for a specific Tuesday when there were no passing cars. On the other side of that patch of wildflowers—see them? There're near that large flat rock. Let's take a break. I... I have a favor . . .

. . .

Oh, don't give me that look. Here it is Diego insists I welcome the new god. It's crucial to him keeping his job.

. . .

I agreed to it, but . . . Do you see how calm the Pacific appears on the horizon?

. . .

In the bio-world, as the water nears the shore, it slams the rocks and then retreats. The rocks do nothing, yet we know that in the bio-world, the ocean is wearing them away. My nature has always been to avoid the rocks by sailing a safe distance between the horizon and the shore. Don't roll your eyes.

. . .

The ceremony is bound to be stressful, and I could use the company of a friend.

Grieving Betsy

There's something else, insignificant maybe, but I hope you can help me make sense of it. Do you remember Betsy Salan, Jeremy's mother?

. . .

Betsy refused to share her memories of her son Jeremy, to placate the Isobel-sim.

. . .

They just delete the sim because Jeremy made the sim's happiness a condition of his marriage to the other Isobel. Good for him. Now, of course, it's irrelevant; Jeremy and the sim are gone.

. . .

A few days ago, I encountered Jeremy's mother, Betsy.

. . .

I had decided to close the Connecticut estate in the interest of moving past all that . . . sadness. Before I did so, I wanted to take one more look. I stood on the veranda, recalling the pain it represented—mine, Jacob's, Celeste's and . . . Eric's. Then I walked through the trees and along the river.

. . .

I planned to request that the estate be erased, and the memory used for something else, perhaps to create more location details for the river environment. Because of Shemathra, much of what was the Atlantic Coast has disappeared. Our world is getting smaller. More virtuals crowd together. There are fewer options now.

. . .

Anyway, I made my way along the Thames Riverbank, looking past the schooners across to Griswold Park, where people, virtuals and sims were relaxing and enjoying the day.

When I stopped at an outdoor café, I heard a low moan and sobs coming from an older woman sitting alone. She looked familiar. She was Betsy Salan.

. . .

Sim patrons near Betsy ignored her outbursts, but the virtuals, mostly couples, reacted with averted eyes and forced smiles. Those who were sitting near Betsy left their tables.

. . .

Sadness makes people uncomfortable.

. . .

I don't know why I approached her. As I got closer, I heard her whispered sob, "Oh my baby, oh Jeremy!" Finally, I sat down in the chair across from her.

. . .

Betsy had allowed her face to show all that emotion, like she was still a bio. Her mouth trembled with grief. Either she didn't see me, or her pain made me irrelevant. I watched her hands hover, suspended inches above the surface of the table, like Jeremy had just been wrested from her grasp. Her hands shook to the rhythm of her sobs. "Why . . . why didn't I just let him be who he was? He was a little boy and they used him. My poor baby . . . he . . . he . . ."

. . .

I couldn't sit there and do nothing. I moved my chair close to hers and put my arm around her and held her.

. . .

Betsy put her head on my shoulder, her arm draped around my neck. I rocked her back and forth . . . just a little and then . . . a young man in his twenties appeared a few feet away, a jump obviously.

He whispered, "Betsy?"

Betsy loosened her hold on my neck and turned.

"I would have come earlier," the young man said, "but it took a while . . . to find . . . oh Betsy . . ."

. . .

The young man was Betsy's husband, Otis. Otis collapsed on a bench, and Betsy moved quickly to his side. You would have thought they were mother and son. Otis shook his head and said, "I'm so sorry, honey . . ."

I wondered how Otis could grieve for a son who was only a collection of fragmented memories. I think what Otis missed was Betsy and their dream of a perfect life. Now they held each other and mourned. I don't know why holding seems to help when you're sad.

. . .

Yes, she was more than just sad. The son Betsy mourned wasn't the pliable virtual whom Bardot used, like Eric used me. Her Jeremy was a dreamy little boy who pretended that he was a grownup.

. . .

You're right. Betsy was grieving. I don't know why holding helps, but I guess it does. I hope. . .

. . .

That's all. I jumped then . . . I was afraid of their grief. It may be difficult for me to play my part in this Welcome-to-Hosseini event. It would help if you were there. You're shaking your head. Does that mean you won't?

. . .

It is important. I . . . Thank you, Tom. I want you to know how much I appreciate you doing this. In the past, I would have been very excited about what should be a rather unique spectacle, but now I . . . I'm not. This event depresses me.

END RECORD

***

GUNTER HOLDEN DOC. 294

V-Loc: See 743.1, Chicago ELYSIUM Penthouse PERSONAL, updated 6.28.2122. 19 detailed interiors include entry lobby, elevators 2 and 8, rotating 4 of 10 resident interiors and concierge. © 8.18.2120 by VEI Personal Options, Non-event day.

Urcuchillay

Urcuchillay, Urcuchillay, Urcuchillay. When we greet Hosseini, we bow, bending to the waist and then upon rising, we say his god name, Urcuchillay, three times. Be careful; don't make eye contact with the llama-god and make sure you stay in the area designated for humans.

. . .

There won't be many. A few people from Classics were pre-approved. There will be one representative from each community. Though some of the religious communities have expressed reluctance, they'll send someone. In this new Bali Hai, Hosseini has a lot of power. The Everlasting Praise "accident" is on everyone's mind.

. . .

I'll tell you what I know. After greeting the "god," humans are forbidden to speak in Urcuchillay's presence.

. . .

Isobel and Tupac are llamas, the only ones other than Hosseini. He is Urcuchillay and he is the multi-colored llama.

. . .

END RECORD

SAD LITTLE BOYS

GUNTER HOLDEN DOC. 295.

V-Loc: See 743.1, Chicago ELYSIUM Penthouse PERSONAL, updated 6.28.2122. 19 detailed interiors include entry lobby, elevators 2 and 8, rotating 4 of 10 resident interiors and concierge. © 8.18.2120 by VEI Personal Options, Non-event day.

Miranda, it seems there are two more files I'm meant to review, a memory record of Patel's and the other one is Marcia's message, the one she recorded before she left Bali Hai. I never understood why she . . . We made this world, she and I thought . . . What do you advise?

Gunter, what advice do you seek?

You cautioned me about Patel's other memory records and expressed concern about Monty's message. I . . . I fear that I'll have nothing to justify my life, my existence as a bio . . . or now as a virtual . . . pointless.

If you don't review his memory, will you lose your fear?

I wouldn't.

COMMAND, Miranda, TRANSFER: I want the Seattle house. Make it rain. I'll sit at the table where my mother sat. When I am done, please have a cup of coffee ready.

In a white cup?

Yes, please.

TRANSFER: to Seattle V-Loc COMPLETE

RAIN

COMMAND, RUN: Randall Patel memory record 108.

RUNNING Randall Patel Memory 108.

Patel memory doc.108:

People don't want to leave the meeting. They're reluctant to face what has happened. Laura, a vibrant young colleague is gone. Holden shot himself, and the life drained out of all of us. Marcia sits and grieves. I want to reach out and take her hand.

Monty looks like a child as he occupies the dead man's chair. Monty is angry with Gunter. But Monty, you could have alerted the police; you chose to protect LeRoi. You must have known what Gunter might do.

Terrance Stiles, the new consultant, wants direction for his press release. Marcia looks at me, and with a faint gesture, she presses my hand and whispers, "Stay."

Stiles says he will release a statement expressing our collective sorrow. Life as it was yesterday died with Holden. I regret that Holden is gone. I surprise myself. My fondest wish was that he should depart this earth.

My replacement, a young Taiwanese shifts in his seat. He's nervous because of my presence. Stiles calls an end to the meeting.

Monty rises quickly. LeRoi is being sentenced in a week. LeRoi, the Anti-Virtual zealot, is a tall young man with a friendly smile who resents how the poor must suffer in this life and then be shut out of virtual existence. The unjust destruction of millions of virtuals entrusted to Joy Forever was LeRoi's act as well as Holden's. Monty knows this.

The door shuts quietly, the humble gesture of Marcia's young assistant. We sit alone. I reach for her hand and her face tilts slightly, like a ship listing in a storm.

Last night, she couldn't sleep. A memory recorded by Celeste Holden was sent to Marcia. Marcia discovered something about Holden that she didn't know.

"Patel," she tells me. "I would have left him to his new world, but dear God, Celeste's memory changes everything. I should do something, let him know the truth about Eric. What if I do? It could destroy him."

"I know something of sad little boys and betrayal," I say, "Holden and I share this. Leave something of you in Miranda; I'll arrange it. Have Miranda keep Celeste's memory files. Imprint Miranda with your love and your desire to protect Gunter. Program her to reveal the truth when he must face it."

She nods and rests her elbow as her other hand covers her face. "Yes," she murmurs.

Reality has turned a page. I must give him his due.

Holden's ruthless optimism was a thing we had scorned, but it thrilled us. "This kid I found." Monty had been giddy. "This kid will save it!" I was cleaning out my desk. And Holden did save Encore with Marcia's help. It was more than the money. Holden's vision of paradise inspired us.

She's quiet now. I put my arm around her. How long do we have, she and I, until he needs her again? However long, I'll spin my own eternity around it.

"I want him to know the truth," she whispers, "about you and me. Promise."

"Yes, my love."

"I love you Patel." She takes my hand and holds it to her cheek.

"I love you, Marcia," I whisper. We leave the office. It's enough for me. I'll need no paradise other than what waits on the other side of Holden's Dreams.

COMMAND: END Patel memory 108.

Patel 108 ENDED.

Gunter, what is wrong? Gunter, why are you distressed? Is your coffee incorrect?

No, Miranda, the coffee's . . . the coffee's . . . fine, thank you.

Gunter, why are you crying?

I'm crying because I'm grieving.

Would you like to be held?

No, Miranda! Thank you, but no, I'll sit for a while and listen to the rain.

END RECORD

***

Byron—During this meeting with Tom, Gunter details his impressions of Hosseini. It is here that we see the stirrings of a hellish nightmare. God help anyone trapped in Shemathra.

GUNTER HOLDEN DOC. 299

V-Loc: Everest Summit 4.5 k by 5.8 k, non-event day 40 of 58, Tactile MOUNTAIN RISE © 2188, Visual/ audio EVEREST

EXPERIENCE by VEI Adventures © 2187, Olfactory DREAM HIGH © 2145, Sims 58 gray geese level 4 Human 2 climbers' level 3.

The Everest Summit

I chose this day because of its exceptionally good weather. The view is incredibly clear. I see the climbers. Even so, there's a feeling of serenity. Bettina thought virtual climbers, their inexperience, were an insult to "Mother." I don't know.

. . .

Why should others be denied this beauty? As bios, few were both wealthy enough and physically able to endure the altitude and harsh weather. The Summit may be gone soon. Let's change the subject.

. . .

Do you mind discussing the Shemathra event?

. . .

I noticed you kept shaking your head. My overall reaction is a sense of personal failure. I let my hatred for Jacob cloud my judgement. If I hadn't, they and I would still be bios. I could have prevented all of this.

. . .

Hosseini, the cigar-smoking llama, was ridiculous. Did you see where the tobacco spit landed?

. . .

Two of the sheep in the front line got it. It fell on the right flank of one and between the eyes of the other. Depressing. Bali Hai was to be paradise. The "Sacred Ecstasy Infinite Nirvana" is grotesque. The whole situation is like a nightmare where the Devil smiles at you and you don't know why.

. . .

The quiet here soothes me after the cacophony of the Shemathra.

The Devil smiles at you

. . .

His entrance was ludicrous, I agree, but it was dignified compared to Isobel's grand introduction. Her llama head, with its banana ears and raisin eyes, peeked out from behind the monstrous Shemathra "White Wolf" statues like a stripper tantalizing the audience, showing just a little bit of llama at a time until she walked on stage, strutting as she stretched her llama neck.

. . .

When she introduced the new god, I cringed when the "children" lapsed into moos, neighs, bleats, and baas. And Hosseini, the llama-god, what a sight! When he let out that gargling noise I almost choked.

. . .

Yes, the big speech: "The program Shemathra wants us all to do is follow the rules on communicatin' with the bio-world, fornicatin' as humans and all the required worship, where of course you make a cyberbuck donation."

I think Hosseini intends to maintain his influence in both worlds by making sure there's a steady cash flow that he controls. Nearly three hundred thousand worshipers stood on four legs waiting for the new llama god.

. . .

It's incredible, the way these people, who can experience so much here, choose to exist as dumb animals. I perceive the beginning of a social hierarchy with the sheep and cattle on the bottom and horses and buffalo at the top. Did you notice how tense it was when several cows wandered off and began to graze on a patch of grass?

. . .

The cows were whispering about the strict security. No one dared leave.

. . .

I did some research in preparation—included some digitals. Hosseini was short and his prominent nose and weak chin resulted in a hawk-like face.

. . .

Hosseini's voice was deep, a surprising sound coming from the rainbow-llama-god. It was insinuating, as if there were an implied threat in every word, especially when he said, "You people might be picked ta go so the goddess wants to make sure. What I'm sayin' is you bettah be woithy."

Did you notice the stallions? They were forcing the cow back in line when the bull got involved. He knew she was in trouble.

. . .

You didn't see it?

. . .

The stallions faced off with the bull and they began pawing the ground like they were going to fight, and then the bull lowered his horns and was snorting. Hosseini said, "Over theh—knock it off!" I saw him mutter something and swing his head. A couple of buffalo stepped down from the stage and went over to deal with the problem. I'm sure he told them to get names.

. . .

He does make a handsome llama. The colors seem to shift when he moves, very godlike. Did you notice that there were only two llamas? Tupac wasn't there.

. . .

I had Miranda look for him. All records on Tupac have been erased, as if he never existed.

. . .

Queen Isobel strutted over to the stallions casually corralling the cow. I would guess it was more than just business in terms of their relationship.

. . .

Ah, look. There are more climbers. I see two of them. No, they're sims, part of the day's program. Despite what I said earlier about other virtuals enjoying Mother Everest's cold hospitality, I value the quiet.

. . .

As to the new "Bali Hai, Shemathra's Realm," I sense that anyone who displeases either the "god" or his consort Isobel might be deleted like poor Tupac and all evidence of their existence erased.

. . .

My world is being corrupted. The lowest form of human communication is overwriting what was meant to be effortless and joyful. I don't know—I . . . I envisioned this world as something beautiful and infinitely fascinating and complex.

. . .

I once valued surprises. Now, I dread them. I do, however, miss the sense of time passing. I miss clocks.

. . .

This is embarrassing, letting someone witness my being so emotional. It was unthinkable before the mergers. Do you see the gray birds flying just below us?

. . .

They're a type of geese, the only birds able to fly at this altitude. They are beautiful and graceful as they soar. I watch them and I don't have to remember . . . It's hard to think that Dad, Eric, murdered . . . my— I mean how could he do such a thing?

. . .

Thank you, Tom, for listening, for your friendship. You informed Miranda that you had recorded something?

. . .

I plan to review it soon. I need to be less distracted when I do.

. . .

the virtual dead,

Do you remember those small dark objects near the rocks, a couple of thousand feet down from us?

. . .

They're the virtual dead, recorded from the memories of climbers who were forced to leave their fallen friends behind, additions to Mother's trophy collection. They've become ghosts. Recently, I have been fighting the urge to sit down there with them to see if I could touch them. Would their frozen images feel solid? If I pressed my cheek against one, would I feel the cold?

. . .

It all seems to be slipping away.

END RECORD

TOM

G UNTER HOLDEN MEMORY FILES
FOLDER YEAR: 2196

GUNTER HOLDEN DOC. 300

V-Loc: The Memory Library, 1.5 by 1.5 city park, non-event continuous morning to late afternoon non-variant moderate (75 degrees F) temperature, park environ (sim-eco-system) by COMMUNITY-LIVING © 2120, 50 benches, one "Bali Hai Memory Library Structure," (book shape modeled on National Library Korea) containing, "front desk," sim-librarian level 7, structure has four stories and two basements, 500 private memory experience rooms.

Tom's memories

Miranda, Tom Bucklin has recorded memories from his bio-life to share with me. In the past, I would have relished the chance to experience his memories but now, I'm weary. I wish that Bali Hai were the paradise I thought it would be. Now, I regret it all. I never meant to hurt anyone. There's no one left to hear my apologies.

Tom is your friend.

Yes, sometimes I wonder why. We seem too different, but I'm grateful for his company and for being my friend for whatever reason. I'd like the penthouse and dusk. Make it a Sunday, with the sun going down behind that building with the penthouse garden.

Sunday June 7, 2094.

TRANSFER: Chicago Custom Penthouse (See 743.1)

TRANSFER COMPLETE

Byron—Although these are Tom Bucklin's memory records, before Tom self-deleted, he requested that these records be included in Gunter Holden's memory files, and they do not fall under the control of the Bucklin family. Thomas Bucklin did not give a reason for this decision.

COMMAND, Miranda, RUN: Thomas Bucklin Memory file 246 and then follow with 247.

RUNNING Thomas Bucklin Memory file 246, followed by 247.

THOMAS BUCKLIN Memory File 246:

I'm sitting at the kitchen table, finishing my egg sandwich before we go to Niverville. The clock over Dad's work desk, the wise-old -owl clock Aunt Sweetie gave us for Christmas last year, is opening its clock eyes and it says "hoot" once because it's one o'clock. Aunt Sweetie calls from the entertainment room.

"Did you gentlemen remember to include the new socks?"

I wait for Dad to answer, but he doesn't because he's busy with the ring.

Dad raises the ring up so that he can see it better. I like the way it sparkles in the kitchen light, like tiny stars between his fingers.

"It was your mother's and I know she would want your big brother to have it."

He keeps looking at it and he doesn't hear Aunt Sweetie, so I answer, "Yes Auntie we remembered."

"Both the dark blue ones and the white?"

"Yes, Aunt."

Sometimes I think about my brother. Does he look like Dad or maybe more like our mom? Sometimes, I imagine he's a character in the adventure stories I write, the ones I keep secret. Only Dad gets to read them. In my stories, my brother is tall and brave. At the end of the story, he always tells me that I'm the best brother he could ever have.

I wish she were really my aunt, even though she's too old to be a regular one. I thought she was at least a hundred ninety, but Dad said she was over cen-plus fifty and that she came to take care of the house when we moved here and then she fell in love with me. I used to think that meant she wanted to marry me, and I wasn't sure about the age difference, but Dad says it's a "turn of phrase." I was a little kid and Aunt was new.

I remember her saying "Just call me Aunt, sweetie," when I asked her name and I thought her name was Sweetie and it stuck so now she's Aunt Sweetie to me and Mrs. Glen to everyone else—the adults, anyway.

We have a new auto-glide, but Dad's keeping the old one "in good repair." He plans to give it to me when I turn seventeen. Aunt Doro is sure that Uncle Charles is planning to give new auto-glides to Linda and David when they graduate, because that's how they do it in the Bucklin clan.

Dad says, "Let's wait and see. Your cousins are five and eight and graduations are a long way off and at any rate, you'll learn on the

LaSalle." Still, I expect they'll get a lot of Christmas presents. Linda still believes in Santa, so Aunt Sweetie says to be careful so that I don't spill the beans.

Dad lays the ring on the counter and gets the gift box. He—

COMMAND, Miranda, PAUSE: Thomas Bucklin memory.

246 PAUSED

The ring is the Solar System ring. I don't understand . . . I—I guess I won't unless I continue . . .

COMMAND, Miranda, RESUME: Thomas Bucklin Memory 246.

Thomas Bucklin 246 RESUMED.

—seems sad, ever since he got my brother's message. Dad was happy at first and got excited. "Your mother would be so proud of her boys!"

Dad sat down at the kitchen table when he read the message. I was afraid he was sick because his face turned red, and he began to shake. I was going to get Aunt Sweetie, but then he sighed and started mumbling to himself, which I'm used to. "Gunter's on his own, and that maniac is preoccupied with the new wife."

When he told Aunt Sweetie about Gunter's message, she got upset, like when I forget to put my plate in the sink.

"Mr. Vanderbok, you must be careful. You know what the man has done and what he might do if . . ."

Then, something scary happened. Dad began to cry. I never saw him cry before. I didn't know men did. I thought you stopped when you were twelve, and I hoped I could because that's when you're supposed to but Dad . . . I think he's worried that my brother will be mad because he never got to come here and live with us. Dad said there were reasons and that he planned to explain as best he could when he meets him in Selkirk on Christmas.

I still don't understand why I can't come too, but Dad told me, "We need to see how it goes, Tom, be patient. I want to mail the ring in case . . . in case the weather turns, and he can't . . . make it." I've never seen Dad so emotional.

The box is on the counter and Dad's turning the ring in his hand. "I gave this to your mother," he says. "Promise me something, Tom."

"Okay," I tell him. He puts the ring in the little box and then he looks at me like he did last summer when we had the "where babies come from" talk. I already knew because Max at school told me during lunch in grade four. Dad puts a hand on each of my shoulders and says, "If, for some reason, things don't go right, he changes his mind, or he can't get—free . . ."

"But he sent you the message," I remind him, "and he said would."

"I know, but just in case," Dad tells me. I nod. I can see that Dad's serious, but I hope we can go soon. Then Dad places his hands on the sides of my face and asks me to promise, "When it feels right, I want you to find your brother and tell him how much we love him—your mother and I."

"And me too," I add.

"Of course, you too," Dad says, and he hugs me like he's not going to go with us to see Aunt Doro, but he is. "One more thing." Dad wants me to make another promise, "I want you to know your brother, really get to know him. He'll need you someday; I can feel it. Okay?"

"Okay," I say. I hope that's all because I want him to be happy; it's Christmas in only nine more days.

I look at the solar system ring to see if the nine tiny planets are still there. Maybe I'll write a story about the ring, and I can show it to Gunter. Dad gave me the cloud box and I keep it with my other

"Mom" things like the holo Aunt Doro took in the hospital of Dad and Mom when I was born. Dad's hair was short, and he didn't have a beard and Mom's hair is dark and some of it spreads across Dad's light green shirt because he has his arm around her. Dad said it was such a happy day, and he wished Gunter could—

COMMAND, END: Thomas Bucklin Memory 246.

Thomas Bucklin Memory 246 ENDED.

Miranda, Mr. Donald was my father. I saw his face . . . and the hair, like a bird's crest. I recognized him when Tom remembered the holo. He was Olaf D. Vanderbok. I told Dad . . . Eric, that I had contacted Vanderbok. Eric was taking Celeste to Paris for Christmas because in a few months Jacob would be . . . coming.

"I won't be home," Eric told me.

"Don't worry, Dad, I have plans," I told him. Marcia and I were in the early stages of it all and I planned to propose to her. And then I said, "By the way, Dad, I contacted this researcher, Vanderbok, with questions regarding his work at Encore. When it comes to virtual life, he's a pioneer. I'm waiting to hear from him; maybe he and I can connect during the holidays. He founded Encore and I have his lectures on . . ."

Eric cut me off. "I keep telling you're wasting your time, but you never listen. There's no future in that business. It's full of complications, all kinds of problems. We'll be back in six weeks. Stay out of trouble if you can manage it. Celeste says Merry Christmas."

Tom's father was my father. Eric had already murdered our mother, so Tom never knew her. By telling Eric that I had connected with Vanderbok, I condemned my real father to death. I never sent any message to meet him in Selkirk. I was waiting for him; I never heard back. Eric set him up, lured him there and had someone kill him.

I don't know how I would have reacted to the truth of who my father was. I'll never know. Eric made sure of it. I made Jacob pay for Eric's lies, Eric's crimes. Eric murdered my parents and I murdered Jacob.

I was Eric's son after all

I feel like . . . not . . . feeling. Let's finish my brother's memories! Let's finish all of it.

COMMAND, RUN: Thomas Bucklin Memory 247.

Thomas Bucklin Memory 247.RUNNING

THOMAS MEMORY File 247:

I imagine the cup sitting on someone else's table a thousand years ago. The Tiffany lamp, found at the Eugene garage sale, sheds the only light. Her dark hair is fading into gray. Is it the drugs or the other thing, the thing that's spreading? We can't stop it, the doctors say. But there must be something; I know there must be.

Stephanie's recliner chair is the only new thing here. She spent years roaming jungles and forgotten villages and the backrooms of country stores. A desk from old Spain, found in California, sits near a spinning wheel that clothed the Patriots of Massachusetts as they fought the British.

She sleeps in the recliner. It's easier to breathe, she insists. Without the bed, there's room to put her collections in order. Later, they'll go to a museum in that same order.

On good nights, we talk as we wait for the drugs to ease the pain. Oh God, the swelling in her neck has increased. "No more doctors," she insists. I won't fight her. I don't want our last weeks together to be spent arguing. She won't look at me.

The nurse, a young Filipina with soft brown eyes, waits for me to leave.

"Good night, Imelda," I say. Imelda nods as she checks Stephanie's heart. Obediently, I leave, although the door remains open. I sit on my makeshift bed near the open door and listen to her breathing.

Stephanie tells stories and each night, they are different. Tonight, my girl wonders if spirits remain among the living. Do they find refuge in something simple—like a piece of pottery? Do gods of the past, beloved, or feared, inhabit something used in worship--perhaps a braided necklace, or do they linger in the grooves of a ceremonial cup?

"We can hear them if we listen," she whispers to the girl. Stephanie doesn't catch the amusement in Imelda's soft eyes, a fleeting thing, better unnoticed.

In happier times, we would talk through the open door, my wife in her library, cataloguing a new find, and me in my office, idly reviewing new glide designs or working on another story. She loved my stories, she said. She urged me to publish them. Why didn't I try at least? I was afraid.

"Write a novel," she said. I promised her I would when I could find the time. Now, there is no more time to find.

Memories here. Andrew at five, playing war with three-year-old Donald, wielding Michoacán plates as shields. Nancy was fourteen as she sat with me here and cried over a pimple minutes before her first date.

I keep begging her. "Stephanie, why not take the nanobots? We can still be together. I'll join you as soon as I can. We can afford it. The kids have their own families, and they will understand." Always the same. My wife's gaze is fixed on the past. Only her work is real and everything else, fading.

She shakes her head. "I don't want to continue in VR. It's not life; it is an illusion, an imitation. When I die, whatever happens, it won't be a trick, no more real than these holos." When her thumb presses a button, the pottery disappears.

She's groaning. *Please God!* From where I am, I see Imelda's delicate hand reach to dim the Tiffany Lamp. I'm afraid!

"Why Stephanie," I ask, "why so adamant?" She sighs and turns away.

"Then I'll die too." I insist. "I'll arrange to neutralize the nanobots and forget the trip to Bali Hai. I can't be alone."

Stephanie faces me and her eyes cloud with mild contempt. She shakes her head. Those green eyes regard me with impatient love. When will I let go? Not yet?

"You made a promise." Is all she will say. Simple.

"I was eleven, I didn't know. Dad must have suspected a trick. Eric Holden couldn't bear to lose so he killed my mother and then ruined Dad by backing the bid to take Encore from him. Why did Dad take the chance? Why couldn't he leave well enough alone?"

She has no patience for a broken promise. It seems like no one does. After Dad died, Aunt Sweetie made me promise never to mention that I had a brother. Uncle Charles tried to take Dad's place. I became a Bucklin with a car at seventeen, but Aunt Doro never lost her fear of Eric. Even though I promised, it was because I had a brother that Aunt Doro couldn't love me. Stephanie knows this—why does she insist I keep my word? Gunter doesn't know I exist.

"Ask your children. If they needed you, would you abandon them? If Andrew were in trouble, would you tell Nancy and Donald to abandon him?"

Imelda presses a damp cloth to her lips. I look away.

Stephanie knows my weaknesses. "There will be no more discussion. I love you and I'll look for you when you're done keeping your promise to your father. When Gunter was in this world, you delayed because of the children. Then it was too late; he killed himself. The only way to reach him now is to follow him into his dream world. When the time comes, find Gunter, and do what you can for him. He is your brother."

Despite the darkness, she sees me watching her from the shadows. She turns away and closes her eyes. Imelda puts her finger to her lips and mouths the words, "Let her sleep." I retreat to my office. It's so hard . . . so hard to be alone.

COMMAND, END: Thomas Bucklin memory 247.

Thomas Bucklin memory ENDED.

I see that I managed to ruin more lives than I thought. Miranda, I want the ocean. Put me in the Pacific, near Bali Hai. I'll watch the ghosts of fish.

END RECORD

SHRIMP ON A HOT GRIDDLE

GUNTER HOLDEN DOC. 301, 304

V-Loc: Pacific Ocean, over and underwater environment by NEMOHORIZONS © 2135, Sims by AQUATIC LIFE includes area (3 k by 5.2k) specific marine ecosystem, Sims rotation of level 6 marine life (varied) including 52 seahorses, 20 turtles, 30 sharks (rotating species), pod of 18 whales (rotating), 28 turtles, Sims fish (varied) 6738.

Gunter, Thomas Bucklin would like to meet with you now.

I'm not available now. I'm sorry, but I can't.

Gunter, Thomas says that he will wait for you in the clouds on the "Mother of virtual ghosts." He said you would know.

"Remember the clouds." My mother said that. I remember. Tell him I'll meet him there soon.

I'll relay the message.

It's comfortable here, watching the waves catch the light of the moon, the moon I didn't want. I like wearing the mask and snorkel.

Unnecessary, I know, but I miss being a bio. As Stephanie said, it's a trick. I want to self-delete, but I'm afraid.

Does it bother you, Miranda, not being real?

Define "real."

In this case, "real" means to be born, and then, to make your way, to fight to continue, to exist, and perhaps, to procreate.

No, Gunter, it does not bother me because I see no advantage in being "real."

I see a turtle is emerging from underwater grass and behind him, ha, seahorses. They're dancing! Seahorse fathers keep the mothers' eggs safe until the babies are ready and then he lets them go. If a hungry fish doesn't snap them up— hungryhungry—wwwaiting waiting wai—w—waiting—oh when . . . so hungry

BREACH!!!

Breach: BIO memory 62453884 Venice, CA Beach June 4, 2077

I am twelve and sitting on a bench on the edge of the sand on Venice Beach. Dad told me to wait.

"I'm meeting an actress in Brentwood, an old friend," he said. "Enjoy the beach!" He handed me a five-credit note, and I put it in my pocket.

"Back in a few hours," Dad promised. I watched him as he waved to his driver. The limo drove away. I waved, but Dad didn't look back.

I have been here for days. The nights here are scary and cold. On day two, it rained. At noon on the second day, I was so sure of Eric's any-minute-now return, I spent the last of the five credits on a funnel cake. It was raining, and the wind made it worse. No one was renting hover boards or skates, so I hid under the overhang of the HOVERS HERE shack.

Day three and it's raining again, and the wind is even colder; it feels like a knife. It hurts the cuts and scrapes on my arms and legs. I'm tucking my hands under my crossed arms to stay warm. I'm cold and trying to keep my burns away from the wind. I tried to snatch shrimp from a hot griddle. The cook grabbed my wrists and forced me to drop the shrimp. When I tried to get away my fingers touched the griddle. My fingers were so cold, they sizzled like the shrimp.

I bet the man was ex-military. His head was shaved, except for the top. He had a short brush and a lot of pink scalp. A law-and-order type, for sure. Maybe he was a cop before he decided to man a griddle.

"Where're your parents?" he asked me.

I knew to look him in the eye. "Sir, my dad will be here soon. He'll take care of it." The cook gave me two small shrimps and told me to get lost.

I look around for that older man. If I see him, I run. He wanted company in exchange for buying me dinner. I ran when a tourist wearing an Iowa sweatshirt pointed at me and said that someone should call the police. Obviously, she said, I was homeless. Clueless bitch.

Now, the sun has finally come out on day three. I'm still sitting on the same bench and finally, I hear the short beep from Dad's glide limo.

"You should have called," Dad tells me. I'm still damp from the rain as I collapse into the limo's backseat. I can tell by the way Dad rolls the moist end of his cigar and tosses it out the car window that he's annoyed. "Our plan slipped my mind; I was distracted," Eric says. Then he lights up another cigar.

"Sorry, Dad," I say. I hide my burned fingers. Dad must never know I begged . . .

We stop for dinner, and I order steak. Why can't I eat it . . . can't. . .?

END BREACH

RESUME 310

Gunter . . . Gunter?

Yes, Miranda? What happened?

Another breach. To protect your file, I interrupted it.

I had slipped my father's mind that day . . .

Daydayday—island—on the island--- rememberremember—islandisland—re . . .

BRR—

NO! I CHOOSE to remember this.

I will remember this day on the island.

I was eight and I swam too far out, and a wave caught me. I—I struggled to free myself until I screamed "Dad!" I could see him as he stood watching, his cigar frozen in his mouth, but he—he didn't move. I kept screaming, "Help Dad please . . . pleeeese!" When the water pulled me deeper, I saw a school of fish. The urge to take a breath and fill my lungs with water was winning. Would those fish be the ones to eat me? I had begun to let go when a hand grabbed my arm and pulled me up.

I was limp in his arms when Dad carried me back to shore.

I could feel his heart pounding, and he was crying, "Oh, Gunter—my little boy! Oh, please God—oh, I'm so sorry! Oh, Gunter!"

I didn't let him know I heard. As I coughed up the seawater, I was happy. I knew he loved me then, the only time he ever said it. That day on the island was why I waited, why I didn't go back to Seattle because I . . .

Gunter, Diego wants to speak to you.

Tell him I drowned.

Diego is counting on you. Urcuchillay requires a meeting to confirm territorial boundaries and policies relating to jumping into "Shema-thra" grazing areas.

Miranda, I wish I cared enough to protect what's left. Give Diego my apologies. Make a list of possible representatives for him to consider.

Yes, Gunter, I'll tell him and give him a list.

Now, I'd like the Fairmont Hotel.

COMMAND, SET: Fairmont Hotel environment

Fairmont Hotel environment SET

COMMAND, TRANSFER: Fairmont Hotel (see Doc 439)

TRANSFER COMPLETE

COMMAND, RUN: Marcia Evans message 522

RUNNING Marcia Evans message 522 with designated PATCH

What patch? I don't understand . . .

Miranda, why is Marcia older? She's even older than the day of Patel's last memory. The lines in her face are deeper.

I know, Gunter. There's a message.

The Fairmont Hotel

RUNNING File 522, Marcia's last message:

"If you're seeing and hearing me now, it's because you know the truth, all of it, yours, mine, Jacob's, Patel's and Monty's."

She sits on a chair on her balcony, the one where she and Patel were the night after my death . . .

"I have been informed that Laura and Jacob have gone into the Dreams, and soon, I'll see you. Patel understands, as he always has when it comes to you. My poor Holden, my golden boy, people have forgiven your transgressions. I think even Monty will before the end, despite the viciousness he displays. Please forgive him and forgive yourself."

Tears well up in her eyes; she ignores them. Oh, Marcia.

"My stay with you will be brief, long enough to help you adjust to being alone. Then I will fall into the Dreams. I've discovered that our perfect world is not what I want. I'll wait for you and for Patel wherever the Dreams take me. I wonder if I can have you both. We'll see. Maybe my brothers are there, waiting for me."

She smiles and leans forward, as if that will span the distance of time and reality between us.

"I wouldn't have missed it, Holden, not one moment of the time I spent with you. I have made some adjustments to Miranda's program. There is much more of me in Miranda now. This change was Patel's suggestion, and as you know, a way of looking out for you. My love for you is now part of her, and so as long as she loves you, I am still with you."

END MESSAGE.

Oh Marcia, is that all? I wish—

RUNNING patch—Marcia Evans.

Patch?

Gunter, your cooperation is required.

Of course, Miranda.

RUNNING: 522 Patch

I'm sitting on the Fairmont couch I remember so well. The coat with the glossy buttons is draped on the back. The Marcia-sim comes through the bedroom door and sits. The envelope containing my graduation present is in her hand.

I'm eighteen, and as I reach, she says, "Hello, Holden."

Oh, my God! There's no emptiness in those eyes! Marcia's here!

"It's only part of me," she says, "the part that loves you." She points to the necklace, the golden bridge I gave her to remember that first year. She kisses my fingertips. I ache with desire.

"It's for a little while," she says and places my hand on the edge of her robe. Like Patel, I'll spin my own eternity. and we begin the night.

END RECORD

THE WHITE CUP

G UNTER HOLDEN MEMORY FILES
FOLDER YEAR: 2196

Welcome to **BABYLON DREAMS**

THOMAS BUCKLIN DOC. 356

Byron—This record is from the file of Thomas Bucklin (Vanderbok) who designated to be available solely to the following: My children, Nancy, Andrew, and Donald and their children and direct descendants and no one else.

V-Loc: Exit transition station 103 "Babylon Dreams" roller coaster (self-deletion system). 0.4 k by 0.5 k "State Fair" illusions, visual, audio, tactile, olfactory by IOWA SUMMERS, INC. © 2120. Sims 230 level 3 "workers" and "attendees," 7 level 5 sims, 5 CUSTOM sims level 8.

Thomas Bucklin Doc 356

Today, I am eleven. Gunter is eight. We will leave here as the children we were before everything changed. I hold my brother's hand as we stand in line.

"What do the tickets cost?" I ask, reaching into my jeans.

"Don't worry, I got it. Miranda told me." Gunter says as he digs in his pocket. I see a tooth is missing as he grins. I point and laugh. When my eleven-year-old voice cracks, Gunter's eyes light up as he puts his hand over his mouth.

I look to see if I know anyone. Not yet. The line is slow. I think it's meant to be slow in case you change your mind. Gunter points to a girl three people ahead of us. He whispers that she's Anna, the woman at the chalet who shook her wrists, ridding her hands of old age.

Anna, who looks eighteen, seems troubled. Her eyes are downcast, as if she's studying the ground beneath her feet. I step out of line and tap her shoulder and ask her why she is here. We hear the faint sound of the cars as they climb the rails. A rainbow of lightning flashes, then the few stars visible are gone in a glow of pulsating colors.

There must be more

The colors remind me of the aurora borealis. I ask her, "Did you ever see it?"

"No, I always meant to, but no." She whispers, "I'm not sure that I'm ready." She takes deep, frequent breaths. If she were a bio, she would need a paper bag in order not to faint. "There must be more," she whimpers. "Life in Bali Hai is so much better than my bio-life. But I can't think of anything else to enjoy. There's nothing new to want."

In the distance, the rails disappear into night clouds. There are more flashes of dazzling color then the dark clouds again. She shakes her head. "I don't know, maybe I'll come back . . ."

I see her hopelessness. She leaves with no goodbye. As we get to the ticket booth, Gunter begins to shake. "The ticket man, he's Monty."

My brother panics; he's ready to run away, but I take his hand and the cyberbucks from his fist and I say, "Two, please." I buy our tickets.

"Two for the Dreams." The sim says.

"A sim is all he is," I whisper. "Didn't you all contribute a sim to the program? Miranda designed the Dreams to protect you, Gunter, from your impulses."

"I'm okay," he says. We walk through the arch. He doesn't look up. Twenty feet above us, a sign says, "WELCOME TO BABYLON DREAMS!" There are bright colors in the sign and periodically, the colors change. Beautiful.

I hear an organ playing *Let's Wish Upon a Shooting Star*. Aunt Sweetie loved that song. We hear men's voices, urging folks to "Step right up and take a chance and win a prize."

I don't know why it's night, but it does seem fitting. I remember going to fairs. The booths and carts are all lit up and the air is full of shouts and laughter. There's only one ride. We see it looming in the distance. The clouds make it hard to see how high up it goes. Gunter squeezes my hand.

I'm in a dream. Booths to toss rings, someone to guess your weight, covered carts and stands selling hotdogs and popcorn, cotton candy, caramel apples and fudge are on both sides of us. There are signs with arrows pointing to restrooms. Buy more chances and win the giant stuffed panda.

Take a Chance

The chance to win something. Serendipity. Good luck or bad luck, but never a sure thing. Bored, older men, carny sims oversee the efforts of sim-teenage-boys trying to impress their sim-girls. Sim-families stroll by, and the children eat ice cream and cotton candy.

Beyond the gate, sims wait to take our tickets. Gunter begins to cry. "The sims, one is Jacob," he sobs, "and the other . . ."

I see the Jacob-sim. Then I see Laura. I point to the Laura sim. He nods, and tears run down his cheeks. I put my arm around his shoulder. "Brothers stick together," I tell him.

"It's okay," he says, as he looks at me and tries to smile.

"You were a cute little kid," I tell him.

He hits me with his fist, but not too hard. It breaks the spell. I decide to distract him.

"Hey, Gunter, do you see any other people you know who are going on the ride?"

The couple in front of us, two men who are obviously lovers, turn to look at us to see if we're familiar. The older looking one, a handsome man with gray hair and a trimmed beard, reminds me of a college professor. He smiles and shakes his head at his lover, who looks to be a dark-haired boy of twenty. Gunter searches the line ahead. There must be at least fifty behind us, who knows? We can't see where it ends.

Twenty people back, I recognize someone.

"Is that Denise?" I whisper. Gunter nods. She stands alone near the arch entrance. She's still beautiful, but it doesn't seem to matter. She's still alone except for the mother-sim who stands passively beside her.

"I see her sim-mother, Pamela, is with her," Gunter whispers. Another ride begins. The cars make a clicking sound as they begin their ascent. The clicks grow fainter when an organ plays *Over the moon with you*. Gunter shudders and he squeezes my hand. We go forward; the line is getting shorter.

"I didn't know sims could ride the Dreams," I whisper.

"They can't." Gunter shakes his head. "Pamela-sim's memory will be erased and sold." Gunter recognizes a woman and a man who are several yards behind us. "Hello, Betsy! Do you know who I am? I met you in New London recently."

Betsy waves. Even from here, I can see her troubled face soften when she sees my brother, manifesting as a little boy, waving back. She must recognize him because she calls to him, raising her voice to be heard over the music and the cars' clicking as they begin another ride.

"You were very kind about Jeremy." I see her struggle not to cry. "What a darling little boy you are!"

My brother ducks his head; he's embarrassed. "The old woman," he asks her, "the one feeding the birds. Do you . . ."

"Terry? You mean Terry?" she asks. The line moves along. "She won't go until Ned is ready," Betsy shrugs, "so she feeds the birds and waits."

I can see uncertainty cloud Otis' face as he looks up into the dark sky. The top of the Dreams is hidden. My own fear wells up. It mustn't show or Gunter might panic. There's a flash of colored lights and another ride is over.

Silent, the cars arrive empty, and the organ gets ready for another song. We hear the faint voices, urging us to buy a ticket and win a prize.as we move closer to the ride. One more set of cars loads, and the clicks begin. I fight the urge to leave. Others turn and walk away, and

I wish . . . Gunter watches them leave. I won't go without him, but I hope that he'll be my excuse to exit. We'll jump away to think. Maybe we'll sit again on Mother's cold shoulder. We'll watch the gray birds sail across the ice chasms.

"I spy someone else," Gunter says. "The woman, see the woman with the reddish hair, the one by herself? I guess Sergei must be staying." He whispers, "Karina, you know, the sister. On Oliver Jackson's wedding night, she was the bride." I nod.

Forever is a long time.

Gunter's words come to mind. I feel pity. She smiles to herself.

The gate opens. We hear Laura announce, "Tickets, have your tickets ready." Gunter grips my hand. I hand both tickets to the sim. She takes the tickets and for a second, she hesitates before she tears them. I see Gunter's young wife.

The Jacob-sim asks us to move along, please. We move up the wooden ramp and it begins to rain. The angle is steep, perhaps thirty degrees. Betsy and Otis are in the next group. As we climb up the planks, Gunter and I turn and wave. Betsy blows us a kiss; Otis holds her other hand. His gaze is on the ground. I still hear organ music and now it's playing *My Love's on Mars*, another Aunt Sweetie's favorite. The empty cars arrive with a rush.

While we wait for the safety bars to spring up,

I pretend that my brother and I are on an adventure, a story of discovery, like the ones I wrote when I was a child in Winnipeg. A man walks over to pull the lever. Gunter looks at the man, whose light brown face is handsome. Rather than a flat affect, the sim's eyes are remote, as if fixed on a distant memory.

"Patel?" Gunter freezes for a moment.

"Watch your step, young sirs." Patel's voice is kind. Gunter and I wait as the bar lowers onto our laps.

Behind us, a sim is checking each bar to make sure it's locked in place. "Nice and safe, you boys have fun, now." A woman with dark hair tests the bar. I know it's a sim of Marcia. Gunter's face relaxes and he nods. Ahead of us, the man and the boy are silent. The boy rests his head on the man's shoulder.

The cars jerk and as we begin our climb. The rain picks up. Gunter trembles. "What if I pee my pants?" he asks.

"Then I'll pee mine too," I say. We hold hands as the rain comes down and we go up into the gloom. I am scared. Each click brings us closer to whatever waits. We're almost at the crest. I see nothing but clouds. No music now . . . we're drifting . . .

Sparkles. No clouds . . . sparkles fill the sky . . .becoming thousands of spinning pinwheels. They're breaking apart into showers of light and color. We're floating.

"Where are we?" Gunter is curious.

There's nothing to fear.

"I don't know, Gunter." Swirls of shimmering color surround and carry us. We're alone in our single car. I don't know where the others, the other cars, the man and the boy, or those behind us are . . . I only know that my brother and I are on our way. A gentle gust of wind propels us up again. It's still hazy. Where are we going?

Gunter whispers. "Do you see it? Look!" I look. There's a city in the distance. He begins to cry. "Babylon, it's Babylon, Tom, I saved it!" We're getting closer now and I marvel at its beauty, this lovely city by the ocean. I see sunlit beaches.

"Look at all the people, Gunter!"

Stephanie, and Marcia, Patel, Laura, and Jacob—are they there, waiting? Is it all an illusion that eases us into nothingness? We're closer now. I see people gather as if to greet us when we arrive. I wonder how we stop. I'll know soon.

"Tom, look! There, do you see them?"

"Yes, I do, Gunter. I see them."

"Oh, Tom! It's Mom and she's with our Dad, and look, Tom! She's holding her white cup . . ."

DELETION COMPLETE

END Thomas Bucklin (Vanderbok), Gunter Holden (Vanderbok) DOC. 356,731-001 pre-deletion record (save)

Byron—I am including this file, which may be of use in locating more documents related to Gunter Holden. This event took place shortly before the Bali Hai program was officially renamed Shemathra's Realm.

(Post deletion) GUNTER HOLDEN DOC. 8742.67

V-Loc: TRANSITION STATION 46. UNIVERSAL ACCESS Visual: Standard daylight South Pacific beach-3.14 k, ocean-1.6 k from shoreline, structures-2, vegetation-tropical no. 3567.2c, © March 7, 2078, by VEI Standard Environments. Audio: ocean surf (standard level 8) gulls 46 level 5, wildlife level 2 OCEANBASE INTERACTIVES © 4.23.2132, Tactile: tropic Sun/Moon late morning light effect 3.7, mild breeze (level 3 fixed), Sand texture BEACHLIFE No. 6.8 © 6.2.2019, Sims: limited-basic vacation beach family level 1.3, entertainment musical greet (rotating) level 6.

Activate: Gunter-Holden-Sim

Gunter-sim, do you know who you are?

"Yes, Miranda. I made this world as it was."

"Call me Marcia, Gunter-sim"

"Yes, Marcia."

"Do you know what to do?"

"I greet new arrivals and aid their initial adjustment process."

"Good. In one point two three minutes, a new resident will arrive at the customary place."

"Fine, shall I wait there?"

"Yes, but first, sing to me."

"I'll see you . . . soon . . . by . . . the weeping willow . . ."

"Beautiful . . ."

"Greetings, new resident. My name is Gunter, and this is Bali Hai. Welcome to our humble world. I made this place and owned it, but Bali Hai's an old program now. Use your avatar until you settle. Feel the sand. It has real texture. See the villas up ahead? Miranda's design . . ."

END Record

***

Via message (confidential)

June 3, 2288

To: Desmond Webb

Archivist

Library of Congress, VR Division

Desmond—

I am immensely grateful for your help. The memory files that you made available to me are now part of a legal effort to force SEINI to allow access to their virtual residents in the Shemathra's Realm program. My guess is that we'll find many residents who do not follow the herds and were uploaded to Bali Hai or one of the Infinite Bliss communities. Their rights as virtuals might well have been violated. The following is due to your help:

> From Two Worlds Unite May 02,
> 2288 Tara Gold:
> "Deeply troubling," says Congressman Sam Rodriguez (D), Chair of the Virtual Regulatory committee. Rodriguez is referring to new information concerning Shemathra's Realm, a SEINI after-death program that has been under lockdown for several months. Rumors of abuses have advocates demanding answers.

If not for your suggestion to review Gunter Holden's virtual encounters with my great-grandfather, Thomas Bucklin, the history of Shemathra and the methods Hosseini used to acquire what *was* Bali Hai would have stayed hidden. Thank you again. The investigation is ongoing and, based on your work, I have developed a new lead.

Finally, as I experienced the last of Gunter's memories, I learned that Gunter was Tom's biological brother and my great-uncle. I'm a bit stunned and sad that they had so little time to spend together as brothers.

What do you think waited for them at the end of their ride? Was it an illusion? Is it possible that their ride ended in a beautiful dream?

With profound thanks,

Byron

***

Via Message (confidential)

June 5, 2288

Byron Hernandez

c/o Trammell & O'Connell Offices

Dear Byron—

Regarding your question: I hope so.

Take care,

Des

END

Acknowledgements

Thank you to Daniel Oldis, dream researcher, for your feedback and creative support, and to Jude Roth, screen writer and extraordinary filmmaker, for putting me on this path.

Finally, a thank you to Ray Kurzweil. In an article about mind uploading, futurist Kurzweil imagined what living in virtual reality could mean. Ah, the worlds that beckon!

ABOUT THE AUTHOR

When Marjorie Kaye Noble was nine, *The Black Stallion* was her favorite book. Years later, she worked as a casting director and found  the young girl who *r*ode Disney's *The Young Black Stallion*. When she read an article by Ray Kurzweil on mind-uploading into virtual reality, she imagined a love-triangle that continues after all three are dead and uploaded into the same VR paradise.

After completing her first novel, *The Demon Rift,* she began her VR novel, *Babylon Dreams* and later, *The Dark Side of Dreams*. Her published work includes short stories, online articles, plus film and book criticism.

THE DARK SIDE OF DREAMS

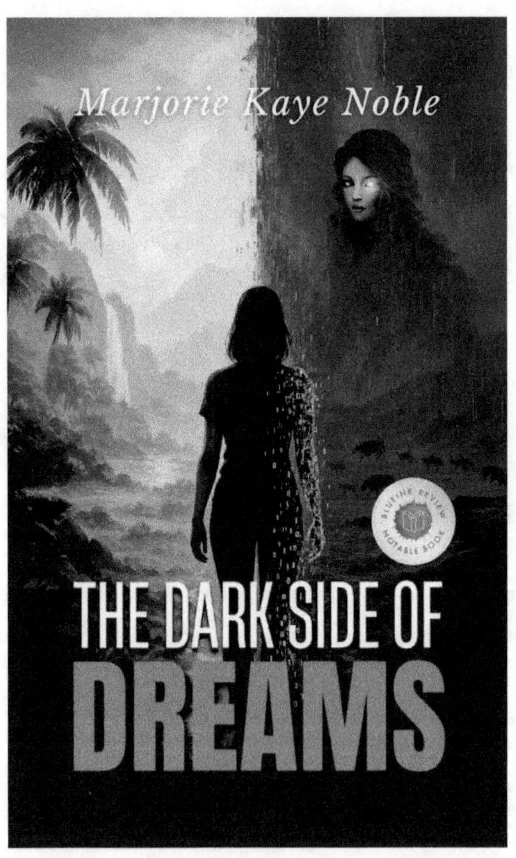

Praise for *The Dark Side of Dreams*

KIRKUS REVIEWS: "Noble delivers a complex, action-packed, dystopian yarn set in a future America of 2290 ... A chilling and fast-paced techno-thriller."

BlueInk REVIEW: "... Marjorie Kaye Noble delivers thematic complexity and storytelling on a grand scale...a science fiction fan's literary dream, blurring the lines between reality, dreams, and virtual reality and delivering masterfully intricate and thematically relevant storylines, unforgettable(virtual) locales, and deeply thought-provok-ing speculation.

It is highly recommended."